50¢

This book may be kept

A LIGHT IN THE WINDOW

By Margaret Lynn

A LIGHT IN THE WINDOW

TO SEE A STRANGER

MRS. MAITLAND'S AFFAIR

The figure of a man lurked in the shadows below, staring up at her darkened windows and Rosanne is certain it is her husband —the man who had ended their three years of blissfully happy marriage with a single phone call. Her immediate reaction to Robert's apparently motiveless decision to leave her is one of shock. Her world topples around her.

Numb and bewildered, she reaches out for help to the "Colonel," kind, sympathetic, always ready to listen and advise, and even to an old school friend of her husband's who secretly frightens her. But in the end, Rosanne is alone as she pursues the shadowy, elusive figure of the man she loves into a world of intrigue and deception, and alone at the end of the trail as she faces a cold, calculating killer.

SCENE: England

 DAMSEL IN DISTRESS

A Light in the Window

Margaret Lynn

Published for the Crime Club by
Doubleday & Company, Inc.
Garden City, New York

25, 634

Library of Congress Catalog Card Number 68–10582
Copyright © 1967 by Margaret Lynn
All Rights Reserved
Printed in the United States of America
First Edition in the United States of America

A LIGHT IN THE WINDOW

1

Now that I was here, now that I had made the decision at last, I knew it was the wrong one. It was a mistake to go back. It is always a mistake to try to recapture anything of the past, even when there has not been disillusionment besides loss.

I should have left well alone; put the whole affair into the hands of an estate agent and remained remote from it all. And that was what I had intended to do at first.

It was only gradually that the hurt nostalgia for what was irrevocably over and done with corroded my mind, whispering the falsehood that it would be difficult for strangers to sort out which particular articles I wanted salvaging for myself from the sale. It would not have been difficult; I could have been sufficiently explicit. And the truth was that I didn't really want to salvage anything from under the auctioneer's hammer. I didn't want any mementoes, any reminders. That was not why I had come.

Standing by the gate, gazing up the winding flagged path to the cottage I had never wanted to see again, I would admit it now. I had come because there was still a part of my mind which would not accept the use he had made of the place. Not this house. The flat, perhaps, although my mind baulked fastidiously even at that. But not Far End, which had always been more than a house to us; more than stout walls and uneven gabled roofs and diamond paned windows.

It had not been a retreat; the whole concept of the word would have been wrong in connexion with it. A retreat is some place to which you can withdraw and shut out the world, but it had not been like that. This cottage had *been* our world. This was where we had known the full meaning of living and loving; where we had had time for each other; where we had come to know each other best.

We had come here as often as we could. Sometimes during an evening, in response to a whim which could afflict either of us at odd moments, one or the other would suddenly say, "Let's go down to Far End"; and we would go, just like that, motoring down in the cold darkness of a winter's night or the soft lingering twilight of a summer's evening. Occasionally arriving in time to do no more than tumble into bed, rising early for the drive back in the morning. Just for the pleasure of a few hours, spent sometimes only in sleep, at the cottage.

We had neither of us ever attempted to define what fascination Far End held for us. Architecturally, it was not a particularly attractive building. It was old and although to some extent we had modernised it, it was sometimes inconvenient according to present day standards. There was no real old world charm about it. In summer the garden could be a riot of colour, but it was not really well planned and apart from that there was nothing about the entire place to draw a second glance.

You had to go inside to know that it was a placid, contented cottage, with a peacefulness which had nothing to do with the fact that it was isolated from the village. And even today that aura of serenity was still there although I hadn't expected it to be. Perhaps that was why I had come, because I had wanted it to be changed; and I think there was resentment in me, as though from a sense of betrayal that everything should seem the same here.

The sunlight filtered palely through the small panes, across the dark polished floor and the gaily patterned rugs, reflecting in the gleaming copper ware on the old oak dresser. All was neat and orderly; no crumpled cushions, no dirty ashtrays, nothing to show the room had been used since I was last here. The woman from the village who came in each week to clean had seen to that.

I wished now I hadn't come. There was nothing here I wanted. The beautiful little mementoes were in my mind, I didn't need to keep them when I could too clearly and painfully recapture the moments when we had purchased them. Not even the delicate antique musical box with its miniature figurine of a Tudor lady.

I stood with it in my hand, knowing that I couldn't bear to push the catch which would release its haunting little refrain of Greensleeves to torment me with so many memories of happiness. Usually, the first thing I did when I entered the room was to set the tinkling melody into action. I couldn't do it today.

What did you do when three wonderful years ended in nothingness—and less than nothingness because it had all been a lie? All of it?

And why not all of it, if a part, only a small part, had been false? Where did you start to distinguish truth from lie, when that small part tarnished and distorted the whole?

It can be hard, even in the light of later events, to pinpoint the exact minute at which things started to go wrong. Hard, but surely not impossible. There had to be something, somewhere. There was always an unguarded moment in every pretence. There ought to be something I could recollect that I would realise should have alerted me. But even now, in the face of enlightenment, I couldn't find a significance in any little incident, in any sentence. I still couldn't read into any action or word anything but the warmth and love and the deep instinctive closeness which had always existed between us.

I put the Tudor lady down on the table and sank into the chair, gazing as unseeingly at her as she stared at me.

What did you do when the first inkling of anything wrong had come as a bolt from the blue with the ringing of the telephone, crashing your whole life into ruins?

Why hadn't I had some premonition when the phone rang? When the momentous shattering of your world was starting into progress, there should have been some intimation of disaster. The very sound of the ringing bell should have been different, ominous. And would it have been more bearable if I had had warning? Would it have been less of a blow—less devastating? It couldn't possibly have been.

But I had picked up the receiver unsuspectingly, cradling it for a moment on my shoulder to rearrange the green fronds of foliage in the vase of daffodils. Hearing Robert's voice, deep, familiar, with the underlying current of sadness which was always in the tones perhaps a little more pronounced but not noticeably so.

A loved voice which could always send little waves of enraptured contentment vibrating through me, even after three years' close proximity of marriage.

But he should have been home, already changed, and I broke in to say, "Darling, you're late. Henry said seven o'clock and it's nearly that now."

"I'm sorry, Rosanne, I can't make it."

I accepted that philosophically. It was not the first time pressure of work had prevented us from fulfilling an engagement.

"I'll ring Henry and apologise." I spoke lightly as I always did on these occurrences, because I hated Robert to think I was reproachful about such disappointments, but I couldn't resist a rueful glance down at my new, very smart black velvet cocktail dress. "What time will you be home?"

The green foliage had slipped once more, spoiling the symmetry of the arrangement and I might only have imagined the slight pause because I had tucked the receiver between my neck and shoulder again. Certainly there was no change in the tone of his voice.

"I'm not coming home," Robert said. "I'm leaving you, Rosanne."

It was a joke, of course—only Robert didn't make inane jokes of that kind—and although I knew I ought to accept it casually it was so unlike him that all I could think of to say was "Robert?" on a questioning note of uncertainty.

That's all it was, even then; just an uncertainty about the dubious quality of the joke. I think I finished pushing the foliage firmly into place because I can remember noting later, in that curious odd detachment of mind, that the green stalks had finally conceded victory to me and remained as I had put them.

Robert spoke again while I was taking the receiver back in my hand and I missed the words.

"What did you say?"

"I said, I'm sorry. That's not very adequate, I know . . ."

"What is this, Robert? Darling, you're not making sense."

I heard him sigh; only the faintest rush of breath escaping down the wire but reaching me clearly, suggesting distress of mind and a sadness. Giving me the first real twinge of alarm.

"Robert, are you all right? Something's wrong, isn't it?"

There was such a long pause I was filled with acute anxiety.

Robert was ill. He had collapsed. He was doubled over with pain. Nothing else could account for his strangeness.

Robert was ridiculously healthy. He had never had a day's illness. Not even a cold.

"Didn't you hear me?" he asked. He told me again. Badly, harshly, making sure the words really penetrated my mind. "I'm leaving you."

The truth has an undeniable ring of authenticity. The room was cold suddenly.

I heard myself ask, "Why, Robert?" in a strangled complaint.

He was a long time answering. Then, "There's—someone else," he said.

It happened all the time. Sometimes to close friends like the Garveys; to acquaintances; to people you didn't know but read about in the papers. But not to Robert and me! Never to Robert and me!

The same strangled voice asked, "Who?"

"What difference does that make? It's no one you know."

"But I want to know . . . You can't just . . . Don't you see that . . ." I controlled the crushing panic, forcing myself to speak quietly and reasonably. "When will you be home, Robert? We can't talk about this over the phone."

"I'm not coming home. I told you. I've already left you. I'm going abroad tonight."

This wasn't Robert. Hard, callous, implacable. You can't be as close, as completely one as Robert and I had been, and not know what they are like, deep down inside. Robert was gentle, compassionate, understanding.

"Don't do this to me, Robert," I said. "Please don't do this to me," and I had forgotten that I had always despised the weakness of pleading in a discarded partner. One should retreat with dignity.

"I couldn't go without telling you, Rosanne."

"But not like this. Without a previous word of warning—without a hint . . . Where are you, Robert?"

"Does it matter? I shall be leaving—"

"Please tell me where you are?"

"I'm at the cottage," he said with reluctance.

"At the cottage? Far End?" I asked stupidly, as though he could possibly mean anywhere else when he referred to the cottage.

"Then if you won't come home, let me come to you. I can be there in—"

"It wouldn't do any good, Rosanne." He sounded desperate.

A woman's soft laughter reached me clearly, even before the words she uttered froze me into a paralysing silence.

"Darling, you're only prolonging the agony. I told you it was unwise—"

And then Robert's voice, harsh, savage, "For God's sake—" before it was cut off, as though a hand had clamped suddenly over the receiver.

It seemed a long time until I heard him say, gently, inquiringly, "Rosanne?" and he repeated the name again, compelling me to answer in a very small voice, "Yes?"

"I'm sorry."

The hurt curled round my heart, squeezing it in anguish. It was the regret, the compassion, the utter weariness, the way he said my name, which made me still refuse to accept defeat. He had sensed the wounding hurt of hearing that other voice with him. He had not been impervious to it. Somewhere, still inside him, there was affection for me, a feeling of responsibility which even in the moment of severance had roused his protectiveness. I couldn't accept defeat. Robert was my life. You didn't accept death just because you had been brutally pushed under water.

"Let me talk with you, Robert. I'm coming to the cottage."

"I'm leaving almost straight away."

"No, wait for me. Please wait . . ."

And then there came the soft click of the receiver being replaced, shutting me away from him with a finality that was shattering. I still went on saying, "Robert—Robert—" into the dead instrument in my hand, at first with a stupid plaintiveness which gradually gave place to a rising panic, so that in the end I was screaming the name futilely.

After that, I don't know how long I had stood there, just staring numbly at the telephone. Not long, perhaps, but too long.

If I had gone earlier . . .

He had said it would be no use for me to go, that he would be gone before I could get there. And even if he should still be there —with her—what could I possibly say to him to make him change his mind?

I had known it was useless to go. But still I went.

Robert's car was still there in the garage, so that briefly I was tempted to take it. It was more powerful, I could cover the road faster; but I was not used to it, so I took my own familiar Mini.

How long would the journey take me? An hour and a half at night, perhaps, if the roads were reasonably quiet and I took risks. I took risks.

Ninety minutes. Perhaps he had only said he was leaving right away to deter me from going. He could still be there—they could both still be there. Both . . .

I couldn't feel outrage. Not then. Later, perhaps, that of all places he should have used for a rendezvous the cottage—our cottage. Now, the numbing sense of loss had retreated beneath the frantic desire to reach him. I could find something to say to him.

What? What use to remind him of the precious years we had shared, of the happiness, of the oneness, of that very special something there had been between us? What use, if it all no longer meant anything to him? If what there had been between us he now shared with—her. If? How could I question it? The question was how long. And would it help to know the length of time he had lived with me in deceit?

How could I never have suspected anything? But how can you suspect, when nothing had changed? When there had been only love and tenderness, as there had always been? There ought to have been a gradual coolness, a constraint, a sensing of indifference. An intuition. Not one moment the door of love opened wide and inviting, to welcome; the next, the brutal slamming of it in the face. How could he have done it like this to me?

If it had been I who had changed, I would have broken it to him gently, talked it over with him. I would—

The idea was too preposterous to contemplate farther. I had never loved anyone but Robert. I never would. I wouldn't know how to face life without him. I had no separate identity.

Why couldn't I be consumed with jealousy? Or resentment for betrayal? Or despise Robert for his cowardice? Why couldn't pride come to my rescue?

I tried to think of Robert with his arms around—her, holding her close with the strength that held such infinite tenderness; his mouth laughing and gentle and full of loving possession in the darkness; of the whispered nonsense which could so soon turn to demanding passion. I couldn't. And it wasn't because I couldn't put a face to the body he held. It was because it just wasn't *me*.

It was all some terrible mistake. Robert had had no opportunity to indulge in an affair with anyone else. When he was not working, we had been together—always. He had no separate interests. There had been times when pressure of work had kept him late but they had been genuine excuses. A wife could be easily fooled but if the results of work were not there, a man could not deceive his superiors. I had met them. Robert was held in high esteem, regarded as a promising man who would go far. To the top. He was not the man to casually throw away his career through scandal.

Robert was at the cottage even now, with some other woman! If he had not already left. He couldn't leave before I got there. He mustn't! When I saw him, when I talked to him . . . And if I made him see reason, what then? How could anything be the same between us after this? Could I ever completely eradicate from memory how casually, how callously, he would have thrust me out of his life? Would I ever have trust in his love again, or would I forever be searching for a word or a sign that proclaimed disinterest?

I wanted Robert. Under any circumstances, under any conditions. If Robert came back to me . . .

When Robert came back to me.

That church clock in the small town I had just passed through was wrong. It had to be; but I couldn't risk a glance at my wristwatch even if I could have seen it in the dark. I was driving too fast. I would have been terrified of the risks I incurred if my mind had not been too occupied with the desperate urgency of time.

If I took the longer way round, would it prove quicker in the end? The roads were narrower and more twisting, but they would be almost devoid of traffic. Or would it be better to stick to the main road which was so busy?

I should have to make the choice soon, but I was still torn with indecision when the signpost indicating the turning loomed up, and on impulse I swung the Mini sharply across the road, without any previous warning, right across the path of a huge articulated lorry. If it had not swerved violently it would have hit me broadside, but I careered off down the dark lane, not caring that I did so to the accompaniment of loudly protesting horns behind me.

The road was even more tortuous in the dark than I recalled. We didn't often come this way. But at least I was no longer dodging nerverackingly in and out of heavy traffic.

There were several turnings. I hoped I would remember them. Robert always said that I was capable of losing my way on a straight road that had no branches.

Robert . . .

I saw the headlights in the distance, long before they reached me; sometimes disappearing from view on the undulating road except for a suffused glow ahead, sometimes cutting a brilliant path of light into the night. It was coming fast, even allowing for my own speed lessening the distance which had separated us when I first saw the lights. I remembered that stretch, some half a mile which had been repaired and widened, converging suddenly onto the right-angled bridge and the narrower road I was on. There was a sign, warning of the bridge and the narrowing road, but either the driver of the other car did not see it or he was driving so fast that even a swift reduction of speed was not sufficient.

I had decreased my own speed until I was almost crawling, not wanting to meet the other vehicle head-on on the bridge, but either he had not seen my lights approaching, as I had seen his, or he had misjudged my closeness.

I was glad I was not on the bridge when the other car met it. Neither of us would have had a chance. Even so, I think that if I had not been on the other side of it, he could have controlled the car. As it was, he had not a hope of regaining his own side of the road.

For brief moments of terror I was blinded by the bright glare of headlights bearing down on me. There was nothing I could do to avoid the impact. I couldn't even shut my eyes as I waited for the crash.

I couldn't believe it when it didn't happen. Above the shrill squealing of brakes came another louder sound—the harsh rending of tortured metal. And then silence.

When I found I had in no way been involved in the collision to my shame I was momentarily tempted to drive on. It had been sheer lunacy which had caused the accident. Whoever was in the other car had no one to blame but himself for driving in that reckless fashion. I couldn't delay. Robert would be gone. I would miss him. If he had left Far End before I arrived, where would I find him? I wouldn't know where to look for him. I couldn't take the chance of missing him . . .

I climbed out of the Mini, consumed with rage for such incompetent idiocy; reaction from shock for the narrowly averted disaster to myself minimised by despair and frustration.

I had been too blinded by the glare to see what had happened. I still didn't know how the other car had missed me until I saw that it had made no attempt to do the impossible and regain its own side of the road, but had continued in its swing right across the front of me, passing me on my near side, to end up in the shallow ditch. One headlight was still alight, canted crazily into the sky. The other, like the front of the car, was shattered hopelessly against the tree which had finally brought it to a halt.

I fell, scrambling across the ditch. Luckily, it was dry, but the fall incensed me further, awakening the temptation to abandon the occupant of the car to the results of his own foolhardiness.

I couldn't see very well. There was a pool of darkness between the lights of the Mini and that one beam that remained of the crashed car. I hoped what I found in the wreckage would not be too gruesome but it wasn't fear of such a discovery as much as impatience for the waste of precious time that troubled me, making me call angrily. Bringing relief, when the voice that answered sounded normal. A little shaken, but with no real weakness in it to betray serious injury.

I was adjusting to the darkness which was not as intense as it had seemed at first; sufficiently at least to find my way round the far side of the car without further mishap. To see that the door had been wrenched open and that the occupant was sprawled half in and half out of the driving seat. Asking with more irritation than concern, "Are you hurt?"

"I'm not sure," he answered. "If you could help me out . . ."

I felt more like flaring furiously at him, but I had no time for recriminations. I wasn't very gentle as I got a grip round his shoulders and started to heave, but even impatience had to yield to humanity when I heard the sharp gasp of agony.

"It's my leg," he said. "From the feel of it, it could be broken."

He was in an impossible position, his head and shoulders suspended in the air. I couldn't leave him like that. He knew it himself; he must have been most uncomfortable, apart from any injury his leg had sustained.

"If you could drag me right out," he said. "Slowly, if you can . . . I'll try to help . . ."

I could hear him gritting his teeth but he couldn't prevent the groans from escaping as between us we manoeuvred him from the car. I think he lost consciousness as the final heave brought his legs clear. He had gone suddenly limp and quiet; such a dead weight that it needed every ounce of exertion to complete the task. But it could only have been a momentary lapse because as I propped him with his back against what looked like the stump of an old tree he murmured weakly, "Thank you."

I looked helplessly up and down the deserted road. If only someone would come past . . .

"I thought there was a car following me." He had raised himself slightly and although the effort brought a long, drawn out gasp of pain from him, he still continued to scan the unrelieved darkness of the night in the direction from which he had come. His voice was stronger again, almost cheerful as he subsided back against the stump. "I must have—it must have turned off."

I waited, thinking acidly that if there had been another car it would not have been travelling at his maniacal speed. When there was no sign of anything approaching I said, "I'll have to leave you. Will you be all right?"

"Sure," he replied. "Do you know these roads? I haven't passed a house or a garage for some time."

"There was a turning back there to some village." I spoke reluctantly. I didn't want to go back. I could phone from the cottage, once I had arrived there in time to catch Robert. How much further yet to Far End? Ten or twelve miles? Fifteen, perhaps. I would *have* to go back, find the nearest telephone.

I hated him in that moment. I could hardly see him, but I hated him. And he didn't make me feel any more kindly inclined towards him by saying, "Will you be as quick as you can? It's rather important . . ."

He didn't know how important haste was, I thought bitterly.

I was turning to leave him without a word when he said, "Will you do something for me? Will you phone—" He hesitated, and then in quick decision, "No, don't bother. Just notify the police, they'll send an ambulance." He stopped me once again. "Could I trouble you to find my cigarettes? They seem to have got mislaid."

I fetched my own; it was quicker than searching for his. Handing them to him in stony silence. Seeing the small red glow of the lighted cigarette as I reversed the Mini, still hating him as I drove back down the road.

I didn't wait, after I had reported the accident. I didn't go back to him. The police would attend to him, the ambulance already alerted. There was nothing more I could do if I returned. Instead, I continued through the village, cutting back into the road farther on from the scene of the accident.

I wasn't sorry about his injury; about leaving him alone there in the dark. I wasn't sorry about anything but the knowledge that for certain now I should have missed Robert.

If I hadn't been held up so, I might still have caught Robert before he left.

But I knew that wasn't true. It had been futile to even attempt the journey.

2

I hadn't gone into the cottage that night. Although I had sat in the car outside it for some time, I couldn't go in. There had been no need to. The cottage was empty, in darkness. There had been no lights flickering through the trees as I had driven down the lane but I had kept on until I reached the gate. Cutting the engine and just sitting there in the deep, empty silence; all sense of haste and panic gone, now that it was too late. Letting the loneliness flow over me in overwhelming waves. Not knowing where to go or what to do.

There *was* nowhere to go, and nothing to do—without Robert. Even now, after three weeks, there was no purpose in life any more.

I had never come down to Far End alone before. Without Robert, the cottage was empty, a shell. I ought not to have come. But I couldn't go.

I could only sit there, remembering. I wanted to remember with bitterness, to ease the ache of intense longing. But even though the place and everything in it mocked me, the bitterness wouldn't come. If I could have felt violent anger that resulted in insensate smashing of everything within reach, it would have helped. But I didn't want to smash anything. Not even my little Tudor lady. I didn't want ever again to listen to the haunting little tune she played, but I couldn't destroy her. She would be sold, along with everything else. Let it all go. I didn't want any part of it now, even if Robert returned to me.

Why did I still cling to that "if", when in three weeks there had been no word from him; when he had cut me so completely out of his life? I ought to be able to accept the fact now, even if I had been incapable of believing it that first night.

When I had eventually driven back to the flat, I had still been sure he would come. That he would realise the cruelty of severing himself from me so abruptly without warning, without any real explanation.

It had been a long night. The longest I had ever spent, a prey to desolation and anxiety and lost, bewildered hurt. A night of waiting, and I was still waiting long after the first faint fingers of dawn had lightened the sky and the pale sun shone through the windows. Still certain that Robert would come.

But it was not Robert who came finally. It was the police.

Robert wasn't desperately calling for me in some hospital, he wasn't lying somewhere badly maimed; they hadn't come to notify me of his death.

It was not Robert they had come about.

They were inquiring about the accident last night. Last night? Surely that had happened long, long years ago, not just only a few hours . . . ?

They were looking curiously at the black cocktail dress, surely strange attire for that time of morning, but I offered no explanation. I wasn't interested in the accident; I wished they wouldn't trouble me over something so trivial. Why couldn't they see that they were intruding into my private grief; that I was dead tired, in an agony of mind through anxiety and bewilderment over something of paramount importance. How could anyone be so insensible? Why didn't they go and leave me alone?

They didn't go, not until they had asked their questions.

I sat down, without the courtesy of inviting them to do likewise, and lit another cigarette, although the one I had been smoking when I had flown to answer the door bell was still smouldering in the debris of the cluttered ashtray. Saying resentfully, "I explained it all to the police in Rillerby last night."

One of them said, "They would like a few more details, Mrs. Grayson. I think they hadn't expected you to leave just so quickly."

"I'd told them everything. I was in a hurry."

"Perhaps you would be kind enough to explain to us fully just how the accident occurred?"

I did so, impatiently. It all seemed so unnecessarily officious. The one who was not doing the questioning was writing rapidly in his notebook. He didn't ask me to retail the account more slowly although the speed with which I spoke was probably making it difficult for him to put down on paper . . . When I had finished he read the whole account back to me, and he had missed nothing out.

"That's correct, Mrs. Grayson?" the first one asked and when I nodded in confirmation he continued, "Did you know the man? Or did he tell you his name?"

"No. I didn't stop to make conversation. I—"

"You have no idea who he could be?"

"No," I said irritably. "Why don't you ask him?"

"That would be difficult. The man is dead."

I said, "Oh" uncertainly, conscious of contrition for my own impatience, and of faint, shocked surprise.

"He was already dead when the police arrived on the scene."

I said, "Oh" again, adding helplessly, "He didn't appear to be seriously injured."

"We're trying to establish his identity. We hoped you could help us, Mrs. Grayson. You said he was conscious when you left him?"

"I can't. I just dragged him out of the car and went to get help. I didn't know he was so badly hurt . . . Hadn't he any papers on him?"

"No means of identification on him at all. No driving licence, nothing."

"What about his car?"

"The car was stolen. It was reported missing later in the evening. Well, it seems as though you can't be of any assistance to us, Mrs. Grayson. Just one thing more, were you in any way involved in the accident? Was there any damage to your own car?"

"I told you—"

"You won't mind if we take a look while we're here?" He was very polite, gravely courteous; not in the least bit trusting.

I accompanied them down to the garage, unlocking the door for them and waiting while they examined the Mini minutely. They didn't use a magnifying glass. They didn't need one, the way they went over the Mini with the naked eye. When they had satisfied themselves that it was without blemish the one who had done all the talking indicated the Jaguar standing next to it.

"Your car also, Mrs. Grayson?"

"My husband's," I told him curtly.

"You were using your own last night?"

I told him that I had never driven the Jaguar but that didn't prevent them from examining the bigger car with the exactitude they had accorded the smaller one. When he looked up finally and caught my irate eye he murmured, "Sorry, Mrs. Grayson, but this was a fatal accident. We have to make quite sure . . ." There was no real apology in his voice. He was doing his duty whether I resented it or not. As they went he said, "As the only witness, you'll be required to attend the inquest. You'll be notified . . ."

At first, I had thought the man who came later in the day was also from the police. Afterwards, I was not quite sure where he came from or whom he represented. If he had told me, I had been too numbed with misery to remember.

He had said his name was Hirst, it was Robert he wanted. When I told him my husband was not at home he had asked if he could come in.

I had tried to refuse. The ringing of the door bell had been another false alarm, flaring my hopes on high. Robert sometimes misplaced his key and had to ring.

There had been other disappointments during the day, each one more bitter, more hopeless than the last. Robert wasn't coming. He had meant what he said on the phone last night. I had still rushed headlong to answer the door.

Mr. Hirst was a persistent man. Against my will, he had insinuated himself into the flat, closing the door behind him. The insinuation had been unobtrusive, he had accomplished his entry without pushing rudely past me. He chose to be oblivious of the fact that he was unwelcome, smiling winningly when I protested that it was inconvenient right now.

"I won't keep you many minutes, Mrs. Grayson," he assured me. "Could you tell me when you expect your husband back?"

"No—I don't know. I'm not sure . . ."

"This evening, perhaps?"

"I—don't think so."

"Tomorrow?"

"I just don't know. He—my husband—wasn't sure when he would return."

"Oh, I see. He's away for a few days? On holiday? Then if you're unsure of when Mr. Grayson will return, perhaps you can tell me where I can contact him? It's rather important, Mrs. Grayson, otherwise I wouldn't trouble you."

Later, I realised his eyes had been everywhere. If he had missed anything, any little detail of the room, I couldn't imagine what it could be. Taking in the untidyness of the room, the piles of debris in the ashtrays which had grown higher as the day progressed because I had been too sunk in misery to bother to remove them. Searching my face with a keenness behind the casual pleasantness of his smile. He was calm, friendly, but he made me inexplicably ill at ease.

"I—can't tell you that," I said.

"Can't—or won't, Mrs. Grayson?" he asked quietly.

I resented his intrusion, I didn't owe him an explanation; but the probing eyes forced one out of me.

"My husband's movements are—uncertain. He wasn't sure where he would go or when he would return."

"I see. So you're just waiting until you hear from him?" He accepted the explanation casually. "Well, Mr. Grayson has been a man with big responsibilities, one can hardly blame him for wishing to be so carefree now that he's retired."

I looked at him blankly. "Retired?"

"You do know that your husband is no longer at the Foreign Office. That he handed in his resignation a month ago?"

The news shattered me completely. It was only pride that came to my rescue.

"Yes—of course." It was lamely said, I wasn't sure whether I convinced him. I didn't really care. I was trembling so uncontrollably I hardly grasped what he was saying.

"As soon as Mr. Grayson returns, or gets in touch with you, will you let me know at once, Mrs. Grayson—or better still, ask your husband to do that?"

I had broken down after he had gone. It was no wild abandonment to grief. I cried quietly, heartbrokenly; I couldn't remember when I had last wept and I didn't think I would ever weep again, because after this, what else was there to weep for?

Robert had known for at least a month what he intended to do and not in all that time had he tried to break the news more mercifully to me. The cruelty of how he had done it hurt even more than what he had done. I had thought I had known every least thing about him, and he had been a stranger to me.

Because if there was cruelty in Robert I had never suspected it, and so I had never known him.

The shadows were lengthening. Soon the sun would be going down and already what little warmth the pale rays had imparted into the cottage was diminishing.

Normally, we should have had a huge fire in the hearth, with the burning logs smelling of cherry wood. I had always liked best this time of year at Far End, with winter still lingering on but with the promise of spring just around the corner. Coming back from long walks with Robert, the cold air nipping our faces and hands; seeing the smoke spiralling lazily from the chimney, knowing that the cottage would greet us with warmth as we went in. Watching for the first signs of colour from the bulbs which were already thrusting high through the hard ground.

Looking out of the window and planning that for sure, this year, we would reorganise the garden. But the days would go by so quickly and soon it was too late to replant and rearrange, and we would look at the fresh young growth of delphiniums that we knew later would be overshadowing the phlox, and plan happily that next year . . .

Or Robert would fix a determined eye on the gnarled old apple tree behind the cottage and pronounce the death sentence on it once more. Then suddenly it would be bursting into blossom, granting its own reprieve for another year. And I was never sorry. It was old, it was ugly in winter, the apples were practically tasteless; but clothed in dripping spring blossom it was beautiful. No longer a withered old woman but a fresh young bride in the glory of her wedding raiment.

The honeysuckle should be drastically pruned. It was untidy, we had both agreed; it should not be allowed to wander indiscriminately until it almost obliterated one bedroom window. But the honeysuckle still rambled at will, carefreely excluding much of the light. There was another window in the room. And what did it matter, when we could sit out in the twilit garden

bathed in the intoxicating perfume; when the scent of it wafted
to us, even if the light did not penetrate, as we lay in bed?

Our plans for the cottage had been many and varied. Few of
them had materialised, mainly because neither of us had really
wanted to make changes. We had liked Far End as it was. The
flat was modern, expensively furnished; but Far End was home.

Nothing had come of the idea for a swimming pool, although
we had toyed with the notion for a long time. There was room
for one, it would have been nice, guests would have enjoyed it.
Not quite in keeping? Robert had wondered, and the idea had
been shelved, but not dropped completely. We had still thought
our own private pool would be fun. Some day . . .

The summer we had been going to build a barbecue—and the
apple tree would definitely have received its death warrant to
make place for it—that summer had been consistently chilly and
wet, and the project had been deferred.

We had consulted an architect about knocking down a wall to
make a small cocktail bar in the alcove. But we had decided we
liked the atmosphere in the village pub; it was friendly, cosy; why
have our own exclusive bar when we preferred the convivial company we found there? If we wanted a drink at home, what was
wrong with sitting in front of the fire or out in the garden?

And the time when we had planned the enlargement of the
cottage. We'll need more room now, Robert had said. And then
at the end of three months had come loss and disappointment;
with Robert, disappointed himself, refusing to allow me to grieve
too much. There'll be another time, he had said; but the plans for
the enlargement had never gone ahead; postponed until that
other time should come.

And now it would never come. If there were ever children at
Far End, they would not be my children, Robert's children.

The room was growing colder, but it stifled me.

Robert was everywhere. The memories paraded before me, as
inexorable as an army on the march.

Robert, in his dressing-gown, hair tousled, waking me with a
cup of tea in the morning; rousing me gently, with tender amusement for the lingering drowsiness which I always found so difficult to throw off. Whistling cheerfully in the bathroom; coming
in later to drag me ruthlessly now from beneath the covers when
he saw that as usual I had snuggled down once more.

Robert, in old slacks and sweater, tinkering with the car, the refrigerator, the lawn mower, an air of profound knowledge on his face. Saying eventually—as I had known he would from the beginning, he wasn't very good at that kind of thing—saying, " 'Fraid we shall have to get someone in to look at this."

Robert, working on the papers he had brought home, frowning as he concentrated, pulling gently on one ear as he always did when deep in thought; looking up occasionally to flash me a quick smile. Robert, helpless with laughter, when I tried to teach him to twist. Ruefully holding his back, "For God's sake, Rosanne, there must be easier ways of disabling me for life."

Robert, courteously welcoming guests, filling glasses; with inherent kindness making sure that no one was overlooked or neglected from the conversation. Standing in the open doorway when the evening was over; giving my waist the little squeeze which without words suggested it was pleasant to entertain, it was joy to be alone together when guests had departed.

Robert serious; Robert laughing; Robert deep in discussion; Robert joking; Robert with that little air of sadness even when he was amused; Robert tenderly loving . . .

Robert, Robert, Robert . . .

The sense of suffocation was too strong, the room was closing in on me.

I fled outside, with no real consciousness of anything except the need to escape from such memories. Sinking on to the stone seat of the well because my legs were trembling. With no real respite here; this was one of the few plans we had completed.

Robert, in the first flush of potential fatherhood, already looking ahead—"This could be dangerous, Rosanne."

And so he had covered the well with two heavy stone flags, tearing down half the circular wall, levelling the other half up into a back rest; removing the winding gear but retaining the canopy as a shelter from the sun. The result, piled with cushions, made an attractive garden seat in summer.

Today, it was cold, with the chill of the bare flags striking through. The wind had risen, blowing strongly in gusts. If it had not been for that, even tormented with memories which would not cease flooding in, I could not have failed to notice earlier. As it was, it was only when the gusts subsided briefly that I became aware of the smell.

And smell was really too mild a word, even with the wind catching at it and casting it away. It was an unfamiliar odour; one which made my nostrils quiver with repugnance. There was nothing in the vicinity to account for it and it was some little time before I realised that the source of its origin could be beneath me. The fact was unmistakable when I put my nose to the minute crack between the two paving stones, making me withdraw in disgust.

The well was dry, there was no stagnant water at the bottom; not even on the hottest days of summer had there been any suggestion of unpleasantness.

I was tempted to leave it; I could mention the matter to Mr. Jenkins as I drove back through the village, he would see to it. Instead, I submitted to impulse. The flagstones were heavy, too solid to have required cementing into place; I broke a nail as I wrestled with one of them, exerting all my strength in the effort to move it.

It yielded suddenly, moving more than I had intended in that final onslaught on it so that I almost fell over backwards, revealing the aperture.

The stench now was appalling, making me choke; one I had never encountered before.

The well was deep, the light filtering only palely into the depths, leaving the bottom of it in darkness. But not impenetrable darkness. The smell had been indefinable but there was something terribly, unmistakably recognisable in the blurred outline of what lay in that darkness.

The odour of putrefaction was still in my nostrils, making me retch, violently heaving; having to wait until the spasms of nausea abated before I could stagger in to the telephone.

3

New Scotland Yard, intelligence agents, M.I.5., Special Branch—
these were things you read about; you didn't experience contact
with them in real life. And not, especially, in connexion with
Robert. The suspicions, the allegations, could have seemed ludi-
crously amusing if they had not been so frightening.

I had to stand impotently by while they searched the flat,
thoroughly, painstakingly, missed nothing; even my own personal belongings were not immune from their probing fingers.
What did they expect to find?

The cottage, too, had suffered the same careful subjecting to
keen scrutiny. That, I could have expected. The decomposing
body of a man had been found on the premises in a situation
which he could not possibly have attained by himself. The
searching of Far End could have been justifiable, even though
what had been uncovered in the garden had no real correlation
with the cottage itself.

But not the flat, so far removed from anything to do with that
gruesome discovery.

They were uncommunicative when I tried to demand some explanation for such arbitrary treatment, flashing warrants which
proved their rights to the violation of privacy.

The questioning was methodical, tedious, repetitious, when I
had already undergone interrogation from the local police; but
they, at least, had confined their interest to Far End. It was Mr.

Hirst's appearance on the scene which widened the horizon to encompass the flat.

He was not alone, as he had been on the other occasions when he had called during the past weeks, and the affable smile which had been noticeably wearing thinner on each visit was completely absent now. The place seemed to be swarming with men, they were everywhere, but it was Detective Superintendent Palmer who came to the crux of the affair. But it was at length, after a skilful parrying to my indignant questions while the meticulous searching of the flat was accomplished.

He had introduced himself when he arrived, nodding towards Detective Sergeant Mollett as he named him. As they came out of the bedroom I asked in icy politeness, "Have you finished now?"

The Superintendent studied my face gravely. "May we be seated, Mrs. Grayson, while I ask you some questions?"

I was fuming by that time, in no mood to be co-operative.

"I'm waiting to go out."

"Perhaps you would prefer to come down to headquarters?"

I yielded resentfully, but I still wouldn't be seated, and when I remained obstinately standing they did also.

"What do you want to know? If you'd told me what you were searching for, in the first place, I could perhaps have saved you the trouble of prying into everything in this way. After all this, I hope you found what you wanted."

He didn't say whether they had or not. Instead, he asked, "Where is your husband, Mrs. Grayson?"

"I don't consider that any of your affair. That man," I indicated Hirst, "has already asked me several times—"

"And I am asking you now. You were vague with him. Purposely so, Mrs. Grayson? Have you some reason why you're so reluctant to disclose his whereabouts?"

"Where my husband is has nothing to do with—all this." I lifted my hand in a movement to include the searching of the flat and their presence here.

Superintendent Palmer exchanged glances with Hirst before saying, "Perhaps it would be better if you accompanied us to headquarters, Mrs. Grayson."

The threat worked again, as he had probably intended it to do. I didn't know whether they had the authority to insist but I decided not to take the risk. I couldn't help wishing I had left that wretched man where he was, if reporting the discovery meant involving myself in this way.

"My husband is still away," I said.

"Where?"

"I told Mr. Hirst—I don't know."

"It's more than three weeks since he left. A man doesn't go away on holiday for that length of time without communicating in some way with his wife. Are you telling me you have had no word at all from him in all this time? Not even a postcard, Mrs. Grayson?"

I shook my head. "No."

"Or is it that you haven't troubled to notify Hirst, as he asked you to?"

"I haven't heard from him."

"You still can't even hazard a guess where he is?"

He was probing at raw wounds, inflaming the still unbearable hurt. The agitation showed in my hands but I couldn't hide it even by clasping them tightly together. It was probably in my face, too, but I couldn't control that, either, especially under such close scrutiny.

"I think you do know, Mrs. Grayson," Palmer said quietly.

"No, I don't. I . . ." In desperation I said, "I won't answer any more questions about Robert until you tell me why you are asking them."

The two men exchanged glances again and small, almost imperceptible nods.

"I think we should sit down, Mrs. Grayson," Palmer said, and this time I complied with the suggestion, grateful for the support of the chair. Outwardly more composed, now that I could hold my hands more steadily in my lap.

The other man took charge of the conversation, launching into the explanation without preamble.

"Over the past few months there have been certain leakages at the Foreign Office. That isn't unusual. I regret to say there are always leakages occurring, of one degree or another."

"Leakages?" The word was an ejaculation of surprise for the introduction of the subject rather than of ignorance of his meaning, but he didn't betray any impatience.

"The passing of information, Mrs. Grayson. Not always of vital import, but information that could be of some value to—another country, shall we say? Sometimes, when a particular information has been available to more than one man it is difficult for us to sort out our suspects and pinpoint the culprit. Your husband came under such suspicion as one amongst three men who had access to certain facts which we know to be now in the possession of this other country."

It was fantastic. For a minute I was too dumbfounded to do anything but gape incredulously at him.

Then, "You think that *Robert* . . . ?"

He couldn't, seriously. Not even for one moment.

"Robert was ambitious," I said. "He wouldn't do anything to jeopardise his career."

"Ambition for position—or for wealth? Promotion can be slow, and not too remunerative. It would be better," he said, "if your husband came forward to defend himself. You're not really helping him by withholding information of his whereabouts."

I couldn't think of anything else to say, so I objected weakly, "I thought you were here investigating the death of that man at Far End. Not Robert . . ."

"Mr. Grayson was being watched. One of our men, Keith Forrester, was detailed to follow his every movement."

"Then he will know that Robert is not mixed up in anything like this. If he's been watching Robert—"

"Nothing has been seen or heard of Forrester since the night your husband disappeared, Mrs. Grayson," he said. I waited, knowing with fatal certainty what he was going to say but even foreknowledge could not detract from the deadly paralysing effect of his words. "The body in the well has been identified as Keith Forrester's."

I looked from him to Superintendent Palmer and back again, helplessly; reading nothing from either inscrutable expression but a grave intentness. But the implication had been there. There had been no mistaking it.

After the first shock, it was almost laughable. But I didn't feel like laughing. Death in any form, however remote, is not amusing. Remote? When they talked of it in the same breath as they mentioned Robert?

It was grotesquely absurd. To even think of Robert in connex-

ion with what was in their minds was impossible. If they had
known Robert as I knew him . . .

But how well *had* I known Robert? Would I ever have believed,
if I had not experienced it, that he could treat me with such cruel
callousness? And if I hadn't known him capable of that, what
else . . . ?

I cast the insidious doubts contemptuously aside, despising myself for entertaining them for even a moment. Whatever he had
done to me, however he had done it, his method of doing it could
only have been motivated by what he mistakenly considered the
kindest way. Robert was incapable of deliberately inflicting hurt
of any kind on anyone.

"Are you seriously suggesting my husband is a—traitor?"

"It's a strong possibility."

"You're not even sure . . . ? Have you any real proof?"

"There isn't much doubt, Mrs. Grayson."

"And because you think that's true—which it isn't—you think
he had something to do with that man's death?"

Palmer answered; a grim statement of facts. "Forrester didn't
fall down the well shaft and pull the flagstones into place after
he'd done so. He died from the result of several savage blows on
the head and was thrown down there in an attempt to conceal
his body. He was murdered, Mrs. Grayson."

"But not by Robert," I cried.

"I didn't say that. But if he has nothing to hide, and you are
convinced he has nothing to hide, why has he disappeared like
this and why are you so unwilling to tell us where he is? You
could be charged with withholding vital information."

The warning didn't scare me into the admission. It was knowing that sooner or later now they would have to know the truth.
I enunciated the words slowly, forcing them out. I had never
voiced them before, because the very act of putting into words
seemed in some way to make the deed completely irrevocable.

"Robert's left me," I said.

It was ironical that they didn't believe me. Scepticism was in
both their faces, even though Hirst asked, "When?"

"Some weeks ago. The day before you were first here."

"Mr. Grayson was at the Foreign Office that day. That was the
date his notice of resignation expired. He left this flat in the

morning, was that the last time you saw him? Did you know then he was—leaving you?"

"No, he rang up in the evening to say he—wouldn't be back."

"And what explanation did he give?"

I told him in a very small voice. "He said there was someone else."

"Another woman?"

I nodded wordlessly.

"Who, Mrs. Grayson?"

"I don't know, he wouldn't tell me."

"But you must have some idea. Even if you hadn't believed it was serious, there must be someone now whom you can realise had held your husband's interest?"

The scepticism was still there, scourging me into angry bitterness. Couldn't they appreciate the mental torture of trying to convince them when I couldn't bear to convince myself? But when I burst into impassioned protest, "This is my private affair," Palmer changed the subject abruptly.

"He gave you no inkling of where he was going?"

"No," I said sullenly, and then, "Except he said abroad."

"I doubt that, Mrs. Grayson. His passport is still there in his writing desk. Unless, of course . . ." He raised his eyebrows inquiringly at the other man.

"Could have," Hirst agreed. "Very probably, perhaps, if he'd become aware he was being watched."

Palmer studied thoughtfully for a few moments, shrugged and then abandoned whatever possibility they had been discussing.

"Where was your husband phoning from, when he rang you up that evening?"

"The cottage."

"So he was definitely there that night. As, of course, he would be, otherwise Forrester wouldn't have been in that area himself."

"Robert wouldn't have had anything to do with his death," I burst out. "How can you be sure that man was killed that night? The police said he had been dead for weeks—"

"It's difficult to be too accurate, after all this time, but the time of death is given as being approximately at that date. It's safe to assume that Forrester was killed the night he disappeared," Hirst said. "If he had been alive, he would have reported in later that night. And certainly he was not alive at your cottage the following day, Mrs. Grayson, otherwise we would have found him. Unfortunately, your well is not obviously a well—it's a garden seat, and we had no reason to suppose it was anything other than what it appeared to be. At the time we were there, the day after Forrester failed to report, it was too soon for us to detect the presence of his body in the well by the means that led you to the discovery."

"Robert had nothing to do with it!" I asserted. "I know Robert —I know he wouldn't—"

"Would you recognise his cigarette lighter, Mrs. Grayson?" Palmer asked.

"Yes, of course—" He was holding the object extended on his palm for me to see and after staring at it for a moment in surprise I said, "Where did you find it?"

"In Forrester's pocket."

"But it's mine," I said.

"It has your husband's initials on it," he pointed out.

"They are my initials, too. They are the same. That's my lighter —Robert's is silver, not gold . . ."

"Really, Mrs. Grayson?" He was very polite, conveying incredulity for the assertion only by the faintest inflexion of voice. "Then perhaps you can explain how it came to be in Forrester's pocket?"

"I lost it—"

"When?"

"I can't remember. Some time ago."

"Then perhaps your husband found it and used it himself?"

"Why should he? He had his own. He would have given it back to me."

"If you ever lost it, Mrs. Grayson. And if it was ever yours, in the first place."

"Why should I say it was, if it wasn't?"

"For the reason, Mrs. Grayson," he said bluntly, "that I think you are being as obstructive as you can, in every way you can."

"I've told you the truth—"

"Have you? I doubt if any word you have uttered has been the truth, excepting the admission that your husband was at the cottage that night."

"I don't know what right you think you have—"

"Then I'll tell you. We're investigating a case of treason and of murder—a brutal murder of one of our own kind. A policeman like ourselves. That gives us the right; and if that isn't sufficient reason for you, Keith Forrester was also Hirst's friend."

He had spoken with a cold intentness; silencing me. And they both let the silence endure for several minutes. I broke it finally to say in a very quiet voice, "And Robert is my husband."

I was not sure what effect the reminder had on them. I wasn't looking at them, I was gazing down at my hands. They were still now, no longer trembling. My whole body, my mind, was curiously calm. None of this was really happening. It was a nightmare. It would end, eventually; and I found it easy to remain unagitated once I had finally realised that.

When I became aware that Hirst was speaking again I met his gaze serenely.

"Did you know, Mrs. Grayson, that your husband had been married previously?"

I wasn't even surprised at the turn the questioning had taken. I answered him calmly, evenly. "Yes. His first wife died some years ago."

"Do you know any details of this first marriage, or the circumstances of her death?"

"Robert didn't talk about her very often. It had been a happy marriage and her death was tragic. She was Hungarian, very beautiful, Robert said—and intensely patriotic. She was killed in Budapest in the 1956 uprising, mown down in the streets by a tank."

He nodded in confirmation. "Tragic, as you say. Have you ever had any reason to believe that your husband had communistic sympathies, Mrs. Grayson?"

"Is it likely," I said quietly, "when his first wife died so terribly at their hands?"

They left soon after that.

The strange, illusory tranquillity lasted until morning. I slept well that night; the soundest sleep I had had since I picked up the telephone receiver that evening and heard Robert's voice announce the fateful words that were the commencement of the nightmare.

4

Robert's face stared at me from the pages of the paper when I opened it in the morning, and the false feeling of security was gone suddenly. Swept away in an avalanche of tormented apprehension.

It was not a particularly good photograph. The photographer had captured nothing of that faint yearning wistfulness which underlined every mood of Robert's.

The wording was discreet, there were no accusations; but this was real, shocking me back into actuality. I could no longer pretend that the moment of wakefulness would banish it into a dimming memory.

Had Robert seen this picture of himself? Was he right at this very minute gazing incredulously at it? If he was, what was he thinking; what would be his reaction?

And for a brief time the uppermost feeling in my mind was one of profound pity. He had started a new life with someone else; seeking to find a happiness which, whatever I had mistakenly believed, he had been unable to achieve with me.

But if Robert hadn't seen it, others had. I became aware that Mrs. Lloyd, the daily help, was looking curiously at me. She was clean, efficient, reliable in her work, but there had never been any degree of intimacy between us. I couldn't bring myself to confide in her or offer her any explanation.

Mrs. Lloyd was not the only one.

The phone and the door bell never ceased ringing. Many of the callers were friends; shocked, sympathetic. Curious, for all that, and who could blame them. It would not have been difficult for anyone to sense previously that something was wrong. I had avoided everyone during the past weeks, been evasive on the telephone. And however discreetly worded in the papers, even the most obtuse could not miss the imputation.

I couldn't stand it any longer, and because I had nowhere else to go, I went to Far End. But it was questionable whether the emptiness of the cottage was preferable to the curious telephone calls and reporters at the door.

I flung myself into an orgy of housework that didn't require doing; polishing, dusting, anything to occupy the time. Washing ornaments that were not dirty; sponging the little Tudor lady with a damp cloth so that the water would not get into the mechanism and ruin it. What did it matter if it did, when I never wanted to hear the refrain again? But someone else . . .

Could I really bring myself to sell her? If not, how could I keep something that was so inextricably linked with memories that were too painful.

We had found her in an out of the way antique shop in Austria. How strange that Robert and I had never been able to recall to mind the name of that small town. It was somewhere we had passed through on our honeymoon. Robert had said many times that if he retraced our route on the map he would be able to find it. But he had never got round to doing so.

The melody had been lingering in the little shop as we went in, captivating both of us. All three of us, because the wrinkled old man who owned the shop had been listening with the same delight. She was not for sale, he said; it was sentiment alone that made him persist in the assertions that she was antique, irreplaceable. We had known from the beginning and he had, too, that he would let us have her. He had been happy to let her go to someone who was as obviously charmed with her as he was himself, proving it by asking only a nominal price for something that had a far greater value. It had been Robert and I who had finally been reluctant to insist on the purchase; conscience stricken at the thought of parting him from something he treasured so highly. My small smattering of the language had not enabled me to know what he was saying, as he tenderly packaged the Tudor lady and handed her to me.

Robert had translated. "I am an old man," he had said, "she will give you many more years of happiness than she can give me now."

How long was many years? Surely more than three.

The sound of footsteps approaching up the garden path wrenched me out of the deep reverie. They were firm, military; easily recognisable. I didn't need to glance out of the window to know that it would be the colonel.

I shrank from the meeting. I didn't want contact with anyone who knew Robert; who would question, however sympathetically, or, even worse, studiously refrain from any reference to a painful subject. In particular, the colonel. We had spent too many pleasant hours in his company, he was too poignantly associated with Robert's and my life at Far End. But there was no avoiding him. His knock was as peremptory as his footsteps. He knew I was here; he couldn't have missed the Mini parked outside the garage. I had no option but to admit him.

Colonel Gregory Haldane was not really a colonel. In fact, I doubted whether he had ever been in the army. He owed the title to his misguided parents having inflicted it upon him as a Christian name. Everyone in the village, from the postman to the vicar, called him "Colonel", the majority of them doing so without realising they were not conferring entitled rank upon him but addressing him personally.

He was a tall man, so tall that the breadth of his shoulders was unremarkable until he stood framed in a doorway, with dark hair already greying at the temples. No one knew; it was generally assumed that he was in his middle forties, but I had more than once had a suspicion that he could be younger than the impression he chose to convey of more advanced years. Handsome, perhaps, in a rather severe way, but the lines of his mouth were a little too sternly set, the blue eyes too hard and withdrawn; although I had seen them strangely gentle when the strong tanned hands had dealt with a sick horse or dog.

It could have been that he was capable of feeling more tolerance towards dumb animals than for his fellow men, or, as I had sometimes shrewdly suspected, a defence against undesired intimacy. He was amiable enough, well liked and very deeply respected in the village, but no one really knew him beneath the surface of that brisk, military exterior. However curious, one didn't question the colonel about his private affairs. Not even Robert or I, who had been so close in friendship to him.

He was a blunt man, wasting no time in preliminary conversation. His greeting was characteristic.

"Where's Robert?" he demanded.

I motioned him vaguely inside, moving some magazines from a chair so that he could sit. Conscious that he checked sharply as his eyes adjusted to the darker interior of the cottage and dwelt briefly on my face, holding for a moment that gentleness I had previously seen reserved only for animals. But he made no comment about my appearance, although, if anything, his voice was more brusque and clipped than usual.

"Was coming up to London to see you this afternoon. Good job Victor saw you pass through the village. Knew nothing of this until I read it in the paper. Goddamn thing never comes until nearly lunch time. Still, good thing for once, otherwise I should have missed you." He didn't accept the proffered chair but stood towering over me, demanding bluntly again, "Now then, where's Robert?"

I shook my head, causing him to give an exasperated exclamation.

"My dear girl, you can tell me. How am I going to help you if you keep me in the dark? Promise the knowledge will go no further if that's what he wants. But it's a mistake. Best thing for Robert to do is to come forward and refute these implications."

"You don't believe there is a possibility he could be guilty?"

"Never heard such utter rubbish in my life!" he asserted, warming me suddenly towards him.

I had been reluctant to admit him; resenting his intrusion, whatever his motive for coming. Now his presence was oddly reassuring.

"I know you're not fond of tea," I said, "will you have a whisky?"

"Tea will do," he said. "I doubt you'll bother making it for yourself if I don't join you. Looks to me as though you've been neglecting yourself all day."

"Longer than that," I said, but quietly, so that I don't think he heard.

He followed me through into the kitchen, watching me in

silence as I filled the kettle and set the tray. Not offering to help; he was not a domesticated man. I doubted if he knew one end of a teapot from the other.

The water was boiling before he asked, "Are you going to tell me where Robert is?"

"I'd tell you if I knew," I said.

"You don't know?" He obviously found it hard to believe. "What the devil is he about, leaving you alone at a time like this?"

I filled the teapot and picked up the tray before answering. "Robert and I have parted." That sounded too much like a mutual arrangement. More honestly, I said, "Robert has left me."

The colonel uttered a rather rude word. Robert had once told me that the colonel may never have been in the army but his epithets had certainly originated on the parade ground, but although I had heard him swear often enough, they had been the more common expressions of profanity. It was a measure of his perturbation that he should use the word in front of me without even noticing he had done so.

"It's true," I said quietly and carried the tray through on to the table.

I had never known him at a loss for words before. He accepted his tea, still without speaking, and sat drinking it slowly. His cup was half empty before he said finally, "He will come back to you." It was spoken uncertainly, a question more than a statement.

"He hasn't, in more than three weeks."

"Because he has been hiding—in trouble over this?" He gestured in the direction of the back garden and the well, one corner of the canopy of which was just visible from where we were sitting.

"If Robert is not guilty, until the body was found he wouldn't know there was anything to fear from the police. And there's more to it than that." I told him about the leakages of information and the colonel listened intently; not interrupting, but his face grew noticeably graver. "But that is not the reason why Robert left me," I finished. "He hasn't disappeared because of any of this."

He waited and when I didn't add anything more he prompted gently, "A woman?"

I nodded and he took a deep breath, expelling it before he got up and began slowly pacing the room.

"This is worse than I imagined, Rosanne. Much worse. I

thought the main reason why Robert was wanted for questioning was because of the discovery of the body in your garden. The newspapers hinted at the other, but vaguely. Very vaguely, which could mean that as yet there is no definite charge against him on that score. Which in turn could imply an element of doubt. . . . But I won't pretend things don't look bad for Robert. The murder of this man who was shadowing him . . ."

It was unusual for the colonel to leave his sentences trailing in the air. And his indecision didn't last long. He came to a halt in front of me, gazing down at me with gravity and deep concentration in his face. For all that, looking very reassuring and confident, and speaking with his customary crispness.

"I must have time to think about this, Rosanne. I am not without a little influence, I have slight contact with people in high places. Whatever there is to be done to help Robert, I shall do."

I thought he was probably being over modest. The colonel was not one for casual name dropping but he was essentially the type of man who would be able to claim at least an acquaintanceship with exactly the right man at exactly the right moment of an emergency. I didn't know what he could do, but his confidence was contagious.

"How long are you staying here?" he asked abruptly.

"I'm not sure, a day or two. Until things quieten down at the flat. There were reporters, people ringing up all the time. . . ."

His expression conveyed distaste. "All the same, you shouldn't be here alone. You'd be very welcome to come and stay at Coplands, you know." He grinned suddenly; a grin that confirmed my suspicions that he was younger than he made himself out to be. "Too unconventional, eh? Even if I arrange for Mrs. Cooper to stay overnight?"

He didn't wait for me to shake my head. "All right, I won't try to persuade you. But I'll expect you for dinner tonight."

I tried to demur. "No—please excuse me. I—"

"I'll send Victor with the car for you at seven o'clock."

I gave in, knowing it was useless to argue with him. The colonel was a determined man. I hadn't known how I was going to get through the long evening, anyway.

His last words, thrown over his shoulder as he strode purposefully down the path, were, "Seven prompt. Gives us time to enjoy a drink before dinner. And don't worry."

Renshaw was not a pretty village, although at one time I think it must have been. There were houses of charm and distinction but they were cheek by jowl with buildings which had been erected without discrimination in the Victorian era. Buildings like the chapel, the police station, the school; all ugly, square, and of a red brick which had not mellowed with age.

Coplands was one of those which had added nothing to the attractiveness of the village. Isolated on the outskirts, it was squat, typically Victorian at its very worst.

It was too dark for me to see anything but the vaguest outline as Victor brought the car to a halt before the front door, but I knew what it was like. The lights were on in the entrance, flooding the driveway; a sure sign that the colonel was expecting to entertain. Usually, except for the room he was occupying, the house would be in a darkness that was calculated to repel the casual caller. The colonel was hospitable, but you visited by invitation only.

He was at the top of the steps, warned of my approach by the crunching gravel, as Victor opened the car door and handed me out; coming down the steps to meet me and usher me inside.

The interior of the colonel's home was not as austere as his own general appearance and manner would suggest. It was, without exception, the most beautiful house I had ever entered. There was nothing unnecessary cluttering his rooms. To that extent, he had allowed the qualities of his own nature to govern him. It was expensively furnished, in exquisite taste. He had an unerring eye for what was essentially right; everything chosen with care to blend with its surroundings, with no piece of furniture outstanding, so that you saw each room as a complete and perfect unity.

The sense of luxury was there as you went in at the door. An atmosphere which encased itself around you immediately you entered, with the warm envelopment of a cloak. I never went to Coplands without sensing an instinctive desire to purr with the pleasurable satisfaction a cat derives from kneading a silk cushion.

The colonel was attentive; making a great fuss over me, but unobtrusively. Taking my coat and installing me in a chair drawn close to the fire, offering his own specially blended brand of cigarettes.

It was only knowing the uselessness to attempt further protest which had kept me from phoning during the meantime to decline the invitation. I was glad, now, he had been insistent. I hadn't realised how much I had missed all the little attentions a man offers; the flame held in readiness to light my cigarette, the remembering of how I liked my drink. I couldn't recall whether he had ever before known how to mix it to my satisfaction without asking, but he remembered now.

I leaned back and closed my eyes, savouring for a moment the little glow of well being that comes from being indulged, of being made to feel of importance to someone—even though that someone may not be the right one.

"You're tired," the colonel said, and even the little note of concern was comforting.

"Not really." I roused myself and took a sip of the drink, looking at him over the rim of the glass. "I was just thinking how kind you are."

"Nonsense!" He sounded embarrassed. "You've been too much alone. Haven't you anyone, any family?"

"A sister in Johannesburg. She doesn't know . . ."

"Couldn't she come and stay with you for a while?"

"She has young children."

"Then the best thing you could do would be to go to her, until this affair sorts itself out."

"I couldn't," I said. "Not now. Not knowing . . ." After a moment I asked, "Do you think it will sort itself out?"

He was deliberately evasive. "If it doesn't soon, you're going to have a nervous breakdown," he said bluntly. With abruptness he asked, "What do you think about that?" pointing to a small landscape painting above my head.

I had admired the colonel's fine collection of paintings on previous visits. I didn't want distracting from something that was of paramount importance to me. This one I had not seen before and I offered my opinion in cool politeness.

"It's very nice."

"My own work," he claimed.

He had caught my attention now whether or not I resented the deliberate change of subject.

"I didn't know you painted."

The colonel smiled faintly. "Don't usually advertise the fact. But I like to dabble at it occasionally. This is mine also and this . . ."

I looked at them with renewed interest. They were good, even to my inexperienced eye. It was a side to his character I had never hitherto suspected, surprising me. I was still admiring them, as he had intended I should, when Victor announced dinner was ready.

Victor was chauffeur, valet, butler, handyman . . . As the colonel once said, "You name the function, Victor fulfils it." As a servant, he was the acme of perfection, making his employer the envy of the entire village. His proficiency in any capacity was unquestionable; it would have to be, to satisfy the colonel's exacting requirements.

I think Robert and I were the only people of any standing in the village who, at one time or other, had not attempted to bribe Victor away from Coplands. Some of the offers of remuneration had been good, too, even by present day standards. It said a lot for Victor's loyalty to the colonel that he had turned them down without even batting an eyelid.

It was generally assumed amongst those who had been disappointed in their efforts, that the colonel must pay on a lavish scale to keep Victor so faithfully entrenched in his household, but I had never thought so. Colonel Haldane was a man who, if he was unsuccessful in commanding unmercenary loyalty, would never seek it by too generous payment. I could easily imagine that he would pay an adequate reward for adequate service, and nothing more.

I didn't care very much for Victor, even while knowing that the faint aversion was unreasonable. I had to admit he was a rare treasure; he ran the colonel's household on oiled wheels, with an unobtrusive effortlessness that left you hardly aware of services rendered. He was adept at having ready your exact want, before you had even quite realised your need of it. He was courteous without being in any way servile.

He was also an immensely strong man. Deceptively so, because his build and appearance gave no indication of such power, but I had seen him perform prodigious feats at the colonel's instigation to show off his capabilities. Even in a man of extraordinarily fine physique such colossal strength would have been astonishing; in someone of Victor's build it was as abnormal as a crippled body. His face had expressed implacable concentration on the task in hand, a vicious fixation that had seemed to lay bare the inner-most essence of the mind behind the contorted features.

Robert had laughed when I had mentioned it later; all heavy weight lifters looked like that when they faced their moment of truth. The thought of it still made me vaguely squeamish. I could never see his hands competently serving at the table without recalling that dormant, frightening strength behind their dexterity.

We were seated once more by the roaring fire, with the coffee tray before us, when the colonel dismissed him.

"I shan't need you again tonight, Victor. I'll run Mrs. Grayson home myself." He waited until Victor had cast a keen eye over everything, checking that nothing we should require had been overlooked before wishing us a quiet, "Goodnight, sir. Goodnight, madam."

"Now, Rosanne, a brandy with your coffee? No, I insist. You're too pale for my liking."

There was no gainsaying him. He put the brandy firmly down on the table in front of me.

"You ate practically nothing," he accused. "I shall have complaints about it from Mrs. Cooper in the morning. Takes it as a personal affront to her cooking."

"The dinner was excellent." I had surprised myself at how well I had eaten.

"I'll tell her that. She likes to be praised." He lit my cigarette, making sure my coffee cup was filled before retreating to the opposite chair. Looking suddenly grave as he settled into it and drew slowly on his cigarette.

Saying with startling abruptness, "Village gossip served its purpose over dinner but you've more pressing things on your mind."

I stirred apprehensively. For a little while he had made it all seem so far away, so unbelievable.

"I've been making a few inquiries, ringing up various people." His eyes were very serious. "I'm sorry, my dear. Things don't look good for Robert."

I waited, still not speaking.

"Robert has been under surveillance for some time," he said. "I'm afraid that when he is found he will almost certainly be charged under the Official Secrets Act, if not of spying then of conspiracy to spy."

"If they are so sure, why wasn't he arrested earlier?"

"They weren't ready to prefer charges against him. For one thing, he has never been caught in the act. And Robert could have been regarded as small fry. They could have been holding their hand, hoping to catch bigger fish through him, or at least his contact. But there seems little doubt of his guilt."

"Robert wouldn't," I started to say, trailing into silence as he slowly shook his head.

"Doesn't help to shut your eyes to facts, Rosanne."

"But why?" I appealed helplessly. "Why would he do such a thing?"

The colonel shrugged. "Who knows? Money, probably. Was Robert in any financial difficulties that you know of?"

"He wasn't desperate for money. We lived within his income; and we have some savings, investments and things like that. Those men went into all that. They went through all the accounts and bankbooks—even mine—and there wasn't any trace of any unaccountable sums of money. They even tapped the walls of the flat and measured them against the corresponding length and width of the other rooms."

The colonel looked faintly amused. "They wouldn't be looking for buried treasure, my dear. They would be searching for any concealed equipment, radios etc. I hardly think they would expect to find anything of the kind, Robert is only a very small cog in a very large wheel, but they wouldn't overlook any possibility. Far End will have received the same treatment."

"Well, they didn't find anything. How can they have any real evidence against Robert? They can't find proof he was paid for what he did. And he didn't need money—not enough to seek it by that means."

"He could have spent it as he got it."

"On what? I would have known."

"Not necessarily. Not if it wasn't spent on you or himself. He could have needed the money, Rosanne," he said gently, "if he was interested in someone with expensive tastes. Or if he had been planning for some time to leave you, the money could have been deposited in some foreign bank for him under a fictitious name, in readiness for some future date. Or he could merely have been influenced by her, perhaps not just for the money. Who knows where her sympathies lie? A man can act very foolishly for a pretty woman without the inducement of monetary gain."

That wounded too deeply. He had known it would; he had said it deliberately. He had warned me it was useless to ignore facts but I still flinched violently away from the hurt.

"Was it—vital information that Robert passed?" And I realised now that one small part of my mind was accepting the possibility of his guilt. I had not believed the men from Scotland Yard but I could trust the colonel to the point of knowing that if there had been any element of doubt concerning Robert's innocence he would have given him full benefit of it.

"Not atomic or military secrets, if that's what you have in mind. Robert hadn't access to top secrets of that nature. But information of one kind or another is being passed all the time, both from and into the country. It isn't all one sided. Some of it is very trivial. It could be information regarding the movements of certain people; nothing more serious than that. But spying for a foreign power in however small a degree is still treasonable activity. So far I have not been able to discover just how serious these defects of Robert's are, but for your sake, Rosanne, I hope Robert is safely out of the country."

"He's not. His passport—"

"That wouldn't present any real difficulty. The people he was working for could have issued him with a false one. I hope so. If he is still in this country I am afraid it will be only a matter of time. But I am confident he won't still be here. If he suspected he was being watched he would take the necessary precautions of making arrangements to get out. I think that is what happened."

The idea of Robert involved in such clandestine business as forged passports was ludicrous. But the colonel hadn't finished. His glass was empty and he got up to replenish it, pouring the brandy with a steady hand; adding just a little more before saying quietly, "I'm afraid Forrester's death can only be connected with his investigations into Robert's activities."

I swung round to face him, knocking my coffee cup flying, spilling the coffee down my dress and on to the carpet. Scarcely noticing in my agitation.

"No! You know Robert. He's not a violent man!"

"Violence can depend upon circumstances, my dear. If Robert was desperate, if he panicked . . . Or it could be that he knew the man had been killed and, if he knew he could not prove his own innocence, was afraid of becoming involved. It could be circumstantial evidence only. But don't build up too much that it *is* only that."

"How can you say that?" I cried. "You are Robert's friend . . ."

"I *was* Robert's friend," he contradicted me, and as he continued there was an edge of controlled anger in his voice. "Nothing of your marriage to him has conditioned you to withstand a blow of this sort. Robert sheltered you, protected you too much. I can think of nothing more barbarous than his abandonment of you under such circumstances. And his complete silence since. You have held up better than I would ever have imagined."

It was curious to hear the views of an outsider on the aspects of my marriage and relationship with Robert, but what he had said was true. I had been the little helpless woman, to be cherished and sheltered from the practical and more sordid actualities of life. Robert had been the cottonwool which served as a buffer to shield me. Without that protective layer I was as exposed and vulnerable as a chick newly hatched from its shell.

The colonel was asking, "How would you feel about Robert if he were found guilty of treason."

A little helplessly I said, "You don't stop loving someone . . ."

"But what are your reactions?" he insisted. "A traitor to one's own country is regarded by most people as one of the lowest forms of animal life. You're not shocked? Disgusted? Outraged?"

"Whatever Robert did, he must have had some motive."

"Even if his motive was his infatuation for another woman?" I didn't answer and after a little pause he said, "And what about murder?"

"It has to be proved."

"And if it is proved?" He added gently, "I wouldn't be doing you a service by encouraging you to keep your head buried in the sand. These are facts that have to be faced. Even if there is not sufficient evidence to arrest Robert in connexion with Forrester's death, he would be held on the other charge while inquiries are being made. But if Robert has a satisfactory alibi he will clear himself."

"He can't give himself up if he knows he will face a charge of treason."

"As I say, I think and hope he is out of the country—and, for whatever reason, I think he had to leave in a greater hurry than he anticipated. But the police are efficient. If there is any other trail leading to Forrester's murder they will get on to it."

The coffee had sunk into the carpet, leaving a dark stain on the cream pile, but the colonel ignored that, concentrating on dabbing at my dress with his handkerchief.

"I'm sorry," I said, but he waved the apology aside, throwing the sodden handkerchief into the fire before retrieving the cup from the floor.

"I'll ring for another," he said. Waiting briefly, and when there was no prompt response to the bell he had pressed he got up with a little movement of impatience. "I'd forgotten. Victor won't be there. I'll get one."

I stopped him. "Please don't bother."

"You're sure?" He probably wouldn't have known where to find one, anyway.

When he was seated once more I watched him in silence for a little while, breaking in at last to say, "This afternoon you said it was rubbish. Now you're not sure. You think Robert could have killed that man."

"This afternoon I didn't know Robert was guilty of doing something that was detrimental to his country. I would have thought that impossible. If I could be wrong in one thing, I could be wrong in another. I don't say I am. I say I could be." His cigarette had smouldered to ashes while he had been occupied with cleaning my dress. He got another and lit it, contemplating the glowing tip in such deep thoughtfulness that he seemed almost to be talking to himself in an attempt to clarify the reasonings of his own mind. "While not condoning, without overmuch difficulty I can conceive of a man betraying the secrets of his country either for personal gain or because of alien sympathies. I can understand the need in a man to kill, and kill violently, if his own safety was at stake, or for several motives which at the time could override all other considerations. What is entirely beyond my comprehension—candidly my mind boggles at it—is that any man who had you for his wife could be fool enough to throw you so lightly away for any reason on God's earth."

The tone of his voice even more than the words arrested my attention. When I looked up it was to see him regarding me with a very wry smile.

"You never guessed? Why, indeed, should you?"

Why, indeed, should I? I had been so secure in the world of my love for Robert, I hadn't looked for anything from anyone else; neither expecting nor desiring anything. There had been no occasion to take into account the emotions that any other man was experiencing in relation to myself. Least of all the colonel. I didn't know what to say.

But the colonel was shrugging it carelessly aside.

"My dear girl, don't look so distressed. Forget it. Should have realised my feelings are of no interest to you. Years too old for you, anyway. Ought not to have mentioned it. Can't imagine why I thought it might help."

I had never known his speech to be more clipped, more crisply military—and yet, curiously, more human.

And he was wrong. It had helped. For the first time in weeks I felt a little warmth creeping into my heart, making the icy hand of loneliness relax its grip. It is always comforting to feel esteemed, to be wanted. Deep beneath the hurt had been humbled pride which had writhed at being so casually discarded. It had been of only secondary importance yet but it had been there, a corroding wound in the background. That, at least, he had helped in some measure to mitigate.

I could almost wonder if I had imagined it. Whether he was regretting his momentary lapse of weakness or merely wishing to spare me any discomfiture, the colonel had obviously done what he advised me to do—forgotten it.

"Whatever I feel about Robert, I am *your* friend, and for your sake I would do everything in my power to help you both. Robert I can do little for at the moment, but you—what are your plans?"

Rather helplessly I said, "I haven't any—except to sell Far End."

"Because of too painful associations?"

"That, too. But I shall need the money," I explained simply.

The colonel's brows knit sharply together. "Robert hasn't left you provided for?"

"He didn't make any arrangements. What money there is, is in his name. I can't touch it. Robert always saw to the financial side of everything. I have a small personal income but it isn't much. But the cottage is mine, it was Robert's wedding present." I faltered a little, making myself add with a false cheerfulness, "I shall have to get a job before long."

"Let me help, my dear. For a time, at least. If it distresses you to sell the cottage—"

"It's better that way. I don't want it now. The flat is on lease, I should be able to keep it for the time being. After that . . ." I couldn't look so far ahead. "Colonel . . ."

"Wish you would call me Gregory," he interrupted. "I'm Colonel to my milkman, I would prefer some distinction." He waited. "You were saying?" he prompted.

"I wanted to thank you."

"Thank me?" He snorted. "When all I've done is confirm what was previously only an unpleasant suspicion?"

I don't think I had really meant that. I wasn't sure exactly what I had meant.

He drove me home later, hurrying round to open the car door for me when he had stopped outside Far End.

"Are you nervous?" he asked. "Would you like me to come inside and peer under the beds and into the wardrobes for you?"

I could barely see his face, the gas lamps didn't extend to the full length of the lane, but beneath the humour I could detect a touch of concern. I let my own answer be in the same light vein, passing the concern off jokingly, but I was reluctant to part from his company.

I stood, running a finger idly along the handle of the car door; recalling what I had noticed when Victor had called for me earlier in the evening, that the colonel had indulged in the extravagance of another new car.

But the remark I had been going to pass about it became suddenly lost in the stark world of unreality into which I had been so precipitately plunged.

"When will it end, Gregory?" I asked plaintively.

His mind was sufficiently attuned to mine, he didn't pretend to misunderstand the trend of my thoughts.

"It *will* pass," he said. "No matter what you think now. Remember that. It's the only way you can live through a time of great unhappiness and keep your sanity."

I wondered if he spoke from personal experience. He had sounded so positive, so undeniably certain. The grip of his hand as he shook mine in farewell was strong, determined, carrying the same conviction.

I wished now I had sought him out earlier.

5

I slept late. There was no Robert at the cottage to waken me now. The bed next to mine was neat, unused. I had become accustomed, if not reconciled, to the unoccupied bed at the flat but I had never previously spent a night alone at Far End. The first waking inclination had been to turn over and settle down once more into sleep, but the unruffled state of those bedclothes was too bleak a reminder, forcing me out from beneath my own sheets.

The morning was a depressing one, matching my mood. Low banks of cumulus clouds loomed greyly in the sky, carrying more than a hint of approaching rain.

I shivered in the cold. I had forgotten to attend to the kitchen stove when I came in last night and the place was like a tomb. There was no hot water for a bath and in a thoroughly disgruntled frame of mind I shrugged into a warm dressing-gown, hugging it tightly round me as I switched on every electric heater in sight. Lighting the boiler never presented much difficulty for Robert but it always behaved with beastly stubbornness for me. This morning was no exception. Even the first cigarette tasted foul in my mouth as I waited for the kettle to boil. I had smoked too much last night. For that matter, I had smoked too much altogether in the past weeks. From the way I felt I had a strong suspicion I was developing a cold.

I was definitely not inclined to feel tolerant when I caught sight of the man from the kitchen window. He was standing motionless, his back towards me, the collar of his raincoat turned up against the biting cold of the wind. So motionless that he gave the impression of having been in that position for some time, his interest concentrated wholly on the stone garden seat.

I stormed outside in a fury of disgust for the ghoulish morbidity which could entice anyone to indulge in such unwholesome curiosity even on a day like this. The wind whipped at my dressing-gown as I crossed the garden. He didn't hear my approach; I was right behind him before I spoke.

"You're trespassing," I informed him coldly.

I dragged him out of some deep mental contemplation. Just for a moment the face he turned was blank before it was suddenly split by a very disarming smile.

"I beg your pardon," he said.

The smile had in no way mollified me. "You're trespassing," I repeated.

"I wasn't aware there was anyone at the cottage or I'd have sought permission."

"You wouldn't have got it," I said bluntly.

He raised his eyebrows in polite surprise; then, evidently realising the reason for such distaste, he explained, "I'm an insurance investigator, Mrs. Grayson. You are Mrs. Grayson?"

Still only half relenting I nodded rather stiffly. "I didn't know. I thought—"

"The apologies are mine. Sorry for intruding like this but I have to look into these things. You've been much troubled with sight-seers, Mrs. Grayson?" He sounded sympathetic, revealing a distaste which had equalled my own.

"They were here earlier—at the time . . . I've been in London. I came back yesterday."

I was searching my mind for what it was that was obscurely familiar about him. I had a good memory for faces; I had never met him before and yet there had seemed to be something that had roused a deeply hidden, elusive memory. I was still vaguely pondering about it when the gusting wind brought a sudden sharp flurry of rain.

"You're getting wet," he reminded me.

I said "Yes", moving towards the house. He was still standing there in the rain when I reached the shelter of the doorway, making me pause in indecision.

"You wouldn't happen to have any coffee to spare, I suppose?" he called whimsically.

Now that he had made the decision for me, I was reluctant. "There isn't any milk," I demurred, rather grudgingly.

"Fine," he said. "I like mine black."

He had joined me in a few quick strides, giving me no chance for further objection. I couldn't have left him out in the rain, anyway. It had settled into a steady downpour, bouncing heavily on the flagged path.

He followed me into the kitchen, closing the door behind him. In the act of taking off his raincoat and shaking the beads of moisture from it he shot a quick glance at me.

"If you'd like to go up and change, I'll make the coffee," he offered.

My dressing-gown was wet. I could feel the dampness soaking through but I hesitated, causing him to grin. "I'm competent," he said. "Don't worry, I'll find everything."

As I was leaving he asked suddenly, "Have you had breakfast yet?"

I called back over my shoulder, "I don't want any."

He ignored that. "Like scrambled eggs? I excel myself at them."

I went upstairs a little resentfully. He was very sure of himself. I wasn't certain I cared for the calm authority with which he had taken possession of the kitchen.

I could hear him whistling cheerfully as I dressed, the sound mingling with the quick rattle of dishes and the opening and shutting of cupboard doors as he moved about. The smell of toast wafted up the stairs, making me suddenly aware of hunger. When I came down the coffee was made, the table set for breakfast, and he was busily stirring the eggs in the pan.

In a short time he had made amazing progress in a strange house. I had wondered what sort of muddle would face me, but the kitchen was neat. As he had said, he was competent. And he certainly liked his coffee black.

"Too strong for you?" he asked, pausing with the pot half poised.

I shook my head, watching rather helplessly as he deftly dished the scrambled eggs and put the plate in front of me.

"You're not having any?" I queried.

"Just coffee. Mind if I smoke while you're eating?"

He sat down opposite, lighting a cigarette and taking care to blow the smoke away from me, watching me as I ate.

"O.K.?" he asked.

I would have rather liked to deny it but I couldn't.

"I'm Dale Merrick," he said. He was fumbling in his pocket, producing papers from it. "My credentials, if you'd care to see them?"

I waved them aside. I was taking stock of him as I demolished the meal he had prepared for me. Wondering again what it was about him that caught at my memory; deciding finally that it was his very mediocrity that was familiar.

He *was* a very ordinary man. About thirty, I guessed, although he was of the type that would change little with age. He had probably looked very little different ten years ago, and wouldn't, ten years hence. Medium height, medium build, brownish hair, good white teeth which showed fleetingly when he turned on his disarming smile. Hazel eyes that were rather deceptive, because they somehow conveyed an impression that they could be humorous, and yet were not. There was something rather odd about his eyes, I thought—the only point of any distinction in his entire features —but I couldn't decide what it was.

For the rest, he was dressed very unoutstandingly in a plain grey suit which could have been expertly tailored to fit or not, because with his measurements he would have had no difficulty in buying an off the peg suit. His shirt and tie were neat, unobtrusive. There was nothing whatever about him or his clothes to make him remarkable in a crowd.

I finished summing him up, unabashed by the quizzical expression in the hazel eyes which told me he was aware of the assessment. A little pushing, perhaps, but not really objectionably so; and I had to admit that where scrambled eggs and crisp toast were concerned he had justified his intrusion.

"I also make a very good omelet," he said gravely, reading my thoughts accurately.

I inclined my head politely, accepting the cigarette he offered as I pushed the empty plate away.

"Do you make a habit of cooking breakfast at every house your investigations take you to?"

"Very rarely. In fact, practically never. It was done as some slight return for your kind invitation in for coffee."

I gave him a rather oldfashioned look which he interpreted correctly.

"Oh, well," he said, "it was raining hard."

The charming smile was somehow just too spontaneous. I felt a faint dislike for it without quite knowing why.

"It isn't raining now," I pointed out.

He glanced out of the window. "No," he agreed, but he made no move to acknowledge the hint. Instead he reached across for the coffee pot. "May I?" he asked, but he was already refilling his cup.

I let the irritation drift away. The kitchen was warm now from the combined heat of the stove and the electric fire. I had nothing better to do.

He surprised me by saying unexpectedly, "I knew your husband very slightly a long time ago, Mrs. Grayson. We were at Winchester together."

"I never heard Robert mention you."

"He had no reason to remember me, I was younger. But Robert was so proficient at everything he tackled. I admired him tremendously. A sort of hero worship of an older boy."

I felt suddenly drawn to him. Any praise of Robert was a soothing balm to me, especially now. I had had no intention of discussing the present situation with him. If he had broached the subject I should have snubbed him. When he made no mention of it, perversely I wanted to talk about it.

"You know about Robert?"

He didn't pretend to misunderstand me.

"I know details connected with any claims for insurance. Also, I read the papers, Mrs. Grayson. But I don't necessarily believe all I read in the papers. I haven't seen Robert in years, of course. A man changes—but I don't think he changes all that much."

The feeling of warmth towards him grew. He was looking at me sympathetically through a little cloud of smoke.

"You're in a very difficult position, Mrs. Grayson," he added. "The best thing you can do is to persuade Robert to co-operate fully with the police. Going into hiding is no way to convince anyone of his innocence."

"I wish I could," I said quietly.

"He won't listen to you?"

I was silent. I couldn't explain to a comparative stranger, and he didn't press the question. Instead, after regarding me thought-fully for a short time, he began relating incidents from past school days, the admiration he had mentioned obvious. But I was only half listening and I think he realised that finally. His smile was a wry one as he got up to go, offering his thanks as he stood in the doorway buttoning his raincoat.

"I hope I have the pleasure some day of returning your hospi-tality, Mrs. Grayson," he said.

I murmured something in response, but I thought it extremely unlikely. He was curiously reluctant to leave, even to the point of retracing his steps up the path to say very earnestly through the already half closed door, "You know, if there was ever anything I could do to help either you or Robert. . ."

I couldn't imagine what but I thanked him politely.

"You won't forget, will you?" he insisted. "Look, I'll leave you my address."

He searched through his pockets until he found a scrap of paper, holding it against the door while he wrote awkwardly on it. I had no option but to take it when he had gone to the trouble but I couldn't even have remembered afterwards what I had done with the address he had given me. It didn't matter. There was no reason why I should ever need it.

My suspicions regarding the sore throat were justified; by early afternoon it was all too apparent that I was in for one of my occa-sional severe colds. I had no wish for it to develop fully while I was alone at Far End, but that was not the real reason why I returned to the flat. Even the importunities of reporters was pref-erable to the oppressive isolation of the cottage.

But all was quiet when I let myself in. Even Mrs. Lloyd had gone for the day in my absence. The flat was as bleakly lonely as Far End.

Robert had always cossetted my colds, fussing over me in anxious concern. There was no Robert now to switch on the electric blanket and bring me a hot drink after he had tucked me into bed. I heated the milk myself, sipping it slowly while the bed warmed, feeling forlornly alone as a fresh bout of shivering seized me.

I was fully abandoned to my misery when the phone rang and

the colonel barked my name sharply over the wire. He sounded relieved when I answered.

"Just been to Far End," he said. "Expected to find you there."

"I'm sorry," I said contritely. "I should have let you know I was leaving."

I explained about the cold and he was solicitous, concerned whether I had someone to look after me. Not even fully reassured when I told him Mrs. Lloyd would be in, in the morning.

"But you are alone now? You need a nurse. Or Mrs. Cooper has a sister, Rosanne. I am sure I could arrange something with her—"

"It's only a cold," I protested, but his solicitude for my welfare was comforting.

In the morning a huge spray of flowers was delivered at the flat. In the midst of white lilac and mauve iris was one single deep red rose. An odd gesture but rather a touching one, especially coming from someone as undemonstrative as the colonel. A reminder that I was not entirely alone and forsaken. There were no trimmings about the message on the card. It was signed simply "From Gregory"; and probably not even in his own handwriting. He would have phoned through from Renshaw for the delivery.

I had Mrs. Lloyd put the rose in a vase on its own by the bedside. She thought it was a rather peculiar mistake on the part of the florist and I didn't enlighten her. I looked at that rose quite a good deal as I lay sniffling in bed.

The colonel called to see me on the third day. He didn't stay long. In fact, he appeared to be thoroughly uncomfortable at being there at all and wouldn't even remove his overcoat. I couldn't remember his ever having been to the flat before. But when he cast a keen eye round I didn't think it was as much interest in new surroundings but rather to assure himself I wasn't enduring any discomforts.

He had phoned each day but he had made no hint at calling when he had rung that morning. I had been contemplating getting up for an hour or two in a little while; if I had known he was coming I would have made the effort earlier.

As it was, he stood towering over me as I lay in bed, looming even taller than usual from that disadvantage point. Looking also rather grim, but that could have been in an attempt to hide the fact that he was ill at ease at being in my bedroom.

I was surprisingly glad to see him. The hours had been long, lying there with nothing but my thoughts and speculations for company. All the pleasure was not due to the pile of new books he had brought with him.

As he deposited them on the bed I saw his eyes flicker briefly to the fading rose but he made no comment.

"Wasn't sure about your choice in literature," he said. "They're a mixed bag. You might find something amongst them."

He started to light a cigarette and then, recollecting he was in a sick room, put the case and lighter away again even though I insisted it was all right for him to smoke.

"Not stopping long, anyway," he said. He peered at me closely, adding in some dissatisfaction, "Ought to have had a doctor, you know. You look completely washed out."

"It was a bad chill," I admitted. "I'm much better now, though. I'm getting up presently."

"No sense in rushing things," the colonel grunted. "That woman of yours looking after you all right? Anything I can do for you?"

The idea of the colonel being useful in a sick room put too great a strain on credulity. On sudden impulse I asked, "Have you ever been married, Colonel?"

I was greatly daring, knowing his dislike of personal questions. He looked sharply at me, his eyes suddenly veiled so that it was impossible to tell whether he was displeased.

He answered shortly. "No, I haven't. And I thought we'd agreed it should be 'Gregory'." After a pause he said, more mildly, "Why do you ask?"

"Just curious."

"And now you're wondering if not, why not?"

"Well . . ." I let the word hang in the air invitingly.

"What reason would you like? That I don't like women? That I'm a confirmed bachelor? That I've been crossed in love?"

"None of those, if it's not true."

"Or would you like me to say it's because of an undying love for you?"

"You've only known me about three years."

"Meaning," he said drily, "that I'd been knocking around for a good many years before that?"

"I didn't say that," I protested.

"You'd be right. I suppose you could say the reason was that it just hasn't been convenient," he said rather ambiguously. "Too old now, anyway."

"How old are you?"

He grinned. "None of your business, young woman." The grin took the sting out of the words but he changed the subject with deliberation. Question time was over.

He didn't mention Robert. I could well imagine that he would be completely conversant of any new developments; the fact that he refrained from any reference could only mean that there had been none.

His bedside manner left much to be desired, but his abruptness was more invigorating than any soft-voiced sympathy. His departure was in keeping. He left after only a very short time with the final gruff exhortation, "Well, take care of yourself."

I thought it was the colonel once more when shortly after breakfast the following day Mrs. Lloyd told me I had a visitor. The colonel I would have been pleased to see but the name Derrick meant nothing to me and I shook my head.

"A reporter, probably."

"I don't think so, Mrs. Grayson. I told him you'd been ill but he stressed it was very important. He said he met you at the cottage a few days ago."

That piece of information settled it conclusively. "Tell him I'm still ill and in bed."

She was back in a very short time.

"He's very persistent, Mrs. Grayson. He wants to know what time would be convenient for him to call later."

"No time would be convenient," I said flatly.

Mrs. Lloyd hesitated. "He didn't say so outright—I may be wrong in having the impression it could be something to do with Mr. Grayson."

Her curiosity was as admirably controlled as ever. I believe she had been discretion itself with members of the press, whether from a sense of loyalty or merely because she had no real information to give them; and she had been exceedingly kind in her administrations to me during the past few days.

"They were at school together, that's all," I explained as I swung my legs out of bed with ill grace, slipping my arms into the dressing-gown Mrs. Lloyd held out for me. If Mr. Derrick wanted to reminisce once more about Robert I was in no mood to listen to him. I had a feeling that he could be the type who finds notoriety exciting, and highly desirable to be connected with it in any way, however remotely.

I noticed irately that he had made himself as thoroughly at home here as he had at Far End. The way he lounged in the chair, idly flipping over the pages of a magazine, showed confidence that he had not expected to be turned away unseen. The fact that he rose immediately I entered the room, crushing out the half smoked cigarette, in no way mollified me. His smile should have disarmed me, it was intended to, but failed miserably.

"Mr. Derrick—" I said.

The smile faded considerably, turning rueful now as he corrected me. "The name is Merrick. Perhaps you'd remember Dale better."

"Mr. Merrick," I began again, with cold deliberation.

"I'm sorry to hear you've been ill," he said. "Nothing serious, I hope?"

"A cold," I told him curtly.

Mrs. Lloyd cut into his unwanted and unsought expressions of commiseration by popping her head round the door.

"I'm just slipping out to do the shopping, Mrs. Grayson. I'll be back in time to make your morning coffee."

"If you're not," Dale Merrick said cheerfully, "I'll make it. I'm pretty handy around the house, aren't I, Mrs. Grayson?"

Mrs. Lloyd didn't know quite what to make of that. She looked uncertainly from one to the other of us before closing the door.

I decided unequivocal bluntness was the only answer to such presumptuousness.

"Your visit to Far End may have been necessary in pursuance of your line of business, Mr. Merrick, but your call here this morning is an intrusion."

He took it unblinkingly. "You don't like me, do you?"

"Not much." I wasn't accustomed to voicing such brutal candour. In an effort to soften the harshness I said, "It's not really that. I don't know you well enough to either like or dislike you. It's just that I feel you presume too much on what was only a very slight acquaintanceship many years ago with Robert."

"About Robert—"

"You hardly knew him. At a time like this, for you to attempt to claim some friendship with a man who I doubt even remembers you . . . Some people react strangely to—other peoples' misfortunes . . ."

He knew what I was trying to say. Just briefly a little flare of anger showed in the hazel eyes and then he said very quietly, "About Robert, Mrs. Grayson. Would it be likely that I saw him near this flat last night?"

Still shaky from the effects of the cold, my legs refused suddenly to support me any longer. I sank into the chair, weakened by the possibility that Robert could have been so close and I had been ignorant of the fact.

"He didn't come here," I said at last, breathlessly.

"I didn't expect he would. He'd never take that chance, in his right mind. The risk would be great enough in being anywhere near here." I looked uncomprehendingly at him and he explained with the faintest touch of irritation, "Surely you realise that the police will be keeping this flat under surveillance?" Still impatient for such obtuseness he added, "Robert will be aware of that, if you are not. He is a wanted man. The police will anticipate that sooner or later he might try to get in touch with you."

I shook my head. "He won't do that."

"Why are you so sure? If he needs help . . ." After a long careful scrutiny of my face he asked, "Who else would a man turn to, but his wife?" When I didn't answer he said very gently, "Even if it was only money he needed from her now?"

I glanced up, sharply suspicious. "How do you know . . ."

He looked vaguely uncomfortable for a moment before he said, "The papers hinted at the possibility—I wasn't sure. I'm afraid that question was rather in the nature of a feeler."

"Then you know now that Robert wouldn't come to me for help."

"I *could* be wrong about the man I saw at the corner of the square last night. It was dark and he was keeping in the shadows. I couldn't find anywhere to park the car or I'd have gone back to find out for certain if it was Robert. But I *am* pretty certain in my own mind, even though I couldn't swear positively to it. That's why I asked if it was likely he could be there."

"I don't think it would be Robert."

"Why? Because you know it couldn't have been? Because

you know where he is and that he couldn't possibly have been near here last night?"

"Why are you so concerned whether or not it was Robert?" I asked.

"I told you the other day that if there was anything I could do . . . I didn't sleep much last night, wondering about it. Because if Robert was hanging around in this area it could mean that he needs to contact you and dare not."

I was touched suddenly by his concern. "Robert could have rung up," I said.

"He would perhaps not risk your phone being tapped." I looked the blank stupefaction I felt and he explained, "Amongst other things, he is wanted in connexion with a case of murder. The man who was killed belonged to a branch of the police, which makes other police especially keen."

"There is no reason why Robert should want to see me." But I knew that even while I demurred my mind was clinging wildly to the hope that it could be so.

"Could he need money?"

That could be true. So far as I could tell, Robert had made no provision for a sudden departure by withdrawing any unaccountable money from the bank. Unless, as the colonel had suggested, he had accepted payments of money that I knew nothing about, it could be extremely likely that Robert was desperately in need of cash.

"But he would know he couldn't get it through me," I said.

"Well, certainly he can't lay his hands on it by walking into his bank. The police will have seen to that. Have you anything he could hope to convert quickly into ready cash—furs, jewellery."

"A few things—nothing especially of value. We don't even know that Robert is short of money."

"We don't," he agreed. "But it could be a very likely possibility. Money is essential for a man on the run. Without it, he is lost." The hazel eyes searched my face very thoughtfully, very thoroughly. "You didn't answer my question," he said quietly. "I asked you if it is feasible that it could have been Robert I saw last night?"

"How should I know?" I protested.

"You would know," he said, "if you knew for certain that either he is no longer in England or he is so far away from here that it would have been impossible for it to be him. If you know that, there is no point in wasting time and anxiety on wondering *why* he should have been in the square last night."

"I can't tell you where he is."

"I wish you merely to tell me whether I spent a sleepless night concerning myself for nothing that a man on the run should be so desperately in need of contacting perhaps the only person who could help him that he risked venturing on to dangerous ground. I don't expect you to trust me to the extent of giving me your full confidence. Although you could, you know. Hero-worship dies hard, especially when it is implanted at an impressionable age."

He disturbed me oddly. He seemed embarrassed himself by the depth of his sincerity. His eyes wavered briefly to meet mine before he sought refuge in occupying his hands with the business of lighting a cigarette. Belatedly, with a muttered apology, he extended the packet towards me and when I declined he pushed it back into his pocket again and sat smoking in silence.

I broke it finally, to say, "I don't know where Robert went, or where he is now."

He found that hard to believe. "But you could make a guess, if you needed to? You must have some idea . . ."

"Why would I? Robert, it seems," I said with a trace of bitterness, "had another side to his life that I knew nothing about. He knew—people . . ."

Dale Merrick put it more bluntly than I had been able to. "You don't know who the woman is? Surely you have a vague suspicion in the back of your mind, even if you were entirely unsuspecting before Robert left you?" He still looked sceptical. "It wouldn't have been very difficult for you to find out. Haven't you tried to trace him through her?"

"How would I do that?" I wanted to know.

"No matter how circumspect, no one can carry on an illicit affair for any length of time without there sooner or later being rumours. Even if you were unaware of them yourself, other people will have heard them. Your friends . . ."

"Why should I have tried to find Robert? He left me—he doesn't need me—"

"Perhaps he didn't—at first. But circumstances can change. You've been indisposed these last few days, confined to the flat, but he wouldn't be aware of that. How do you know he hasn't been in the square on previous nights in the hope of contacting you either as you left or came back?" He drew deeply on his cigarette, letting the smoke escape slowly as he spoke. "In my line of business I meet a lot of people. Without going too closely into details of why, sometimes they can be grateful. It *is* possible that if Robert wanted to get out of the country I might be able to arrange something. It would cost money, of course . . ."

"Hero-worship can prove expensive, is that it?" I asked contemptuously, but I was conscious of a little pang of disappointment.

For a moment he looked disconcerted. Where I could have expected a bluster of anger, only a flicker of annoyance crossed his face; and even that, I think, was directed inwardly at himself rather than at me.

In a perfectly controlled voice he said, "It's understandable that you are suspicious of everyone and their motives; and it seems I don't express myself very well. But are my motives so important, after all, if you need help for Robert badly enough? The main thing is that you don't forget it has been offered."

I was ashamed of my outburst. When I tried to offer an apology he brushed it almost brusquely aside. He left soon after, his persistence in offering to make coffee frustrated when he heard the obvious sounds from the kitchen of Mrs. Lloyd's return.

6

Long after he had gone I stood by the window, gazing out into the dull greyness of the morning. Searching the square hopefully and yet with trepidation for a sight of that so familiar figure. He would not be there, of course; in daylight, it would be madness. But had he been there, hiding in the darkness, so close and yet so unattainable? Wanting to see me?

Hope longed to flare high but I wouldn't allow it to. If Robert sought me out it could be for nothing other than any assistance I could give him.

Was it his passport he needed? He would surely be aware that he had no chance of getting out of the country now under his own identity.

Had he nowhere to seek refuge, because the police had already unearthed his hiding place? Was he, literally, on the run; a fugitive without any place of concealment where he could feel safe, as equally unable to trust previous friends as he was to risk staying in any hotel?

Or was it money, as Dale Merrick had suggested, that he was desperate for? He would know I had no authority to draw from the bank, but was he counting on what could perhaps be raised from the sale of personal possessions? I made a swift mental calculation of such assets—there seemed so few items of real value. Would they fetch much at a quick, forced sale?

Robert could have remembered that Far End was mine to dispose of as I wished. He would realise that it would take time but if there was no other means . . .

Except the colonel. He had offered to lend me money.

I suppressed the temptation to ring him up right away. It was useless until I knew how big a loan to ask for. I didn't know whether it was money Robert needed.

I didn't even know whether it was Robert who had been at the corner of the square last night.

Later in the afternoon I told Mrs. Lloyd she could go; there was no point in her staying to cook an evening meal I didn't want.

"I'll make something for myself," I assured her when she demurred, but I knew I shouldn't bother. Repressed excitement had prevented me from doing justice to the lunch she had prepared and disbelief for the assurance showed plainly in her face.

If my continued presence at the window during the day had aroused her curiosity she hid it beneath dissatisfaction over my neglect of myself.

"You ought to go back to bed for an hour or two," she declared. "You'll catch more cold standing there."

Sooner or later, I should have to make the decision about how much longer I could afford to keep Mrs. Lloyd.

I took her advice and did lie down for an hour, but I couldn't rest. The window pulled me irresistibly even though grey daylight still lingered. When it faded at last I didn't switch on the lights. I could see better with the room in darkness behind me.

Search as I would, I could see no one who appeared to be keeping a watch on the flat. Even during the day I had observed no especial person too casually loitering or unobtrusively on guard behind the screen of a newspaper. No one had sought to rest overlong on the seats, pretending an indifference to the raw coldness of the weather. The exchange of cars parking in the square had continued intermittently during the day, but if there had been anything significant about any one of them, my inexperienced eyes had failed to detect it. The scene had been ordinary, everyday, with nothing untoward to focus suspicion.

Now, with darkness enveloping the square, there was even less. The bare branches swaying in the wind cast moving shadows which could be deceptive; but my eyes were sufficiently attuned to define shadow from fanciful belief. The statue in the centre of the square threw a deep pool of darkness but nothing moved in it. Occasionally the telephone kiosk on the far side would be occupied but without exception the user of it hurried away into the night, and if anyone waited in the deep wells of blackness of area steps, their patience and fortitude must have been inexhaustible.

So far as I could see, no one spared even so much as a glance in the direction of the flat. I began to think that Dale Merrick had been over-cautious in his estimation of police circumspection. But if I failed to observe anyone keeping watch I also failed to detect any other figure keeping vigil.

It had been futile to hope. Only selfish thoughtlessness born of desperate longing to see him had made me cling fervently to the prayer that he would be there. Better for Robert that there had been no need for him to endanger his liberty by attempting to approach me. I should be glad for his sake that my hopes had been in vain.

I tried to be and failed dismally; so sunk in abysmal despondency that I studied the shadow at the far corner of the square with unnoting eyes for a long time before I realised with a heart-stopping spurt of excitement that this was no shadow. It had substance.

Even then I delayed, hardly daring to breathe; straining frantically out in an effort to penetrate the darkness and seek some semblance of form from that indeterminate shape. A car was approaching, headlights dimmed, cruising slowly past the flat. I offered up a silent supplication that it would continue until the fringe of suffused light brushed that corner, willing it on when it halted almost below me to assess a parking space that was obviously too small; watching with relief as it gathered speed again on its way out of the square.

It didn't expose what I hoped; but that in itself was proof. Whatever had been there had not dissolved in the car lights, it had moved back to escape from the too revealing glow. There could be no doubt; some person, some man, was waiting at the corner.

Common-sense tried to assert itself. It could be anyone.

But I knew differently. I knew it was Robert.

I must be careful. In all those long hours I had seen no one who seemed remotely interested in the flat, but I must subdue the impetuous desire to rush headlong to him. For Robert's sake I must be cautious; everything must appear normal. To run out on a cold night without a coat would be to invite attention.

I seized the first that came to hand, flinging it on with feverish fingers which fumbled impotently with the buttons. Robert would be gone, while I wasted precious time.

For a few desperate moments as I closed the outer door behind me I thought that he had. The lights in the entrance had spoiled my ability to probe the darkness of the shadows; and then, as they attuned once more, my heart leapt. He was still there.

I forced myself to walk casually; but not too casually. It was not a night on which to enjoy a leisurely stroll.

What would Robert do? Would he risk acknowledging me there, or would he let me walk past and then follow. And where should I lead him, where we could talk undetected? My mind wouldn't concentrate; it was a conflict of sheer happiness at the contemplation of such close proximity and panic for the risk Robert could be taking.

The vague outline stirred as I drew nearer. He had seen me. Had he recognised me? Surely my walk and contour were as familiar to him as his were to me, but I paused under a street lamp, lifting my face to the light so that there should be no possibility of mistake.

The last twenty yards stretched interminably. I could think of nothing now—not the risk Robert was incurring in being here, not of the ghastly charges of which he was suspected, not of the fact that he had left me for someone else—I could think of nothing but the overwhelming longing to be near him once more, to hear him speak, to be able to reach out a hand and touch him. My whole world was centred on that coming reunion to the exclusion of all else.

I would have thought it impossible to hear anything above the tumultuous thumping of my heart, and at first it seemed to be only that I heard. It was the startled movement of the man in the shadow that alerted me into realising that the heavy pounding was rapidly overhauling me from behind.

It all happened so quickly, too quickly, thrusting me so brutally back into reality my mind couldn't keep pace with it. One moment there was the delirious prospect of being reunited, the next, the brittle shell of rapture was shattered into fragments. I was brushed brusquely aside as the pounding footsteps passed me, knocking me off balance. I hardly saw Robert go. There was a blurred awareness of someone disappearing round the corner before the man who had pushed me aside in his pursuit blocked my view, and then both were gone and the pavement yawned emptily in front of me.

I would have stopped Robert if I could. The disappointment was so intense that there was only the sense of loss, overriding all else. I think that for one or two agonising seconds of despair I wanted him to be caught, to be brought back to me under any conditions.

Then reason asserted itself and frantic anxiety came crowding in, filling me with apprehension that made me set off running wildly to the corner of the square. The street was busy, full of a bustling activity which confused me after the calm backwater of the square, but I was in time to see a car farther down the road swinging furiously out from the kerb with a sublime indifference to traffic. I couldn't see the driver, the car was too quickly submerged into the moving stream, but I watched the man who had given chase slow to a halt now that he had realised the futility of running. He stood briefly in an attitude of frustrated indecision before darting into the road in an attempt to flag down a passing taxi. I didn't wait to see if he was successful. The first car was already lost to sight, I was confident there was no danger of it being overtaken.

I turned away, sick with despair and disappointment.

I didn't risk using the flat telephone. The precaution seemed absurd, but if Dale Merrick had been right about the flat being under surveillance he could be right about that, too. He could also be right that Robert's infidelity had been discussed behind my back.

Robert was not an impulsive man. To reach a point of abandoning his entire way of life, his affair with some other woman must have been of some duration. Over a period of time, someone must have seen them together and known who she was.

I wondered before how many of my friends I should have to humiliate myself in seeking such confirmation. I squirmed inwardly, but only briefly, shrugging the distaste aside. The humiliation didn't matter. If Robert needed me and was unable to get in touch with me, then I had to find some means of contacting him.

The telephone kiosk was occupied. I had to stand shivering in the cold until it was finally vacated, grateful of the shelter from the biting wind once I was inside, but the chattering of my teeth owed even more to overwrought nerves than to the cold.

Henry answered the phone. He sounded stiff, a little guarded; as uncomfortable as one can be when unexpectedly confronted with a situation in which it is difficult to find the appropriate words of condolence.

"Oh—Rosanne," he said. "How are you?"

Margot had no such inhibitions. I was a little irritated. It had been Henry I wanted to question, it seeming logical that Robert's closest friend would be the one likely to be knowledgeable about Robert's most intimate affairs, but at the mention of my name I had heard an excited exclamation from the background followed by a slight altercation and scuffling sounds as the receiver changed hands.

"Rosanne, for heaven's sake what have you been doing with yourself these past few days. We've been worried out of our minds about you."

Her voice held excitement, reproach, deep concern. She was as troubled for me as I would have been for her had it been Henry. If there was also curiosity that was understandable.

I stifled the impatience. It was useless to protest, anyway; Henry had probably been relieved to relinquish an embarrassing conversation to her.

"Where are you now?" she was asking.

"I'm at the flat," I said, which was near enough to the truth.

"When I called there Mrs. Lloyd told me you were at Far End. I've tried several times to ring you there during these past few days and couldn't get an answer. I'd have come down to stay with you but I couldn't leave the children."

"I came back the following day . . ."

"Well," she said, "you can't stay at the flat by yourself. Throw some things into a suitcase and come straight round to us."

"I can't do that. Margot, I have to find Robert—"

"You don't know where he is?" She sounded a little incredulous.

"I thought you might know—"

"Darling, we know nothing except what we have read in the

papers. We were stunned—it's all too fantastic. Robert . . .
What's it all about, Rosanne?"

She was as bewildered as I had been myself.

"I thought you might have some idea who Robert is with," I
said.

"Who he is with . . . ?"

"Hadn't you any suspicion he was interested in someone else?
Men talk among themselves, didn't he ever mention anyone to
Henry? Haven't there been any rumours?"

"No, of course not. You're mistaken, surely . . . ?"

"Robert left me nearly four weeks ago. He told me himself. He
wouldn't have given the most cruel reason he could think of if it
hadn't been true." She was silent so long I called sharply,
"Margot?"

"I'm here." Her voice came heavily over the wire. "Robert
seemed always so devoted to you, Rosanne. So . . . We didn't
believe it even when the police questioned us about it."

"The police?" I said, startled.

"I think they were trying to get a lead on Robert's whereabouts.
They've been asking round . . . We told them it was absurd . . ."

"You hadn't heard anything, not even the vaguest rumour?" I
was disappointed.

"Not a word," she assured me earnestly. "I wouldn't have believed it if I had."

"Would anyone else be likely to know?"

"I don't think so." She sounded hesitant, half-apologetic. "In
fact," she added with a little rush, "I'm sure. You know how it is,
Rosanne. We've all been so anxious, we've been frantically ringing one another when no one could get in touch with you. It
wasn't for idle gossip—we were worried, trying to find out if anyone else knew any further news. I'm certain someone would
have mentioned a suspicion if they had had one."

"I was sure someone must know . . . He can't have been *so*
discreet. Not all the time . . ."

"Is it so terribly important? After all . . ."

"I *must* find Robert. I don't know any other way to trace him."
I sounded as dejected as I felt. I ought to have known it would
not be as simple as that.

The silence from the other end continued for so long I thought
she had hung up. I got no response to speaking her name and

was on the point of replacing the receiver when she said, "Rosanne?" and realised that she had had her hand over the mouthpiece. I could still hear Henry's voice arguing in the background.

"Look, Rosanne," Margot said, and she was ignoring Henry's protests, "there's probably nothing to this. Henry is sure there isn't, he's angry with me for mentioning it to you. In fact, he never even gave it a second thought until we were talking after the police questioned us. But a few months ago he ran into Robert unexpectedly. Henry had never been to the place before, it wasn't one of their usual haunts. A business associate, Rogers, took him there. Robert was at the bar when they went in, sitting next to a very glamorous female. Honestly, Henry wasn't even sure they were together, he never saw them speak to each other and Robert left soon after on his own. What just seemed a little—curious—about it was that a week or two after he saw Robert coming out of St. James's Park and a few minutes later that same woman followed him out. She went in the opposite direction and there was no reason to connect her presence there with Robert. Henry wouldn't have remembered it was the same woman if she hadn't been so strikingly beautiful, and he hadn't given it a thought since . . ."

"Does Henry know who she is?"

"Rogers knew her name. He mentioned it at the time but Henry had no occasion to remember it."

"Could you find out from him?"

"I suppose so." She sounded reluctant. "Rosanne, Henry's sure it was the sheerest coincidence. Perhaps he's right, I ought not to have mentioned it . . ."

I hadn't anything else to go on; I had to follow even the most slender lead, improbable though it seemed.

"Please get Henry to ask him, Margot. Please! Even if there's nothing in it . . ."

I heard her speaking to Henry, overcoming his unwillingness.

"I'll ring you back later," she said finally. "But I wish you'd come to us. You shouldn't be alone—"

I cut her short. "I'll ring you," I said. "In half an hour."

Elbury Court was a small block of exclusive luxury flats, the ample spaciousness of the forecourt helping to proclaim its expensiveness. Not for the occupiers and guests of such costly residences the frustration of having difficulty in parking their cars. There were several standing there but it was uncrowded, the Mini looking rather forlorn in the midst of the opulent Rolls and Bentleys and sleek convertibles.

The whole place whispered discreetly of seclusive affluence, of a hushed reverence for the privilege of privacy, of muted bells and thick pile carpets to deaden the intrusion of sound.

I sat gazing up at the façade of the building, at the private balconies overlooking the park; wondering which apartment it was. Wondering, too, whether this place was familiar to Robert. Whether he had known from long usage which bell to ring; or perhaps Robert had had no need of such formality; one of these flats could be as conversant to him as his own home.

He could be here now, even at this moment watching me from behind the concealment of draped curtains. But although I searched each window carefully there was nothing to see. The only sign of any occupation at all was a large Siamese cat sunning itself at a ground floor window.

I shivered getting out of the car. The cold was returning. A splitting headache and aching limbs had made staying in bed a very tempting proposition but I hadn't succumbed. It had been too late last night to do anything about the information Margot had given me but I couldn't wait another day.

The heat met me as I entered the building, stilling the shivering to some extent but not entirely. It was not all due to the cold. My heart was beating heavily as I consulted the name plates and rang the bell of the ground floor flat. I thought it could be the one in which I had seen the Siamese cat but I wasn't sure.

I didn't hear the bell ring; in that place I hadn't expected to, but the door was opened almost immediately by a very pert maid in an impeccable coffee coloured silk uniform. From the wisp of a cream bow on her head down to the incredibly high heeled shoes she looked indisputably French. She was not. Disguise it as she would, her voice was cockney.

The vestibule in which she left me had been designed for the gracious welcoming of guests. My feet sank softly into a carpet of palest blue which it seemed sacrilege to walk on. The chairs were gilt, delicately carved, the silk covered seats of a deeper shade of blue. An arrangement of spring flowers had a delightful artistry. Done by a professional florist, perhaps, but somehow I didn't think so. There was a very personal touch in the way they were displayed.

The French cockney maid came back presently to ask me to wait, before disappearing through another doorway with a quick little flirt of her rustling silk dress. I went on sitting there, feeling apprehensive and more than a little foolish; not helped any by the unprepossessing glimpses I kept catching of the pinched, anxious face and the dark, hollow-ringed eyes reflected in the mirror.

It was a long time before there was any sign of movement. I caught only a glimpse of spaciousness, of pale, softly blended tones, before the door closed behind her, and then she herself claimed my full attention.

She was essentially feminine; the sway of her walk would have been a liquid fluency even without the emphasis of the gently swirling white negligee, and she brought with her a soft lingering fragrance of expensive French perfume.

As Henry had said, she was strikingly beautiful. She was dark, *petite*, her body perfectly moulded. The bone formation of her face was exquisite, the skin translucent and flawless. These alone, without the lovely, darkly luminous eyes and the mobile, softly curved mouth, would have ensured remembrance. The combination was unforgettable.

I felt inelegant and drab, conscious of staring rudely as I got awkwardly to my feet. She was probably accustomed to the effect she created; she waited with a serene patience and when I didn't speak she said, "I'm sorry to have kept you waiting. I am not an early riser."

"I'm Rosanne Grayson," I said at last.

"So my maid told me."

Her speech was rather precise, as though she enunciated each word with great care, but her voice was beautifully modulated. If the name had meant anything to her, she had had time to recover from any surprise before she came out. The tone of it told me nothing.

"You are Mrs. Julya Logan?"

She inclined her head in acknowledgement; a graceful, regal movement.

It was difficult, more difficult than I had imagined. I felt even more incredibly foolish now.

"I'm looking for my husband—Robert," I blurted out.

"Yes?" The word was a question, softly asked.

"You don't know him?"

"Should I do?" She seemed to search her memory before shaking her head and then, as though something touched a chord of remembrance she asked, "Grayson? Surely I have heard that name recently?"

"You probably read it in the newspapers," I said quietly.

The lovely dark eyes studied me thoughtfully. "I am sorry. I can't help you."

She was moving to the door, obviously terminating the visit, when she asked, "What made you think I should know your husband?"

"You once sat next to him—in a bar."

It sounded ridiculous. A flicker of something that could have been annoyance, surprise, amusement—I was not sure which—crossed her face. She was not a woman to make visible play of her emotions.

But she sounded faintly amused. "My dear, in the course of my life I have sat next to a great number of men in a great number of cocktail bars. That doesn't necessarily mean I have known every man on the next stool to mine."

She was cool, poised, sophisticated, but I suspected there was a hard little core beneath that breathtakingly lovely exterior. Whatever she owned now in worldly possessions, I felt she had not easily acquired them. There is something about those born to a natural affluence—something indefinable, but very positive. Whatever it was, Julya Logan didn't have it.

"You were seen later—in St. James's Park," I said.

"That is very probable. Quite often I stroll through one or other of the parks. But not with your husband."

"But Robert was there, too—at the same time."

"And how many other people, I wonder?" she scoffed gently. "The parks are very busy on any fine day. It may even be possible I spoke to him, I wouldn't know. I can't be expected to remember everyone with whom I have passed the time of day."

"No," I agreed miserably.

I started to apologise for troubling her. My head was aching intolerably, I wasn't quite sure whether what I said was adequate. It didn't really matter. She was ushering me towards the door, pausing before opening it to say, "I'm curious as to how you knew my name?"

I tried to explain, not making a very good job of that, either, and finally she cut me off, gently but with finality. "You must forgive me. I have an appointment shortly at my hairdressers."

As I drove off I saw her at the window, stroking the Siamese cat, but she wasn't watching me. The lovely dark eyes were idly scanning the road. I felt somehow that she had no interest in my movements; she had already forgotten the intrusion.

Back at my own flat I crawled exhausted into bed and abandoned myself once more to the misery of my cold.

7

The sunshine enticed me out on the fifth day. After so many long hours confined indoors I would have gone had it been raining, but it was a beautiful morning. The first leaves were unfurling on the trees and the whole square seemed awash with the fresh spring sunshine.

I hadn't anywhere particular to go; but even idle sauntering through the streets distracted my mind to some slight extent from the problem which had faced me during the past days. I had kept watch from the window each evening although I had guessed it was useless. Robert wouldn't take such a risk again after the near disastrous outcome of the other night. I had hoped he would find some other means of communicating with me, if his need to do so was so urgent he had risked arrest by waiting so near his home, but the days had dragged by uneventfully.

I wasn't sure whether my most pressing need was to give Robert any assistance he might require or the overwhelming desire just to see him and learn the answers to all the questions which tormented me so as to how and why things had gone wrong between us. At the back of my mind I couldn't stop entertaining the possibility that his presence in the square could mean not that he was seeking any doubtful aid I could offer, but because he was regretting the choice he had made. It was wishful thinking, but I couldn't dismiss the thought. I dwelt in a realm of speculation in which Robert had foolishly allowed himself to be caught up in circumstances that had gone beyond his control. He could not return openly to me without risking arrest, but I wanted so much just to see him again that even if the outcome of the meeting proved the position between us to be no different, it seemed impossible such intense longing should not be conveyed to him and even reciprocated. We had been so close, he knew my every thought and reaction so intimately, he could not be unaware of the lost bewilderment into which he had so precipitately plunged me.

I was sunk in a foolish daydream in which I had persuaded Robert that the imperative need was to clear himself of the suspicion of murder by presenting the police with a suitable alibi. If by giving himself up he were proved guilty of the charges of subversive activities, provided the information he had passed was not of too serious a nature, the sentence could be light. Two years? Five? More than that? I didn't know; but even that was better than spending the rest of his life a fugitive from justice. Once he had served his sentence he could start again, and I was so deeply lost in a delirious flight of fancy in which I was waiting for Robert, knowing he wanted to start afresh with me—so deeply lost that I didn't even at first recognise the man who had spoken, jolting me out of my fantasy, until he spoke again.

"Hello, Mrs. Grayson. Remember me?"

There was the same ruefulness in his voice which had marked my lack of remembrance on the previous occasion, as though his pride was a little hurt that he had made only so slight an impression on my memory. I looked at him vaguely, feeling resentful at the rude interruption of my fanciful reverie.

If I showed it, he didn't allow it to deter him.

"How is the cold?" he wanted to know, and chatted on, friendly, at ease, about the change in the weather; compelling me to respond to his congeniality.

I had hoped to pass on after that exchange of commonplace courtesies, but when I tried to edge past him he moved too, barring my way. It was done unobtrusively, so that without being deliberately churlish I couldn't persist. It was also intentional, as his question proved.

"Any further developments?" he asked.

I forced back the rising annoyance. The hazel eyes searching my face were serious, troubled; his concern was undoubtedly genuine, but I wished he would interest himself less in my affairs.

I shook my head, still seeking to terminate the meeting, with Dale Merrick as doggedly determined not to allow me. "Did you find out; was it Robert I saw near your flat the other night?"

I barely hesitated. There seemed no harm in telling him. The police had given chase, they knew that Robert had been there; and, after all, it had been Dale Merrick who had first drawn my attention to the fact. If he had been so disposed he could have easily alerted the police without mentioning Robert's presence there to me.

"He was there the following night," I admitted, and he nodded his head in a movement of satisfaction.

"I was sure I wasn't mistaken. Did you manage to talk to him?"

"Someone was watching—Robert ran away before I had the chance." I relived briefly those moments of bitter disappointment and, watching me closely, he said in commiseration, "Oh, too bad. But at least Robert wasn't caught. It was a hell of a risk he was taking, I wonder why it was so necessary to him."

That was the question that had plagued me incessantly during the past days.

I was on the point of excusing myself and leaving him when he said on a sudden inspiration, "I was just going for some lunch when I met you. How about joining me, Mrs. Grayson?"

"Mrs. Lloyd is expecting me back for it." I gave the first excuse that came into my head. It wasn't true. I had told Mrs. Lloyd that if I wanted a meal when I returned I'd make something for myself.

"You can give her a ring. Do come. Please! I hate eating by myself. There's a good place just across the street."

It was the last thing I had intended doing. I didn't know why I allowed him to persuade me. Perhaps it was that too vivid reminder of the loneliness of solitary eating; but somehow I didn't think it was entirely that. This morning he had not treated me to the too-disarming smile. There was something about that smile that had roused a faint aversion, and I liked him the better for the omission.

Whatever the reason, when the hand under my arm urged me gently towards the crossing I went unresistingly. He had guessed the excuse I had given was untrue; he gave me no reminder about the call to Mrs. Lloyd.

The restaurant was an expensive one. That was manifest without even a glance at the prices, and I felt a twinge of uneasiness in wondering if he had been aware of that when he chose the place. But Dale Merrick went in with the assurance of a man accustomed to a sublime disregard for such mundane considerations. Insurance investigating obviously was more remunerative than I would have thought.

He had also, I found surprisingly for such a completely unremarkable man, that inherent aptitude which unconsciously expects, and so receives, a special and whole-hearted attention from those who serve him. I would have supposed that if we got a table at all in that crowded restaurant it would have been only after a delay and then badly sited, but with no trouble whatever we were installed in one of the best positions. Clearly, Dale Merrick had expected nothing less. He was solicitous in his inquiries whether it was satisfactory to me. Equally clearly, had it not been, he would have anticipated no difficulty in obtaining something more suitable.

In the ordering of the meal he was quietly desirous of gratifying my tastes without displaying a too ostentatious fuss, consulting me where necessary but otherwise calmly taking the initiative. I was discovering that he had that rather rare ability of being able to make a woman feel preciously shielded and secure in his presence. Robert had had it, too, but I was surprised to find it in Dale Merrick. I had thought him a brash, too self-confident man who, when he sought to please, would do so in a way to render the recipient of his attentions uncomfortable.

I wasn't sure whether it was because I was the helpless type of female who roused in men the instinctive desire to protect, or whether I ought to mentally revise my first impressions of him.

As we ate, the subject of Robert was avoided. Dale Merrick asked me a little about myself, touching mainly on my earlier life before my marriage, but mostly he talked about himself. Not boringly; I felt he did it to divert my mind and although I was not particularly interested in him he succeeded in holding my attention.

He didn't say so outright, he didn't have to, but when he mentioned his mother and older brother it was obvious that both held a very warm place in his affections. He seemed to withdraw inwardly into some quiet sphere of his mind, untouched by his surroundings; his voice instinctively softened, holding a note of wistfulness. When I asked idly if the brother had been at Winchester, too, he looked at me blankly.

"The same school tie generally runs in a family," I pointed out.

"We're only half brothers. My mother married twice. Dinly followed in his own father's footsteps."

"Dinly . . . ?" It seemed an odd name.

"DINLY." He spelled it out. "From an oft repeated phrase of my mother's—Dale Is Not Like You. I always saw it in capital letters." Seeing me still puzzled he explained, "I never quite measured up to her ideal as a son. She was so full of life herself, I was always too quiet, too studious—too unexciting. Not like Dinly."

It was more revealing than he intended it to be. He had spoken casually, making light of the explanation; I was sure he had not meant me to detect the hurt that so deeply scored his mind. I sat silent, disturbed by that insight into a boy's awareness of his own inadequacies.

After a little pause I said, "She *was* . . . ?"

For a moment he didn't quite catch the implication. Then "She's still living, if you can call it that. Recently, after a bad shock, she had a severe stroke. We don't know yet just how much she will recover from it."

I was murmuring suitable words of regret when I glanced up and saw the colonel walking into the restaurant. He caught sight of me in the same moment and raised a hand in quick acknowledgement, waving the head waiter aside to thread his way towards our table. Briefly, he seemed to check when he noticed I was not alone and his brow knit in a tight frown. I felt that if he could have retreated without being too obvious he would have done so.

He stood looking down at me, still frowning slightly, and his greeting was curtly characteristic.

"Cold better?" When I said that it was he added in some dissatisfaction, "Hope you haven't ventured out too soon again. These spring days can be deceptive."

His nod of greeting had not included the man I was with. He was ignoring him. I had the impression that Dale, too, was not over pleased but he stood passively, politely.

The colonel accepted the introductions stiffly, satisfying himself with a curt gesture of the head when Dale would have extended a hand, and then studiously ignoring him once more.

He sounded disgruntled. "Hadn't expected you to be out. I called at the flat."

"Oh, I'm sorry. I didn't know . . ."

"Course not." He softened a little. "How could you? Came up unexpectedly. Thought we might have lunch together."

"Will you join us, Colonel?" Dale asked.

I thought it was rather nice of him in the circumstances, but the colonel's response to the invitation was ungracious.

"No point in it, you're nearly finished. And the name's Haldane, if you don't mind," he added curtly.

Dale looked slightly bewildered, as well he might.

"Shall I be seeing you, Rosanne?" the colonel asked.

"I suppose so." Dismay for such unwarranted rudeness made me answer stiltedly. The colonel realised it. Belatedly, but on a more genial note he said, "Kind of you to ask me, Merrick. Won't butt in now at this stage of your meal." To me he added, "Have dinner some evening with me, Rosanne? I'm in town for a few days. Or perhaps if you're coming down to Renshaw?"

"I'll let you know."

"Do." Turning away, he hesitated before he said with gruff sincerity, "Glad to see you out and about again."

I noticed he didn't go to another table. Evidently he had changed his mind about eating there because he marched briskly out without a backward glance.

"What was that about?" Dale wanted to know as he sat down.

I took my eyes from the colonel's retreating back.

"What? Oh, the name . . ." I explained, adding, "Usually he doesn't mind. I can't imagine why he was so rude about it."

"Can't you?" His expression was quizzical. "I have a feeling that your colonel took a very strong aversion to me."

"How could he possibly, in those few minutes? Why on earth should he?"

"You tell me," Dale Merrick suggested.

To my utter chagrin I found myself blushing furiously. The hot colour rose in a flood, burning my face, and the glint of amusement in the hazel eyes did nothing to help it to subside. I sat in such complete confusion that finally he took pity on me, signalling to the waiter that we were ready for coffee. By the time it came I had regained my composure although I still wouldn't meet his gaze.

"About Robert," he said as he held a light for my cigarette. "What do you do now?"

"There isn't anything I can do." I was grateful for the change in subject, any subject, that would remove me from the embarrassment of the previous one.

"You're waiting for Robert to make the next move? What if there isn't any move he can make without endangering his liberty?"

When I made a small movement of my shoulders he said, "I should have thought someone in the circle of your friends could have come up with some idea . . . ?"

He was quietly insistent, urging me gently into confidence, but that line of inquiry had proved abortive. There was no point in mentioning it.

"If anyone had known anything they would have told the police."

He guessed it was a prevarication. A faint expression of something that could have been disappointment or dissatisfaction flickered across his face but he answered cheerfully, "You're probably right."

He spooned sugar into his coffee, stirring it with slow thoroughness until it dissolved; adding a little more after he had tasted it before asking with the same bright cheerfulness, "By the way, who were you visiting in Elbury Court the other day? The beautiful Lya Logasi?"

8

The room was whirling round me in a wild kaleidoscope of too vivid colours. When I closed my eyes they were still there, swirling in mad confusion. I tried to pinpoint my mind, to concentrate on the bright red of the woman's suit at the next table. I thought I could even distinguish the sound of her laugh.

From a long way off, from the distance of a long period of time, from more than ten years ago, I heard Dale Merrick saying, in some anxiety, "Rosanne? Are you all right?"

And then the room steadied and the red suit came into focus, a separate entity from the other colours. It could only have lasted a moment; the woman in red had been reaching for a wineglass, it had barely yet reached her mouth. Even Dale's anxiety had been only a first uncertain awareness of something amiss.

"You're rather pale," he said.

I tried to smile. As smiles went, it was probably a fiasco, but I did my best.

"It's so warm in here," I murmured.

He seemed reassured, smiling in return, so perhaps my effort had been better than I thought. I watched him as he drank his coffee.

He could not possibly have mentioned that name so casually to me. Not that name! Not to me!

But he had. His face was bland, the hazel eyes innocent of all ulterior motive. He couldn't possibly know what that name meant to me and still return my gaze so serenely.

My cigarette was smouldering in the ashtray. I picked it up but my fingers shook so much it was impossible to hold it steady; to conceal the trembling I started to smoke with quick nervous puffs, which was equally as revealing. I had hoped he would follow up on the question he had asked. When he showed no inclination to do so, I had to myself, but the effort to speak naturally was almost beyond me.

"Why did you ask if I had been visiting . . . ?" I couldn't force myself to pronounce the name. I hoped he would put it down to the foreignness of it. He seemed to do; he supplied it offhandedly.

"Lya Logasi? Oh, just idle speculation. I saw you coming out of the building and she is the only person I know who lives there. Was it the glamorous Lya?"

I shook my head. "No."

He seemed to expect me to add something to that; when I didn't he asked with blunt forthrightness, "Who, then?"

I told him and he nodded in agreement. "She calls herself Julya Logan now, but she was born Lya Logasi. Didn't you know?"

I said "No . . ." It was not so much an answer as a piteous appeal against acceptance of the truth.

"She changed her name; altered it slightly, anyway, to sound more English."

"But she's—" I caught myself in time. Even with a mind raging in devastating confusion, I remembered caution. For Robert's sake I must be careful. Dale Merrick had been friendly, helpful, but I wouldn't admit anyone into my trust. Not over this!

I knew it was not just a case of trust. It was that I couldn't bear to accept the possibility even to myself. He could be wrong. He *had* to be wrong!

"How do you know this?"

"Oh, a matter of insurance, some time ago." He asked casually as he crushed out his cigarette, "Why, is it important?"

I moved my head numbly. Important!

"More coffee?" he questioned.

I made a pretence of looking at my watch. "I'm sorry, I must go . . ."

He checked in the act of refilling his own cup and put the coffee pot down with a little gesture of resignation.

"What was your business with Julya Logan, anyway?"

His eyes appeared suddenly too keenly probing. I tried to collect my scattered wits, saying the first thing that came into my head.

"Oh—committee work."

"Julya Logan?" He looked his frank disbelief.

He made no demur when I started fumbling for my gloves and handbag but his face was bleak, his voice cool as he said, "My car is some distance away. If you're in a hurry I'll get you a taxi."

He sounded still remote as he handed me into it and asked, "What address?"

His eyebrows rose in faint surprise when I gave him my own but he relayed it to the driver. He must have been wondering at the abrupt termination of the lunch, even feeling resentment. Too late, as he slammed the door and stood back, I remembered that I hadn't thanked him for it but the taxi was already drawing away. I don't think I even returned the action of a hand lifted in farewell.

I waited until the taxi was out of his sight round the first turning before redirecting the driver.

The pert French cockney maid answered the door. She invited me to sit down in the elegant entrance hall before disappearing through one of the several doors that opened from it, but I was too nervously on edge.

Dale Merrick was wrong. Or it was coincidence. It had to be one or the other, it couldn't possibly be anything else. I would have guessed when I came here previously; some instinct would have told me, surely.

My heart thumped deafeningly when the door opened but it was the maid again; not holding the door open for me to pass inside but closing it behind her.

"Madame is sorry, Mrs. Grayson," she said, "but there is nothing she can do to help you. She has asked me to tell you that she would be obliged if you would not call again."

She was well trained. Her face betrayed nothing of curiosity regarding an ultimatum that was curt, however courteously it had been phrased.

"I *must* see her," I said. "It's terribly important."

"Madame was quite definite, Mrs. Grayson."

She was moving to the outer door, certain in her knowledge

of the uselessness of disputing her mistress's authority. I couldn't
be dismissed so summarily.

"Please tell Mrs. Logan that I shan't leave until she has seen
me. Tell her," I added, as the maid still hesitated, "that I want to
ask her about—Lya Logasi."

She complied, but with a faint shrug which conveyed the
futility of such insistence. She was back almost immediately, this
time leaving the door open.

"Will you come this way, please?"

I knew then, with sickening certainty, that it was neither mistake nor coincidence. And now I didn't want to go in. I stood in
the doorway, not wanting to have to look up and see her. I was
consumed with the jealousy which earlier had been subdued beneath too many other conflicting emotions. Previously, the
woman for whom Robert had left me had been a nebulous creature. There had been no face, no figure, nothing substantial on
which to fix my imagination.

With the jealousy came a sense of hopeless defeat.

At the back of my mind had always been the thought that
when finally I met her, I could fight for Robert. With anyone else
I could have used everything in my power in an effort to win
him back from her.

But not this woman. Not Lya Logasi. This face and figure was
one for which I had always subconsciously entertained, if not a
feeling of jealousy, then a sense of wistfulness in connexion with
it.

The slow cool voice was saying, "Will you come in, please, to
allow Cecile to close the door?"

I moved obediently, hearing the quiet click behind me, but
still I couldn't look at her. Not yet.

The room was beautiful, gracious; wholly feminine without being oppressively so. The window at the far end extended the
whole width, framing a delightful panorama of the park beyond.
The sun flooded in, across the carpet of palest silver grey, en-
riching the silk covered walls and the softly muted tones of the
furnishings. It was a room that combined the leisurely elegance
of the eighteenth century with the modern comforts of present
day life.

It was a room that Robert could know intimately. He could
have relaxed on the richly brocaded settee or sprawled at ease,

under a hotter sun, on the balcony. He could have sat writing at the Sheraton escritoire, or enjoyed a peaceful hour of music from the expensive radiogram.

For all I knew—and my heart quickened—he could be here now. He could be living here. But there was no sign of male occupation; nothing around at all that could betray his presence or that of any other man.

The soft, beautifully modulated voice said, "You're very persistent, Mrs. Grayson."

She had not risen; the Siamese cat was on her lap, indolently revelling in the continued movement of her hand over its fur. So much I had taken in without really seeing her.

"You lied to me before," I said. My voice sounded harsh in comparison.

"I don't know either your husband or the Lya Logasi you mentioned."

"But that name changed your mind about seeing me, didn't it?"

"Only because my maid seemed incapable of persuading you to go."

"That wasn't why. The name meant something to you."

"I can't imagine why you should think—"

"If I made enquiries, it shouldn't be difficult to get proof," I said, and the hand paused in its stroking of the cat.

"As you say," she agreed quietly. "It seems pointless to continue to deny it."

I studied her now, minutely; absorbing every detail of that perfect face and the lovely dark eyes which met mine with calm repose. If she was disturbed or annoyed she didn't show it. She bore the scrutiny and the silence which endured with complete unconcern.

It was easy to see how captivated Robert must have been with her when she was a young girl. She was beautiful still. She would be beautiful when she was an old woman because that delicate, finely moulded bone structure was ageless. But as a young girl, with the light of innocence shining in her face, with those fabulous dark eyes sparkling with the bright effervescence of youth, she must have been irresistible.

Robert had never made any secret of the fact that he had loved her deeply and devotedly; that for a time his life had been devastated by the news of her untimely death.

And I could see why he had been attracted to me. There was sufficient in my own appearance to remind him of her. I hadn't her beauty. I had no such perfection. But we were of the same type, the same dark petiteness, the small features, the slightness of body suggesting frailness; that fragility which appealed to the protectiveness in men like Robert.

How alike we were in character was impossible for me to judge; I had only Robert's occasional reference to go by. She was older now but the impression I had gained from Robert of her as a girl was one of glowing vivacity, tinged a little with a haunting sadness.

I wondered desolately how much of Robert's love for me had been rooted in nostalgic remembrance of the dead wife of his youth. I hated her for the lost happiness she represented; for having taken from me not only the present and the future, but the past also. All the pity that had been associated with the tragedy of her name had been unwarranted. In a fit of childish, ungovernable rage I wanted to strike at her, to spoil that lovely face with my bare hands.

"You died," I said. I hardly recognised my own voice. "You were killed . . ."

"Reported dead," Lya corrected gently. "It was perhaps not considered necessary to change the original report when I was found to be terribly injured, not expected to live."

"Robert didn't know—not all this time."

"Robert has known for the past six months."

"Six months?" I echoed bleakly. How was it possible to have still felt so loved during that time when it had all been a deception. "Why didn't he tell me?"

"It is perhaps not easy," she said, still gently, "to tell a woman she is not the wife she has believed herself to be for three years."

That aspect of it was a prostrating blow to my heart. I was not Robert's wife. I never had been. Even that had been taken from me.

"There was—no divorce?" I faltered.

"There was no divorce," she confirmed.

"Why wasn't he informed earlier that you were alive? You could have let him know—years ago . . ."

"I had my reasons—even if those reasons were imposed on me. Sit down, Rosanne. This has been a shock for you. Would you like a drink, a little brandy?"

I ignored both suggestions.

"Why didn't you tell me when I came before? You denied even knowing Robert."

"I saw no reason to, my dear. I would have spared you the knowledge if I could."

I couldn't believe in the consideration her words implied.

"What have you spared me?" I asked harshly. "You and Robert —all this time . . . Six months! You took him away without any warning, with scarcely a word. If you had wanted to spare me, either of you, you would have told me the truth."

"There is perhaps more involved than you realise, Rosanne. But the thing is done now. I am sorry you have had to be hurt, but you are young. You will forget Robert more quickly than you can possibly imagine right now. Believe me. I am older, more experienced. Experienced enough to know that the tragedies of youth are never as irreparable as they seem at the time."

"Is that what Robert thinks?" I choked out. "Or does he only think what you tell him to think?"

"Blame me, if you like. If it helps," Lya said quietly.

"You could have been generous. You had Robert—"

"The result would have been the same. He would still have left you. And I thought it better for you not to know I was still alive."

"I wonder," I said shrewdly, "whether your concern was for me or for yourself?"

"That's a rather ambiguous remark."

"No," I said. "I was—" I corrected myself. "I lived with Robert for three years. He was proud of his position at the Foreign Office, ambitious. He would have done nothing to jeopardise his future there—not until these last few months. Not until you came back into his life. Why should he change so drastically, risk his entire career? Was it because you put pressure on him? Because you wanted beautiful things you couldn't afford any other way?"

She was amused. "My dear child, do you think the information Robert obtained for us was of such value that the purchase price provided me with all this . . ." She waved a small white hand to encompass the apartment and its luxurious contents.

"Us?" I asked quietly, and her eyes returned sharply to mine. The amusement still lingered, but tempered now with an air of caution.

"You're a very discerning young woman," she remarked. "Robert said you were no fool."

It brought a twinge of hurtful distaste that Robert had discussed me with her, in whatever way, but I wouldn't allow it to distract me.

"That's why you didn't want your name associated with Robert's, isn't it?"

I think once over she had meant to deny it; and then she gave a little shrug of her shoulders. With the cessation of her stroking the Siamese cat had twisted its head to fix unblinking pale blue eyes on her, and she bent her head, murmuring softly to the cat as she yielded to the silent appeal.

I sat down now, everything else temporarily submerged beneath a feeling of helpless defeat. Until her confirmation, I had still clung to the hope that Robert could be innocent. Mistakes had been made before, it could have been only circumstantial evidence against him. The act of disloyalty to his country seemed so foreign to his nature, to everything I had believed him to be.

"If it wasn't for monetary gain, why did he do it?" I was talking more to myself than to her, groping blindly in bewildered ignorance for understanding. "Robert isn't a communist."

She told me, simply, starkly. "Robert is whatever I am," she said.

The stressing of her own indivisibility with Robert dissociated me too completely from him. The hurt caught in my throat.

"Don't look so stricken, child," Lya said. She pushed the animal from her lap and reached for the gold cigarette box. I shook my head numbly when she offered it to me, watching her with still anguished eyes as she extracted a long thin cigarette and lit it. Her movements were fluid, graceful. She leaned back, blowing a fine stream of blue smoke from the delicately flared nostrils.

After a while, still struggling for some semblance of understanding, I said, "Robert told me you were passionately patriotic. That what was happening to your country affected you deeply. How can you have turned so against all you believed in, work for the people who have destroyed your country's freedom?"

Lya tapped ash from her cigarette. "You English have a saying

—if you can't beat them, join them. It is a very sensible idea, especially when you are dealing with people who haven't hesitated to apply some—rather unpleasant methods, shall we say?—to encourage the indoctrination. That appals you, Rosanne?"

"But you are in England now."

"I was not offering you an excuse, only an explanation. I neither seek nor wish to justify my actions to you. Your feelings about the work in which I am engaged are not important."

"You need not have involved Robert."

"I was married to a rising English diplomat. The relationship was a convenient one."

She could have been discussing the weather. The fury of hatred for such dispassionate calmness made me stutter.

"How could you ruin his career, his life, like that? If you love him . . ."

"Who said anything about loving him?" She was calmly amused. "Once, yes. But personal feelings are of secondary consideration. I used Robert. I used his love for me."

"You are heartless," I breathed.

"Just practical, that is all. I won't deny I have an affection for Robert. He was my first love—my only love, in fact. But I was young then—empty headed, frivolous."

The core of hardness that I had vaguely suspected earlier was visible now. It harshened her features, compressing the seductive softness of her mouth into firm, determined lines. The allure was gone from the beautiful face now. I wondered if Robert had seen her like this, with the appealing feminine helplessness reduced to a mockery; whether it would have made any difference to him if he had.

She was studying me quietly, unmoved by the loathing I made no attempt to conceal.

"You are wondering why I am so frank with you, Rosanne? Thinking, perhaps, you can convince Robert of my unworthiness?" She had interpreted my thoughts correctly. A faint smile just touched her lips. She was supremely confident. "He would not believe you. Or, possibly, he may even know and it is of no consequence. What Robert did for me, was done willingly. I didn't have to coerce him with protestations of my own love." She was deliberately hurting me now. The intent to taunt was obvious.

"You will not see him again, anyway," she added carelessly. "Forget him."

"Robert is in trouble," I said.

"He doesn't need your help."

"Does he need yours? And would he get it if he did?"

"Our organisation—"

"I'm not talking about your organisation," I said steadily. "I mean you, personally."

"I have given Robert all the assistance he requires. The police will not find him."

"He can't spend the rest of his life in hiding. He didn't kill Keith Forrester. You know he didn't!" I made the assertion with firm conviction.

Lya hesitated, for once unsure of herself.

"I wouldn't believe you if you said that he had," I told her. "I'll never believe anyone who says it. Only Robert, himself."

"You have a rather touching faith in Robert, considering in how many other ways he has deceived you." I let that pass, waiting until she added, "He would have difficulty in proving his innocence."

"You were with him that night. You could prove he didn't do it."

"Was Forrester killed that night? It is impossible to ascertain the exact hour after such a lapse of time before his body was found. He could have died the following day. I was not with Robert that day."

I said, "He *must* have been killed that night. He disappeared then, failed to report . . . The police are assuming it happened then. You could give Robert an alibi, you were with him that evening."

"You cannot seriously expect me to involve myself in this? An alibi is unnecessary, even if I could provide one that would satisfy the police."

"If Robert could be cleared of the murder charge, he could give himself up," I said, and she stared at me incredulously.

"You are very naive to think he would willingly subject himself to the certainty of imprisonment on even a lesser charge of treason."

I said doggedly, "It needn't be a long sentence—with remission. Surely that would be better than having to live furtively, never knowing . . ."

"Can you imagine what prison would be like, for a man like Robert? Not knowing whether I would be waiting for him when he came out? He would never take that risk." Her lip curled. "Or are you hoping he would come back to you, Rosanne? It is a vain hope."

"I want to see Robert," I stated.

"That is impossible!" Her whole body moved in emphatic denial. "As far as you are concerned, Robert is dead. Why don't you forget him? Put him out of your life?"

Why didn't I? Robert had loved Lya enough to push me casually aside, to turn traitor to his country for her. Every instinctive knowledge I had had of him had been false. How did I know he would not commit murder for her? What made me so sure he was incapable of that act, in face of the evidence of all the other of which he was guilty?

"Is Robert protecting someone?"

"Protecting?" Her brow furrowed in a slight frown before understanding came. "That man was beaten to death before he was dropped down the well." She held up her hands, the two magnificent rings which adorned them stressing the frailty of the slender fingers. "You really believe I could have dealt so with a grown man with these? I am sorry to disappoint you, Rosanne; Robert is not chivalrously covering up for me."

"I want to see him."

My stubbornness irritated her. She crushed her cigarette out impatiently, reaching for another and lighting it before fixing me with a cold stare. "It is not possible. To put it brutally—and I know of no other way to put it to convince you—Robert washed his hands of you. He pushed you out of his life. Perhaps he could have done it more gently; but the result would have been the same. I fail to understand how your pride allows you to be so insistent when he has demonstrated so plainly that he has no further use of you."

I had sat stolidly, meeting that hard gaze. Not being too successful in concealing the hurt that the deliberate gibes caused me because suddenly her face changed, softened briefly into a gentleness which showed me clearly the girl she had been whom Robert had loved, and still loved.

"I am sorry," she said, and the precise enunciation contained a trace of accent now, as though with the gentleness she had reverted to the less perfect English of that young girl. "It is unforgivable of me to taunt you so. You love Robert. I loved him once, too, so how easily I can understand your doing so. There is something about him that is—special. I do not know how to define it differently than that. Not just charm, but a rare quality of holding you bound to him whether you would be free or not. He made time seem endless, enduring. With Robert," she said, and suddenly she lapsed into Hungarian, her voice very, very gentle. When she continued I was sure she was not translating what she had previously said in her native language. Her voice had hardened, all trace of accent gone. "But that was a long time ago. You are not much older than I was then. You will get over him, as I did. Remember there is another side to Robert, one you have previously never suspected. He can be hard and inflexible. And mercenary. You are wasting your time lamenting over him. He has no wish to see you ever again."

"Then why," I asked, "has he been trying to do just that?"

She looked vaguely perplexed. "I don't understand you."

"Robert," I said, "has been waiting in the square near our flat. He was there the night before I came here the first time. And the night before that. Why would he risk arrest like that if it wasn't because he wanted to see me?"

"You are mistaken. It was not Robert." She denied it positively.

"How can you be sure it wasn't?"

"Because—he was with me those nights."

The hesitation had been so faint it was hardly discernible, but I knew she was lying. She was aware of my disbelief because she asked in irritation, "What makes you think it was him?"

"Why should anyone else wait there and run away when the police gave chase?"

She moved impatiently, spilling ash unnoticed down the expensive dark blue dress.

"It could not have been Robert."

She had spoken with conviction but the words had been mechanical, as though she had uttered them while her mind grappled with some different problem. I sensed an unsureness in her; she was puzzled, uneasy. There were some things about Robert that she didn't know.

It was a small triumph, but it was mine. It served to strengthen my resolve.

"I insist upon seeing him," I said.

"He would never agree to a meeting . . ."

"Robert? Or you? Why are you so afraid of letting me see him? Is it because you are afraid he will come back to me, eventually?"

The idea was beneath scorn. Her ignoring of the suggestion proclaimed fully how ridiculous it was to even think he would leave her for me.

"I could never persuade him."

"You could, perhaps," I said, "if you told him that otherwise I shall inform the police that you were at Far End with him the night Keith Forrester was killed."

I used the blackmail callously, calculatively.

Lya moved restlessly, rising to her feet and crossing to the window. She stood there, smoking, indifferent to the blatant cajolery of the Siamese cat which leapt with feline grace on to the ledge, arching his back as he rubbed sinuously against her. The bright sunlight framed her, the head poised proudly on the slender neck, the curved outline of the body in the expensive simplicity of the dark dress, the long perfect line of her legs. Apart from the movement of her hand as she lifted the cigarette to her mouth she was still, quiet; but there was a tenseness in her body that implied inward disturbance.

It was a long time before she said, still gazing out on a scene I suspected she was not really seeing, "Rosanne, leave well alone." There was appeal in her voice, and that faintest trace of accent again. "You are not helping Robert . . ."

"Let Robert and me be the judge of that."

"But you are in no position to realise . . . For your own sake. I would not have you hurt more than you already have been. I assure you I have no ulterior motive in wishing to prevent this meeting. It is only in your own interests . . ."

"I'll be the judge of that, too," I said hardly. "Is Robert here?"

"Here? No." After a moment she added with a trace of bitterness, "You are welcome to look for yourself, if you do not believe me in that either."

I didn't avail myself of the invitation. I was sure she spoke the truth.

"When can I see him?"

"You are so stubborn, Rosanne," she said in a flare of anger. "Why will you not listen to reason?"

I remained silent and she swung round to face me. She stood for a while as though seeking further words with which to dissuade me. There was appeal still mingled with the anger in her eyes. When I wouldn't yield to it she made a small gesture of finality.

"It will not be easy to arrange. It will take time." She was coldly practical now, no longer unsure of herself. Her face was empty of all expression.

"How long?" I asked in dismay.

"A few days. More, perhaps. But you will not come here again or try to get in touch with me in any way, in the meantime. You understand that? You have already created extreme difficulties by coming here at all. If you were followed . . ."

I looked mystified. "Followed?"

"The police are searching intensively for Robert. Your movements are naturally of interest to them, in case you try to get in touch with him. You are too innocent, Rosanne." Where I could have expected exasperation for my stupid ignorance she was still coolly detached. "Apart from being wanted for questioning about Forrester, Scotland Yard will be also interested in who Robert's contact was. Previously, to my knowledge, they have had no suspicion of me, but by coming here you may have connected me with Robert. I will not have my work and my own liberty imperilled by your foolhardiness. Although it will perhaps appeal more to your caution in future if I point out that it will also work the other way round. Robert could be traced through me. He would not thank you to be the instrument of his arrest. Do I make myself clear?"

I nodded, and she continued in the same emotionless manner. "I will let you know the time and place. That may not be easy. For a mere whim, you are forcing needless risks upon me that one doesn't take in my profession."

"Would it help," I suggested, "if I phoned you, from a public box?"

Lya's eyes were very cold. "I thought it was clearly understood that you were not to attempt to communicate with me, however long the delay." The cold stare compelled another nod of agreement from me. "You will leave all the arrangements entirely to me. When you hear from me you will obey instructions implicitly. If it is a written note, destroy it immediately. You will tell no one, trust no one. Wherever I decide it best for this meeting to take place, you will make sure you are not followed."

"What if I can't?" I asked helplessly. I was floundering in this alien world of intrigue.

With casual indifference she said, "It is not difficult to confuse someone who is shadowing you. But," implacably now, "that is your problem. You will not see Robert unless he is absolutely certain it is safe."

She stood, waiting, looking down at me. Finally she said, "That is all. Cecile will see you out."

She rang the bell. There was no sound of it in that quiet room. We faced each other in silence. Only in the last moment before Cecile answered the summons did she ask, "When I have told Robert what you wish, will you accept my word if I tell you he refuses?"

I met her gaze steadily, not bothering to reply. I think she had expected what the answer would be.

"Very well," she said quietly as Cecile opened the door.

She was watching from the window, as she had been the last time I left. This time I knew she was not idly interested in the view.

I wondered if her more experienced eyes detected anyone, because search diligently as I would, I could see no one who seemed even vaguely observant of my movements.

9

Lya had said a few days. Perhaps more.

I was filled with such deep thankfulness that I was going to see Robert again, it overshadowed both the desperate anxiety for the trouble he was in and the crushing sorrow that he had never been my husband.

Seeing him once more could be only a brief reprieve from the finality of complete severance. He had never ceased to be inwardly haunted by the tragedy of the beloved young wife who had plunged with fervid patriotism into her country's fight for freedom, whose life he had thought had ended so brutally beneath the pitiless onslaught of the tanks surging across the square in Budapest in 1956. I had always known that the horror of that unforgettable episode had been the cause of the sadness which tinged his memory even in our happiest moments.

Robert had loved me. I wouldn't doubt that. But I hadn't known how much his love could have been a reflected shadow of the deep devotion he had felt for the wife I faintly resembled. Whatever the future held for him, he would never return to me now that Lya was alive.

Still, I could think of nothing beyond seeing him again. Just once more. The days dragged. I didn't know how to get through them.

It would have been easier if Lya had given some intimation of how she would get word to me. I floundered helplessly in ignorance. All the experience I had of such undercover transactions was secondhand knowledge conned from the dubious authenticity of books and films.

I went out for short periods each day. I rode on buses, visited the library, frequented my usual shops. Would some seemingly innocuous shop assistant hand me a message with my change, or would I find a note slipped between the pages of a library book? If anyone brushed against me I expected to find that something had been pushed into my pocket.

I gave anyone who was so inclined every opportunity; I watched everyone with alert eyes, suspicious of every innocent action.

After each outing I hurried back to the flat in case, after all, Lya had decided to risk the telephone by using some enigmatical message that would make sense only to the two of us. On the few occasions when the telephone rang I answered with my heart in my mouth, trying vainly to decipher any hidden meaning behind friendly chatter and inquiries.

The colonel was one of those who phoned, complaining that I had not kept my promise to let him know my plans. I hadn't even remembered I had said I would. His brusqueness barely concealed reproach, filling me with compunction, but he brushed my apology aside.

"I've got tickets for that Russian show at the Festival Hall tonight," he said. "Care to go?"

While I was inwardly debating whether it would be wise to be so long away from the flat, the colonel settled it for me.

"Shan't take no for an answer, anyway. Sure you'd enjoy it. All right if I call for you at seven? We can have a meal after the show."

He was punctual to the minute. I was glad I had gone to some trouble over my appearance because he had dressed for the occasion, looking somehow even more military in the dinner suit and black tie.

His eyes flickered only cursorily over the emerald green dress but they expressed approval even before he said, "You look very charming, my dear. I'm glad you decided to come."

There was no irony in his words. He was a man who made quick decisions. He would have been amazed to be told that he had a habit of making them for others, also. But I was glad, too.

The show was excellent; colourful and exhilarating. Occasionally I was aware that the colonel stole surreptitious glances to see my reaction to it. He need not have worried; he could not have chosen more diverting entertainment than the fantastic agility of the Russian dancers inspired by the wildly pulse stirring music. I suspected his choice had been deliberate.

Afterwards, Victor drove us on to a small, exclusive restaurant tucked away in a back street.

"Best food in town," the colonel commented as he led me in.

He was known there. He was addressed by name by a jovial proprietor who was obviously delighted to see him. They lapsed into a foreign tongue, although still clearly exchanging greetings of mutual pleasure. I had never seen the colonel so animated, or known he was capable of displaying such *bonhomie* towards anyone. If it hadn't seemed too completely incongruous, I could almost have imagined him indulging in genial back slapping.

Belatedly, as though temporarily he had forgotten my presence, he introduced me. Some time I should have to tell him I was not Mrs. Grayson, but I couldn't do so yet without involving myself in too many explanations.

"Joseph is a very old friend," he said, and he spoke with visible affection.

"What language was that?" I inquired when Joseph had personally supervised our order and left.

"Russian." He didn't add "of course" but he seemed surprised it had been necessary for me to ask.

"I didn't know you knew Russian."

"There are not many languages I don't speak, if only a smattering. Languages are a hobby of mine. I have many friends in many countries. It is common courtesy not to expect them to converse only in English."

I felt rebuked; still rather astonished by the revelation of such unsuspected conviviality which had the effect of rounding the customary abruptness from his speech. The colonel was not as austerely reserved as he made appear. I wondered why the façade.

"Some time," the colonel was saying, "I would like to take you to a Turkish restaurant. Also owned by a friend of mine. Tonight it seemed appropriate to have Russian food after the performance we have just seen. I hope you'll like it."

I was not sure whether I did or not. Perhaps it was not the food. Two men in traditional Cossack costumes were playing balalaikas. The soft, soulful music haunted the room; as disturbing, but in a different way, as the passionately gay turbulence we had just heard. The plaintive sadness stirred too poignantly into the mind.

Certainly I didn't like the drink Joseph poured into my glass. I couldn't prevent myself from grimacing.

"What is it?"

"The basis is Vodka. What goes in after that is Joseph's jealously guarded secret," the colonel explained. "It is an acquired taste. Don't drink it if you don't like it. Joseph—"

"No." I was insistent, refusing to allow Joseph to remove the glass. "I'll drink it and acquire the taste."

"What is it about you that is different tonight, Rosanne?" the colonel asked when Joseph had left us once more. He had been watching me for some time, studying my face with a faint air of puzzlement.

"A new dress?" I said, and he shook his head impatiently at the frivolity of the suggestion. He was deeply serious.

"In some way you're even sadder. And yet suddenly you're—" he sought for the right words "—alive again. More as you used to be. Is it because—" he searched for the words again "—because you're beginning to get over Robert?"

I wouldn't meet his eyes. I took another sip of the obnoxious drink.

"Perhaps that's it," I said evasively.

The answer didn't satisfy him. He continued to probe keenly, and I found that those blue eyes could probe very keenly indeed.

The temptation to confide in him was so strong, I almost yielded to it. It would have been a relief to unburden myself to him, to let him shoulder the weight of my problems as he was so obviously desirous of doing.

Lya had been adamant on secrecy, but it was not her warning injunction that made me refrain. I knew suddenly that I didn't want to implicate him in the sordid business. It was a criminal offence to withhold evidence from the police. He had not my implicit faith in Robert; I couldn't trade on his loyalty to me by placing him in a predicament that would be abhorrent in every aspect to anyone of such scrupulous integrity.

"I am not the only one who is different tonight," I said.

The colonel was disappointed, still vaguely puzzled, but he accepted the refusal to confide in him with good grace.

"I presume you mean me. In what way?"

"You've always seemed so uncompromisingly *British*."

"Have I really?" He looked surprised. "Go on. It is always interesting to hear how other people view oneself."

"I didn't expect you to have such a cosmopolitan array of friends."

"But why not? I've travelled a good deal in my time."

"I know, but . . ."

"But you'd expected me to regard anything or anyone that isn't British as undesirable? Keep a stiff upper lip, don't let the side down, salute the Union Jack at sunset. Is that how you see me?" He was really amused now. The lines round his eyes crinkled with suppressed laughter. "Rosanne," he said, "I—" He checked abruptly. "Well, never mind that." Casually he said, "As a matter of fact, I have to go abroad in a week or so. Would postpone going if I could but it isn't possible."

"Business or pleasure?" I was conscious of faint disappointment. I should miss him.

"I have interests abroad that need my attention occasionally. Usually I combine business with holiday, but I shan't this time."

"Will you be away long?"

"Difficult to say. Wish it were possible for you to come with me. It's not, of course, but it would do you good to get away. I was happy to see you have started going out again, Rosanne. Accepting invitations."

It was an oblique reference but an unmistakable one.

"I met him by pure chance—it wasn't previously arranged."

"That makes me even happier," he said rather obscurely. "Someone you've known long? What is the name—Merrick?"

He offered the name tentatively but I was confident the uncertainty was assumed. He hadn't forgotten.

"Dale Merrick," I said. "He was at school with Robert. And you were very rude to him."

"So I was. Does it matter?"

"Not really."

"If you see him again, you could offer my apologies," he suggested.

"You apologised at the time," I pointed out.

"So I did," the colonel agreed with sudden testiness.

It was only later I realised he had been edging cagily around asking the outright question.

He was quiet during the drive back to the flat, sitting upright in his own corner of the back seat. Victor was turning the car into the square before I broke the silence.

"Will you come in for a drink, Gregory?"

"I think not. It's late and—" He broke off to give a startled exclamation. "What the devil—"

Some dozen or more motor cycles had seemingly materialised from nowhere, sweeping into the square behind us and following us round to the far side, giving the appearance of escorting us in a motor cavalcade. The roar of the combined engines made the night hideous.

"Rowdy young hooligans!" the colonel said disgustedly. "Do you get troubled much with this sort of thing round here?"

"No."

We had to shout to make ourselves heard above the deafening cacophony. They had drawn up behind us as Victor halted the car outside the flat, scattered across the road in contumacious indifference to any obstruction they might be causing, with engines revving furiously. They were dressed in the traditional black leather uniform of their kind, faces concealed anonymously behind goggles.

The colonel got out on the far side and stood, gesticulating angrily to them to pass. In the glare of their headlights his face was suffused with contemptuous anger. Rather surprisingly, they responded to his waving commands. As Victor helped me out on the other side, with final bursts of thundering exhausts they surged forward.

I was watching the main body streaming past the colonel. Until Victor grabbed me roughly, pulling me back against the car, I hadn't been aware that one of the riders had elected to roar dangerously through on the pavement. It was a lunatic action in such a narrow space. He loomed terrifyingly close, blinding me with his headlight. Something tugged sharply at my arm, and then they had dispersed miraculously.

One minute, the night had been filled with the raucous sound of engines screaming at full throttle; the next, the customary peace had settled once more in the square.

The colonel came storming round the car.

"Blasted, criminal idiots!" he fumed. "Did you see that?" For a moment words failed him. He could only stand there choking impotently on his spleen. And then, with rage giving way to anxiety as he saw me rubbing my arm, he asked sharply, "Are you hurt, Rosanne?"

"I don't think so," I said.

"Your sleeve's torn. Are you certain?"

The arm was smarting only slightly. I had already started to deny any real damage again when the man who had approached unnoticed broke in to inquire, "Any trouble?"

The colonel took him in in one sweeping glance, his eyes travelling from him to the car which was parked further back with its lights still on.

"No," he said with hostility.

"The lady seems hurt."

He would have reached out to inspect the extent of the injury for himself but the colonel interposed his body between us, preventing him with cold deliberation.

"It's nothing!" he said curtly.

The other man was quietly insistent, impervious to the colonel's snubbing. He tried to address me. It was difficult for him, with the colonel's tall form shielding me completely from view.

"Are you sure, madam? If you need any assistance—"

"She doesn't! And you'd perhaps be better engaged keeping such dangerous louts as those under control," the colonel said with harsh finality.

He turned, drawing me away, deliberately ignoring the man. I thought he had been inexplicably hostile. I saw the man give a resigned shrug of his shoulders before sauntering back to his car. He didn't drive away; instead, after climbing in and slamming the door, he doused the lights.

The colonel was still muttering balefully under his breath.

"Sorry about that," he said as we reached the front entrance of the house. I didn't know whether he meant for his animosity towards an innocent offer of help, or the episode of the motor cycles.

He took my hand, still a little stiff, not yet fully mollified.

"Going back to Coplands in the morning. Not quite sure yet what date I'm going abroad but I'll see you again before then, I hope?" His fingers were moving, exploring uncertainly over my hand. With a little exclamation he lifted it to examine it by the light of the street lamp. "That's blood! You *were* hurt, Rosanne."

It wasn't much. Just a smear from a thin trickle down my arm. I would have made light of it but the colonel was dismayed.

"I will come in, after all. Victor!" He called tersely over his shoulder to the waiting manservant. "If there is any bandaging to be done, Victor is better at that sort of thing than I am," he explained, pushing aside my protests.

It proved to be only a shallow wound, scarcely more than a two inch graze across my forearm, but when Victor had bathed the already congealing blood away the colonel insisted it should be bandaged. He had been right about Victor. I was surprised how gentle and deft those strong, blunt hands could be. I didn't say it, the colonel was almost too ridiculously concerned already, but I felt more pain in my other arm from the pressure of Victor's fingers as he pulled me back across the pavement, than I did from the graze. That arm, I suspected, would show proof of injury long after the other superficial wound had healed.

Victor stood rigidly at attention when he had completed the task. "Is that all, sir?"

"Yes. No—wait a moment." There was an odd note in the colonel's voice. "How did it happen?" A little impatiently he added, "I mean, what did you catch your arm on, Rosanne? Does either of you know?"

"I suppose the catch of the door," I said. "I don't really know. It happened so quickly."

"Or something projecting from the cycle, sir," Victor added. "He was very close."

"Very probably," the colonel agreed after a moment but the odd note was still there. More briskly he said, "All right, that's all, Victor. I'll be down in a few minutes."

I waited until Victor had closed the door.

"What's wrong, Gregory?"

"Nothing," he disclaimed, but there was still a slight frown furrowing his brow. He gave a final inspection to my torn coat before throwing it over a chair.

"Now you're here," I said, "you might as well have that drink." I gestured towards the cabinet. "Help yourself, will you."

"Sure you won't join me?" When I declined he poured a good measure of brandy into a glass, bringing it back to stand looking down at me.

"Do you often get that kind of thing round here?" he asked.

"Cycles? Mods or rockers or whatever they are? I've never seen them here before. But it happens all over the place. It's their idea of a good time."

"And an idiotic one, at that," the colonel grunted. "Wish now I hadn't been so offhand with that man. He belonged to the police, you know," he explained. "He had been following us—you —all evening. That's why I was so annoyed, that you were being subjected to the indignity of having your every movement shadowed. God knows you've had enough notoriety. I didn't want you involved in any more incidents with the police. Maybe I was unwise. It might have been better to lodge a complaint and let the police take further action." He shifted restlessly.

"It's too late now, anyway," I pointed out reasonably. "They'll be far enough away by this time, it would surely be impossible to trace them. And you're right, I should have hated more interviews and questioning even over something as trivial as this."

"Trivial?" He still seemed dissatisfied, looking moodily at the contents of the glass which he hadn't touched yet. "It's the thought of how nearly you could have been more seriously injured." He drained the brandy at one gulp before giving me a rather wry smile. "Shook me a bit, you know. Previously, I disliked the idea of your being under surveillance; now, I think I should welcome extra vigilance."

I was alarmed. It was disturbing enough to know that Lya had been correct in her surmise about my being followed. That would present more than sufficient difficulty when I came to meet Robert. An even closer and more assiduous guard would be fatal.

"You're not still thinking of reporting it?" I asked in dismay.

"Not much use now, as you say," he conceded but he glanced sharply at me. I had been a little too dismayed over something I had described as trivial.

He put the empty glass on the table and sat down beside me, taking my hands.

"Is there something you're not telling me, Rosanne?" The grip of his fingers was forceful, compelling me to look at him. "About —Robert?" he added, but the air of doubt implied that he found the suggestion inconceivable.

Almost, then, I told him. There was something rather pathetic in a man of the colonel's habitual assertiveness labouring in puzzled indecision. Illogically, it was the unusual confusion of mind that urged me into confiding that also refused to allow me to succumb to the temptation. In his own way, he would probably be as lost in the morass of intrigue as I was myself.

"What could there be?" I evaded.

It was easy to deceive him; he had not really expected any other answer. But he still looked vaguely puzzled.

He moved restively, releasing my hands. As he got up to go he said very earnestly, "You wouldn't hesitate to ask my help, would you, Rosanne? You know there is nothing I wouldn't do. You promise? When I go abroad I shall not take Victor with me. You can turn to him as you would turn to me."

"You take him usually."

"This time I shall not. I have to go, it is imperative, but I shall not be away any longer than I can help. Victor can stay in town, if you remain here while I am away, but if you decide to go to Far End he will be at Coplands. Wherever you are, he will be at hand if you need him."

"It isn't really necessary," I said.

"Maybe not." He sounded all at once unutterably weary. The lines of strain were pronounced on his face, ageing him. "I'm being ridiculous and over-imaginative. But this business of Robert's lends itself to morbid, fanciful ideas. God knows what he's mixed up in. I shall be happier knowing I haven't left you entirely alone."

"You'll be lost without Victor," I protested.

The colonel made a wry face. "Is that the general opinion? Probably true. Victor is my right arm. I admit it. But the loss of one limb is unimportant compared to the safety of the whole body," he said, rather enigmatically.

Sleep would not come. I lay awake for a long time, wishing now I had confided in him. Some inner misgiving convinced me suddenly that I had been wrong to withhold the information. I consoled myself finally with the thought that later, when I had seen Robert, when I had heard what Robert had to say, perhaps then I could tell him.

I couldn't know that by then it would be too late. It could have made a difference. One life perhaps could have been saved. But not the other. Whatever I had told the colonel, nothing could have changed that.

10

Mrs. Lloyd handed an envelope to me when she brought in my breakfast the following morning.

"A boy at the bus stop asked me to give that to you," she said.

It was as simple as that. There had been none of the more theatrical methods I had envisaged being employed, after all. Just a sealed, unaddressed envelope, creating only a modicum of curiosity in the woman who had passed it on.

I waited until she had gone back into the kitchen before I tore it open. The instructions were curt, unsigned, but explicit. I read it through twice more even though every word was already committed faithfully to memory.

I was dizzy with excitement and thankfulness. At the back of my mind had lurked the fear that Lya would disregard my threat; that she would surely realise I would do nothing to involve her that would lead the police to Robert. Or that Robert would refuse to see me.

But he hadn't. In—how long? The day stretched interminably. Twelve hours—in twelve hours, I would be with him.

Further than that, I wouldn't think about. For the time being it was sufficient—oh, more than sufficient—that I should just see him again.

The telephone rang as I completed a thorough job of scattering the ashes of the burnt note. I thought it would probably be the colonel but it wasn't. It was Dale Merrick.

He sounded brightly cheerful, as if, even though I couldn't see it, his face was composed in the disarming smile. For all that, I was irrationally pleased to hear from him. I was so filled with goodwill I would have delightedly welcomed hearing from anyone.

"Do you ride?" he wanted to know. "I'm sure you do."

"Not for ages."

"Then how about it? I'm going down to see my mother today —did I mention she runs a farm in Sussex? There are some good horses. We'll ride before lunch—things are rather at sixes and sevens at the house with mother's illness but we'll find somewhere to eat. The countryside's very beautiful round there and the weather's perfect. We could make a day of it."

"I couldn't," I said. "I have—an engagement in the evening."

"Oh, that's all right," Dale said easily. "I have to be back at the office before it closes. That soon enough for you?"

"It would be . . ." But I still demurred.

"Then do come," he urged. "I suspect that you're really a country girl at heart. Confess it."

It was so true, I couldn't deny it. I had always been happier at Far End than in London.

"I haven't suitable clothes . . ."

"You must have a pair of old gardening slacks? Jeans? Anything will do. Shall I pick you up in about an hour?"

Why not? I capitulated suddenly. I would never get through the eternity of the day without something to occupy my mind.

He was round in under the hour, dressed not in the dark grey suit and tie but in an open-necked shirt and sports jacket, and still contriving to appear as completely unremarkable. I noticed that the skin the open neck revealed was not white, suggesting that he spent more time in casual wear than I would have thought feasible for a man who worked in the city.

He drove an Alvis saloon. A rather more expensive car than I would have expected he could afford. It could have been second-hand, an older model in good condition. I wasn't very knowledgeable about such things. It could even have been hired.

If it was, he had soon become accustomed to it. He was a good driver. He drove carefully, but with a sure confidence; taking no dramatic risks but not overlooking any opportunity to manoeuvre skilfully through the traffic. Accelerating, but not excessively, when the road stretched more clearly ahead.

I relaxed, almost happy; appreciating the beautiful morning. The countryside was brilliant with the first fresh greenness of spring. There was a crystalline sharpness in the air proclaiming an earlier frost but all sign of it had dissipated now beneath the increasing warmth of the sun. I was looking forward to riding again.

It had never been a hobby of Robert's, although we had often discussed taking it up so that I could renew a childhood interest in it. It had been one of those things for the future. Some day . . . There had never been time for all the things we had planned.

A thought occurred to me, and I voiced it.

"You seem to have an unconscionable amount of free time. Aren't you supposed to be working?"

He explained airily. "My type of work allows me a lot of latitude. I'm not tied down to office hours." After a moment he asked curiously, "By the way, why do you keep looking back at the road?"

"To see if there is anyone following me."

Dale shot a sideways glance at me. "And is there?"

"I wouldn't know," I said ruefully. "I'm not very good at detecting that sort of thing."

After studying the rear mirror Dale said, "I haven't noticed anyone in particular. There's no one in sight at the moment—unless you have suspicions about that tractor we've just overtaken?"

I laughed, and he risked another quick look at me.

"You're quite lighthearted this morning," he said. "Any special reason?"

The colonel had remarked last night on the change in me, when it had been only prospect that caused it. Now, faced with certitude, I was *really* alive again. Not just a being that responded to automatic instruction from the brain, but a body that glowed with vitality. I was jubilant with anticipation. I couldn't conceal it, even though caution prompted me into the wisdom of doing so.

"Spring goes to my head a little. It always did," I said. "And I'm excited at the thought of being among horses again."

If he was sceptical about the explanation, he accepted it naturally. "I detect a note of affection when you mention horses," he said.

"I used to be mad about them. I entered all the junior show jumping competitions. I saw myself as a second Pat Smythe, but I never quite made the grade."

"I knew you were a country girl," Dale said with some satisfaction. "You can't hide it, even under all that sophistication."

"I'm not sophisticated," I protested.

"You're always very—what's the word? Chic? Elegant? Even in those slacks. Is it correct to call those tight fitting things, slacks?" He ran an appreciative eye down the length of my legs. "Um. Very nice," he commented.

Without really knowing why, he embarrassed me a little by indulging in personal compliments. Dale saw that he did, switching with ease on to safer ground.

"I think there's just the horse to suit you at Merrick. Fourteen and a half hands, just about your size. A roan gelding."

"Is that the name of your mother's farm? Just Merrick?"

"Not originally, but it's been in the family for generations. It's always known as that now."

It sounded rather pretentious for the small holding I anticipated. The actuality proved to be quite different.

I should have been warned by the length of winding driveway after leaving the main road; by the pedigree herds of cattle which studded the grazing parkland behind neatly maintained white fencing. In fact, I hadn't quite realised we were on private ground until the house and farm buildings came into view as we rounded a small copse.

The house was typically Tudor, sprawling mellowly behind lawns of such mature perfection they could only have origin when the building itself was first erected. A house that was part of, and yet still held remote from, the well kept, symmetrical outbuildings which flanked it.

Farmers, the Merrick family might be; but of the category that is referred to as gentleman farmers. I need not have wondered who would be feeding the hens during Mrs. Merrick's illness. I doubted if she would ever have any knowledge of them beyond the produce that appeared on her table. My vision of muddied Wellington boots ploughing stickily through the sludge was very inappropriate for those spotless paved yards.

I was still absorbing every detail of what was obviously an immaculately operated place when Dale drew the car to a halt before the front entrance and came round to help me out.

"Come on in," he said, taking my hand.

"It isn't what I expected."

"Isn't it?" He sounded surprised.

The house was calm and quiet. An old grandfather clock ticking melodiously in a corner of the hallway was the only sound to break the peacefulness. The stillness which could have given the atmosphere of emptiness had quite the reverse. It was a lived-in house. That was the first impression that struck me. A quietly lived-in, warmly pleasant home.

Some of the furnishings in the room into which Dale led me were faded with the sun, a little worn, but it suggested comfortable use, not shabbiness. There was a fire burning in the hearth for all the warmth of the sun steaming in through the windows. I had the feeling that even on a hot summer's day there would still be that blaze of welcome.

"Sit down," Dale invited. "I'll see about some coffee."

He disappeared, leaving me alone.

I had that strange feeling that can sometimes assail one in old houses that this was a place I had always known. It was as familiar to me as my own flat, almost as intimate as Far End.

Dale had said the household was disrupted owing to his mother's illness but there were no signs of neglect or disorderliness. The flowers in the vases were fresh, newly cut, and there was a faint smell of lavender polish on the furniture mingling with another, more aromatic odour which made me crinkle my nose in appreciative conjecture.

"Pot-pourri," Dale explained. I hadn't heard him come back. He had been so quick he could not possibly have made the coffee himself.

The tray he carried was very tastefully set with eggshell china. The silver coffee pot was a good one, and old, in that one or two faint dents showed signs of much usage, but of no particular period of antiquity. The hot buttered scones were undoubtedly fresh from the oven.

"A passion of mother's, pot-pourri," he said. "She has it all over the house. I'm told she's asleep at the moment, so we'll see her when we come back after lunch. You don't mind, not eating here?" he asked in some anxiety. "I wasn't expected down today. It was a sudden impulse."

The thought crossed my mind that a household that could produce such an elegant coffee tray at a moment's notice would perhaps not have been too disorganised by having to provide an unexpected meal, but I refrained from saying so. It was, after all, none of my affair, but I had a feeling that consideration for any inconvenience it may have caused was not his whole concern.

There was something a little odd about his manner. It was all so faint it was almost unnoticeable, but I was sure he was not completely at ease. He sat on the edge of the chair, head held in a position of alertness; as though he listened for a sound he expected to hear but hoped he would not.

It seemed strange. I couldn't imagine a more restful place than this old house.

It could have been that he was impatient to be outside. His offer to refill my cup was no more than perfunctory; there was no polite urging when I declined.

But once away from the house he seemed more relaxed again, pointing out the different buildings as we passed them on our way to the stables.

"I'll show you round this afternoon, if you're interested," he said, "but right now let's have our ride. Will you be all right?" When I looked inquiringly at him he explained, "I thought you appeared to be having some trouble with your arm."

He was unusually perceptive. There was only a slight irritation from the graze. I hadn't been aware of showing any discomfort to proclaim the injury. I passed it off casually, without explanation.

There was no one working round the stables, they were deserted apart from the half dozen horses which poked inquisitive noses out at the sound of our footsteps. Not quite deserted. I had a momentary glimpse of a face at a window opposite. When I glanced back it was only a pale blur, as though whoever it belonged to had withdrawn farther into the interior of the building.

And then the horses claimed my attention. I breathed in the old familiar odour with deep satisfaction.

"This is the roan I mentioned," Dale was saying, but I had immediately spotted the horse I wanted; a chestnut so dark his coat was virtually sable velvet. The alert, impish little gleam in his eyes was a challenge I couldn't resist. When I ran my hand down the length of the soft nose he snickered with contentment, as if he had known he would be my choice.

Dale was already unbolting the door to lead out the roan for my inspection. When he saw that I had no intention of by-passing the chestnut he stopped.

"Not Sabre!" he said, and the almost startled dismay in his voice surprised me.

"Do you mind? Is there some particular reason . . . ?"

"No—of course not! It's just that he'll be a bit mettlesome. He hasn't been ridden much lately."

"Is *that* all?" I scorned the idea but Dale still looked dubious.

"I'd really prefer you had the roan. Or any of the others . . ."

"Sabre knows I've chosen him. I couldn't disappoint him now."

There was no outward sign of it but mentally he gave a small shrug of reluctant resignation.

I snapped back the bolts myself, steadying Sabre when he would have lunged forward too impetuously once the restraining door was open. Taking in the strong clean lines of the horse in appreciative anticipation.

"That's Dinly's horse!"

There had been no sound to be heard above the sharp clatter of Sabre's hooves as he sidled eagerly forward. Dale was as startled as I was. He swung round, dismay plainly in his face. There was apprehension there, too, I was certain of it.

The girl who had approached unheard stood some three yards away. She would perhaps have been attractive had she looked less sullen, but the blue eyes were remotely cold and her mouth was set in uncompromising hardness. When the wind blew the long fair hair across her face she tossed it impatiently aside, but otherwise she remained rigidly motionless.

I wondered if it was the face that had watched us from the opposite window. There was no one there now.

Dale broke the silence. "Oh—there you are, Helen," he said lamely. Her presence was clearly unwelcome. Even more lamely he added, "This is Rosanne."

She made no effort to come nearer, or any sign that she had heard him. Her eyes never even so much as flickered in my direction.

"That's Dinly's horse!" she said again in the same hard voice.

"I know," Dale said. He seemed to have recovered some of his composure. He spoke quietly, but more assuredly now. "He wouldn't mind."

"Wouldn't he?" The blue eyes stared long and stonily into the hazel ones. Dale looked troubled but he met the gaze steadily, and it was the blue eyes that surrendered. "Wouldn't he?" she asked again with the same harsh bitterness as she swung on her heel and ran back across the yard.

The tension that remained in the air was uncomfortably unmistakable even after she had disappeared. For a moment I thought that Dale would follow her and then with an abrupt movement he turned back to me.

"Perhaps I'd better have the roan after all," I suggested uncertainly. I had inadvertently made a wrong choice.

"Nonsense! Take him if you feel you can handle him," he said shortly. More pacifically he added, "The horse needs exercising. Helen is like mother—too possessive about Dinly's property."

He didn't speak as we were saddling the horses, beyond looking up with an inquiring "O.K.?" as he adjusted the girths. Only as we were cantering down the drive did he say, on a lighter tone, "Sorry about that. Helen had really no right to interfere, but she was engaged to Dinly."

"Was?"

"Not any more," he said, "but she's helping to take care of mother." He didn't elucidate further on the situation. Instead he said, "You have an eye for horses. You've got Sabre's measure and he knows it, the old devil."

The disarming smile was on his face. I realised with sudden disquietude what it was that was odd about it—it didn't reach his eyes. It never had, not once. They remained as coolly isolated from that pleasant smile on his mouth as the chill wastes of the Arctic under the sun. In its own way, the realisation struck as jarring a note as the uncomfortable little scene with the girl had done.

But I couldn't dwell on it. It was sheer delight to feel the strong ripple of muscles moving evenly beneath me. I put both episodes from my mind, concentrating solely on the heavy thud of hooves as I pushed Sabre into a gallop and felt the swift rush of wind through my hair. I was in my element now, revelling in a too-longed-for pleasure. I gave myself up wholly to it.

We ate lunch at a small wayside inn which didn't normally cater for meals. While we waited for it to be prepared we sat in the oak beamed bar and chatted to the few local inhabitants who had dropped in for drinks. The fare when it came was plain but good. I discovered an enormous appetite which appeased Dale, who had been rather dubious about my choice of the unostentatious little inn.

We returned to Merrick leisurely, allowing the horses to choose their own pace.

"That was wonderful," I said as I assisted Dale in the unsaddling, giving Sabre an affectionate slap on the rump to send him into his stall.

"I'm glad you enjoyed it."

He didn't suggest, even in politeness, that the experience could perhaps be repeated at some future date. Rather, there was a finality in the way he slammed the bolts home and led me back to the house which held the chill of remoteness.

"We'll go straight up to see mother," he said, but at the foot of the stairs I held back.

"Would it be better if you went up alone?" I suggested.

There was something a little odd again in his manner, now we were back in the house. Not the previous uneasiness, there was no sign of that now. He was abrupt in his movements, abrupt in voice as he said, "No, I'd like you to see her."

I followed him a little reluctantly. The bedroom of a very sick woman seemed no place for a complete stranger to enter. His insistence was difficult to understand. I was beginning to think that Dale Merrick was a very complex man.

The girl, Helen, was emerging from a room on our left as we reached the top of the stairs. She must have heard us but she continued across the landing, closing the door of another room she entered quietly behind her.

Dale led me into the bedroom she had just vacated. It was low ceilinged, dim, the curtains drawn almost wholly across the windows to exclude the brightness of the sun.

A woman in nurse's uniform rose from a chair as we went in, laying down her knitting and nodding with a pleasant smile to both of us.

"I'll leave you," she said. "You needn't be afraid to disturb her. She's awake."

I would have left Dale to greet his mother alone but he drew me forward with him towards the big double bed. It was too dim to see clearly. Mercifully, I thought. In the full light of day, the havoc wrought on the right half of the quietly motionless face and body would have been too pitiful. The shadows were kinder; but not kind enough. It was still a grievous wreck that I saw.

There was nothing of Dale in her. It was possible to see that from the unravaged half of her face. I tried to concentrate on that, and not on the drawn distortion of the other side. Her appearance had shocked me even though I had been partially prepared.

Dale said "Mother?" very softly, as though torn between desire to rouse her to knowledge of his presence and reluctance to disturb her. There was a wealth of love in his voice, and in the gentleness of his hand as he laid it over hers. I was sure that if she had not responded he would not have persisted, despite his longing.

But the twisted mouth moved. "Dinly?" The left eye fluttered open slowly, stressing the disparity between the two halves of her face. It searched weakly to distinguish the features bent over her. Then, "Oh, it's you, Dale," she murmured.

The repudiation of him was there, for all the difficult articulation of the words. As the eye closed again with weary disinterest, I saw that Dale's face was suddenly bleak with harshness.

I caught my breath as the profound pity for him flooded through me. He stood, seemingly uncertain, before he slowly relinquished her hand; even then, I think, hoping that the withdrawal would induce some reaction from his mother.

When there was no response he straightened up, turning to me.

"Well," he said with false lightness, "I think we've just time for a cup of tea before we leave."

The red-flagged kitchen was empty when we entered it, although a pan gently simmering on the big electric cooker proclaimed an earlier occupation. Whose? Helen's? I wondered. Everything was neat, spotlessly clean and shining, the tiled window ledge gay with bowls of daffodil bulbs in flower.

Dale found his way round unerringly, locating all the things he sought without difficulty. By the time the electric kettle had boiled he had everything ready on the blue formica topped table.

I wanted to say something to him but I didn't know of any way in which to express sympathy for the bleak hurt that was still lambent in his eyes. He guessed it. Without any preliminary, knowing that the remark needed no expounding, he said defensively, "She's ill. Only half conscious."

But she had still reacted to the instincts that had dictated to her always. I didn't say it, but he was aware that I knew that, too. As he brought the teapot over to the table he said, abandoning all pretence, "It was always Dinly." But he said it whimsically, without any rancour.

He was a man torn between genuine affection for his brother and the deep wound of hurt for that brother's usurping of all a mother's love.

"I told you that the other day, didn't I?" he said, remembering. He spoke cheerfully now. "You must find me a crashing bore. How do you like your tea?"

"Does your brother run the farm?" I asked, sipping the tea when he had poured it.

"Lord, no! Never had the slightest interest in it. Not the life for him at all."

"Who does run it then—now that your mother is ill? Helen?"

Dale laughed. "Helen scarcely knows a cow from a horse. She's just taking care of the house. But there's plenty of good help about the place and I see to accounts and things at the week-end."

"Isn't it—embarrassing—for her to be here when your brother visits his mother?"

His eyes shadowed briefly. "Dinly doesn't come much, now," he said shortly, but a moment later he was discussing the farm, describing the working and the planning of it with cheerful amicability.

Later, when the teapot was empty, with a glance at his watch he said, "We haven't really time now, but I would have liked to have shown you round. I suppose you really have to get back? It isn't an engagement you can cut?"

"No," I said with such positive conviction that he looked curiously at me, but he didn't pursue the subject. But once again he didn't mention the possibility of a next time. There was no real reason why he should, but in some indefinable way I felt snubbed.

The feeling was still with me when he turned the Alvis into

the square and drew up before the flat entrance. On impulse I asked, "Why did you take me to the farm, Dale?"

"Why?" He was surprised. He twisted in his seat to look at me. "Because I thought a day out would do you good and you might enjoy it. You did, didn't you? I've never seen you so animated before."

He thought my unaccustomed lightheartedness was due to the outing he had arranged. I didn't disillusion him. To be fair, perhaps a little of it was. Even if I had not been meeting Robert that night I think I should have responded, in part, to the unexpected pleasure of the day. Most of the time he had been a calm, companionable person to be with. I had noticed formerly that some of his own relaxation could be imparted to me.

I was grateful to him for the way, although he couldn't know it, he had helped me through that particular day. I was grateful, too, that not once had he mentioned Robert's name. I should have been unable to discuss Robert without completely betraying myself. But he couldn't know that, either.

I forgot him immediately the flat door closed behind me.

11

As I switched off the engine I heard a clock somewhere in the distance striking nine. I checked the time by my watch before dousing all the car lights, knowing that I had an hour to wait.

When I had set out I had allowed myself plenty of time. Lya had told me it was not difficult to lose a shadow but I had viewed that airy dismissal of the problem with some scepticism, partly because I had not her experience but mainly because I had to first ascertain who was shadowing me.

I had seen no one during the day while I was with Dale who had seemed relentlessly intent on keeping me under surveillance. Cars had followed us, cars had overtaken us, but I hadn't been able to perceive one in particular that seemed disposed to keep us in sight. But I hadn't even noticed that I had been followed last night, although the colonel, who would be as unconversant as I in these matters, had observed it.

I had wondered how I could possibly lose someone who was on my trail if I couldn't establish who it was I had to lose. But it hadn't proved difficult. I didn't know whether it was because whoever was following me was becoming negligent or sufficiently indifferent as to not care if I was aware of the fact or not; or whether, and I realised this with a feeling of faint distaste, I was getting the hang of this cloak and dagger business. Whichever it was, I picked out the black saloon car almost immediately.

I had not been absolutely sure at first. Oxton bridge was some five miles from Renshaw; too near for my peace of mind. Even if I temporarily lost someone, once I had set out on that road they would guess my general direction and have no trouble in picking me up again. So I headed east, and although the black saloon remained behind me its journey could have been as innocent as the rest of the rush hour traffic. Not until I experimented by leaving the main east bound route, detouring round side streets to rejoin the road farther along, was I fully convinced. Whatever turn I made, the black saloon made, too; it was there, not too far behind, sometimes allowing other cars to fill the gap between us, but inevitably there. If I loitered, it loitered also. There could be no mistake that this was the one.

Twice I had tried the ruse of indicating I was making a left turn, seeing through the rear mirror the left indicator flashing on the car behind; changing my mind at the last minute and swinging sharply to the right with blind unconcern for any violation of the rules of the highway code. I had been chagrined to see that the black saloon had followed the same lunatic procedure.

I had begun to be a little worried. It looked a bigger car than my Mini. When I cleared the traffic I didn't think I would have much hope of losing it by speed down the open road. And even with time still in hand I couldn't afford too much of it by going too far in the wrong direction. The main paralysis of rush hour was over but I had London to recross. Before very long I should have to abandon this red herring of a trail leading eastwards.

The opportunity came very simply.

I chose a time when the black saloon had allowed another car to edge between us, deliberately slowing as I approached the traffic lights so that I hit the crossing as the amber was turning to red and then accelerating furiously across. Through the mirror I saw that the car between had prudently halted, preventing the black saloon from crashing the lights.

I turned down the first side street to the left, then left again. The third left turn brought me back to an approach of the lights at the same intersection. They changed to red and from the vantage point of four cars back in the queue I saw the black saloon crossing with the green light now in his favour.

I couldn't see him after he had passed. He would make the first left turning as he would have seen me do, but there were many side streets I could have taken. He wouldn't expect me to double back so quickly on my tracks.

I hadn't realised I could be so crafty but I couldn't feel any real satisfaction in my cleverness. What had been necessary had been accomplished but later, when I had time to dwell on it, I thought such furtiveness would sicken me a little. Perhaps at heart I was a strictly law abiding person. I had never previously had any real occasion to put myself to the test. I was glad now I hadn't told the colonel. Loyalty to me would have made him want to do something to help; he would possibly have insisted on accompanying me; but he would have hated such hole and corner manoeuvres.

I had kept a wary lookout for the black saloon but there had been no further sign of it. I had lost him. It had been as easy as Lya had said.

Oxton bridge spanned the main London railway line. The road was hardly more than a cart track, I couldn't remember that it led to anywhere in particular. I had never driven up it before but Robert and I had walked it many times. It was little frequented even by day; it was unlikely there would be anyone in the area at that time of evening. Robert would have realised that when he made the choice.

I had drawn the Mini off the road at a point where the headlights picked out the incline that led to the bridge. At the top of the incline the lane angled sharply to the left to span the railway lines, with another acute bend to the right at the other end down the farther slope. The approach up the ascent was too narrow to park without partly obstructing the road; it also seemed wiser not to draw too much attention to the actual meeting place.

A train thundered past as I got out of the car. I waited until the sound of it had died into a distant rumble before I started walking towards the bridge.

I was early. I had an hour to wait . . . I could have remained in the car until nearer the time and it would have been better if I had. The warmth of the day had given way to a brittle coldness which indicated there would be frost again during the night. The low stone wall I found to sit on struck chill through my clothes within the first few minutes but I was too tensed with expectancy to return to the Mini. At long last I had reached the point which every fibre of my mind and body had ached for so despairingly; I couldn't retreat one step from it, even for temporary comfort.

It was a fool's paradise. There could be no permanency in it. Realising that could not make me any less joyous, any less taut with anticipation; it could not diminish the feeling of portentous fulfilment.

It was so dark I couldn't see my watch and the clock that chimed remotely on the quarter hours had such long intervals I was certain it must have stopped. Occasionally in the sky I could see the faint reflection of headlights from the distant country road, even hear the faint murmur of engines from time to time, but they were more than a mile away. Trains passed at infrequent intervals, vibrating the ground; but apart from those periodic disturbances the stillness was so profound it would have been frightening had I been on any other mission.

The clock tolled out the quarter to the hour when I had given up all hope it would ever do so. It was clearer than before, carried more distinctly as though with some variation of the wind although not even a slight breeze was apparent in the still, cold air. It should have been a clarion declaration of exultation; instead the sound was doleful, full of melancholy sadness.

After that, the waiting was an unendurable eternity. I chided myself for being so foolishly affected by the sonorous tolling of an old church clock, but it was strange that now, as the moment of being with Robert again was imminent, for all the joyous expectation I had never felt so alone. The bright lights of a passing train, its windows steamed with warmth, the carriages filled with people, was a world remote from my own, stressing too cruelly my own isolation.

I had a brief moment of wondering what I was doing here. What had we come to, Robert and I, that we should be meeting in this furtive manner, with fear of discovery in my mind as it must be in his. I was not even a woman waiting for a husband who had deserted her. I had no claim on him, beyond three years of happiness together which had meant so little to him he had discarded them lightly. He had not even had the decency to tell me when Lya came back into his life, to leave me with at least my memories intact. Instead he had embarked into an unlawfulness that had brought us to this.

There had been no sound to warn me. How could I have failed to sense instinctively that he was near? He could have been there some time for all I knew, coming unheard under the roar of an earlier train. There was one approaching now, the sound of it still muted in the distance but ever increasing. It was that, that had made me look up, to see the man standing across the lane against the parapet of the bridge.

He was a vague, blurred outline. If my eyes had not become accustomed to the darkness in all that time I could easily have failed to distinguish his presence there.

The rush of thankfulness made my senses swim, paralysing me. Now there was no bitterness, no reproach; no aversion for the circumstances. There was nothing but Robert.

I hurt with love. It was a deep wound scarring through me, obliterating everything but the fact of his nearness. I no longer knew where I was or why we should have to be meeting here, in this deserted place. There was only an ending at last to all the hopeless loneliness of separation from him.

Not until he stirred did I find power to move my nerveless limbs. I got up then, oblivious of the stiffness from the long, cold waiting. My whole body was flooded with warmth, but cramped muscles made me stumble as I took those first few steps towards him.

"Robert—oh, Robert . . ." The name choked in my throat. I would have flung myself headlong into his arms, not thinking, and not even caring in that moment, that there was not perhaps the frantic longing for closeness in him as there was in me. I had forgotten Lya. It would have made no difference if I had remembered her.

Robert restrained me.

"Sh-sh!"

The train almost drowned the sibilant warning. I could barely discern the gesture as he put a finger to his lips, but the air of caution was unmistakable. I went with him unresistingly when he took my arm.

He was leading me over the bridge. If he had come by road, he had come from the other direction. He could be taking me to a car he had left. And then, as though my own urgency had communicated to him and he, too, could endure the waiting no longer, in the middle of the bridge he halted, gathering me suddenly, bodily, into his arms. Lifting me and holding me closely against him in desperate intensity.

The roar of the train was indistinguishable from the tumultuous pounding of my heart. The vibration of it as it thundered nearer was the wild trembling of my own body. I was drowning in the suffocation of that deeply longed for fulfilment.

It all happened so quickly; there was so little time, I was never sure afterwards whether I knew an instant of terror or not. Or even whether, had there been time, I would have known terror. I wasn't sure of anything.

There had been something . . . In three years I had become as sensitively attuned to the familiar pliancy of the arms that held me as I was to the movements of my own body. It could have been the circumstances, the tension in both of us, which made the difference. There was no real certainty in me that there had been a difference. It was all a part of the hideous confusion.

There was a sharp pain in my back, but even as I gave myself up briefly to the pain searing through me there was another, greater, more unendurable pain.

The sound of the train had died in the distance but the night erupted with the shrillness of police whistles, of men shouting, of pounding footsteps. Above it all, a woman was screaming; in time drowning all other sound so that there was only that high-pitched keening of a name.

I hadn't even seen him go. One moment there had been only the exquisite bliss of closeness, the next I was alone in chaos. I lay where I had fallen, the lights from flashing torches adding to the lost confusion. The disappointment was too intense, too much for me; but I lay quietly now, no longer screaming Robert's name in hysterical hopelessness. I was unconscious of the hardness of the ground, of the cold, of the pain in my back. There was only that great void of emptiness.

When a torch was shone in my face I closed my eyes against the brightness of it, wanting only to be left alone in the darkness. There were voices around me, not shouting as they had been previously. One, I seemed to know, and momentarily, in the confusion of my mind, a feeling of familiarity made me mistake it for Robert's.

Hands that were surprisingly gentle pulled me to my feet, checking when I winced with returning pain.

"Are you hurt, Mrs. Grayson?"

"Probably caught her back across the parapet, sir. She seemed to fall that way."

I felt hands exploring my back, stressing on the point which made me wince again. "Bruised, I should think. You're a lucky girl, Mrs. Grayson." I wondered bleakly how he came to that conclusion. "Can you stand? Better send one of the cars along, Mollett. It'll be warmer for her."

He helped me into it when it arrived, settling me in the front passenger seat before getting into the driving seat himself. It was warm in the car; he left the engine running, with the heater on, but my teeth were chattering uncontrollably now, and not with the cold.

I had seen his face in the headlights, as vaguely recognisable as his voice.

"Yes, it's Palmer," he confirmed.

The name brought a flare of futile anger. "What are you doing here?" But the anger was fleeting, over almost before it began. I was too dazed for any sensation other than despair to last. The shock of the interruption at the moment of ecstasy was still with me, crushing me defeatedly.

"A good thing for you we *were* here," he said with grimness. He lit two cigarettes, forcing me to accept one of them when I would have refused.

The torch lights had dispersed in the distance now, scattered around the area both sides of the railway lines; flickering with the luminescence of glow worms amongst the thick undergrowth. There was still shouting, but it was spasmodic and indistinct.

It was Robert they searched for, and fear of his discovery warred with the longing that he would be brought back to me. There had been so little, when I had yearned for so much. I had exchanged scarcely a word with him, only that choking utterance of his name, and Robert had not spoken at all. There had been only that sudden urgency on the bridge to indicate his emotions. He had had no chance to offer me any explanations, not even to tell me what need had made him risk waiting in the square to see me.

But fear was predominant. Palmer had been considerate; he had also a duty to perform and he would not allow consideration for distress to deter him indefinitely from it.

"Where will your husband be heading for, Mrs. Grayson?"

I shook my head mutely.

He said, "You're not really helping him, you know. We shall find him eventually, it's only a matter of time. But it would be better for both of you if you told me now."

"I don't know," I mumbled.

"I think you do." He was still persuasive but it didn't entirely conceal the hard determination. "And I must warn you, you can be in serious trouble. It's an offence to withhold vital facts from the police. I'm asking you once again where he will have gone?"

"I told you, I don't know."

"You're not being very sensible, Mrs. Grayson. You must have some idea. You've been in touch with him otherwise you could not have arranged this meeting. I think you've known all along where he is hiding out. In fact, I think there are a lot of things you know that you haven't told me. Now why don't you make it easier for yourself and tell me?"

My teeth were chattering audibly above the quiet murmur of the engine but I maintained a stubborn silence. He went on, quietly persistent with his questions, trying to coax some response from me. He was growing impatient with his failure, looking up irritably when a helmeted head appeared at the window.

"Anything?" he asked curtly, and I held my breath.

"No, sir. It looks as though he could have got away."

"What about the road blocks?"

"Nothing to report, sir. But if he knows these parts well and left his car outside the area of the blocks, he'd have no trouble dodging back to it across country through these woods, sir."

"I know that," Palmer said testily. "And you can rely on it he knows his way around these parts. Keep on searching. There's a chance he's holed up somewhere until things quieten down a bit. And send Sergeant Mollett back here."

I let my breath go with a shuddering sigh and Palmer turned back to me, his face grim.

"It's no occasion for relief that he's got away, Mrs. Grayson. Your husband is a dangerous man."

"Please let me go," I said plaintively.

"Presently. When you've told me where he will have gone."

"I wouldn't tell you if I knew," I said, and his mouth tightened.

He looked at me for a long time with bleakly cold eyes before saying, "I don't understand you, Mrs. Grayson. Loyalty, as you interpret it, up to a point, yes; even though it's misplaced. But how can you still feel you owe him loyalty after he has tried to kill you?"

"Tried to . . . ?" I stared at him blankly, uncomprehendingly.

"Didn't you realise? He was about to drop you in front of that train. We had to shout when we realised his intention. But for giving him that warning, we'd have got him. He tried to kill you. Do you still want to protect him?"

"No . . ." I said. "No . . . Robert wouldn't . . ."

I thought I had been trembling previously. It was nothing compared to the ague that seized me now. I couldn't breathe for the violence of it. I was unable to speak. I could only stare at him with piteous eyes that pleaded for a denial.

"I'm not wrong, Mrs. Grayson," Palmer said, more gently. "There were enough of us to see it. You were damned lucky that he decided to drop you on this side of the parapet when we yelled at him. Although I doubt it was consideration of you made him do so. Few people would commit cold-blooded murder in front of witnesses. You've had a very narrow escape. Your faith in your husband very nearly caused your death. You might not be so lucky another time."

"It wasn't Robert," I said pitifully. "He has no reason to—kill me. He wouldn't . . ."

"It was Robert, and you know it."

"I don't . . . I don't . . ." I moaned.

"Then why were you screaming his name?" he demanded.

"It couldn't have been Robert, it couldn't. Robert wouldn't . . ."

"He would and he very nearly did," Palmer said inexorably. "Whatever else is proved against him, when he is found he will be charged with attempted murder."

I was sick, violently and so suddenly that I had scarcely time to fumble open the door handle before the nausea overcame me. The ground rose up to meet me, heaving dizzily with the deep swell of the ocean. I moaned with the pain, with the sickness; but most of all from the hideousness raging in my mind.

The lights were flashing once more, nearer at hand, but I didn't know whether it was from the torches or from some inner conflict of semi-consciousness. Through the heavy drumming in my head there was only vague awareness of being helped, of being held while I retched with the sickness, of someone smoothing the hair gently back from my damp forehead. There was kindness in the touch, but it was impersonal. I was lost in the profound loneliness of the administrations of strangers. I wanted someone desperately . . .

In a moment of lucidity, in the confusion of voices I heard someone say, "She's in no state for further questioning tonight. Better get her back home."

I tried to struggle upright and the lights revolved giddily in vivid flashes of colour that hurt my eyes, threatening further nausea. I had to wait until it subsided before I managed to speak.

"Take me to the colonel."

It was a cry in the dark. I think somewhere, in the dim, lonely recesses of my mind, I had finally realised the hopelessness of ever again turning to Robert. Whatever the reason, it was the colonel I wanted.

It was all I could say now, the only coherent thought in my mind. I went on reiterating it over and over again. "Take me to the colonel."

12

The colonel calmed me. No one other than Robert could have subdued the sobbing hysteria—and not Robert now.

Whatever he had felt about the unexpected appearance of policemen depositing a half-conscious, hysterical girl on him at that time of night, he had taken charge unquestioningly. I was his primary concern. If he had any queries, he didn't demand them of me. He may have had a brief explanation from Superintendent Palmer but I was in no condition to be aware of it having been given.

I know that he gave one small, stifled exclamation as he relieved the policeman of his burden, carrying me through to put me tenderly in his own deep armchair. He organised without fluster, calling for Victor to produce brandy and a blanket to throw over me; putting fresh logs on to the dying fire and kicking at them impatiently to encourage them into activity.

When the brandy was poured he held the glass, coaxing me to drink as he would have coaxed a child, with little murmured words of inducement, not ceasing in his efforts until the glass was empty. He lifted the blanket he had tucked round me to chafe my cold feet until the numbness went, taking over then from Victor who was rubbing my hands with his strong fingers. Between them, they tended to me with gentle care, adjusting the cushions behind my head, pushing the chair nearer to the now blazing logs.

When I opened my eyes I saw Palmer and the policemen still

there, looking oddly ineffectual and a little uncomfortable, as though in some way they would be held to account for my condition. But they had gone a few minutes later when I opened them again.

The colonel was missing, too, and I moved, stirred into alarm. I said, "Gregory?" in a plaintive voice and someone held me back when I tried weakly to rise.

"The colonel will be back in a minute, Mrs. Grayson."

I wondered why I had ever had such an aversion to Victor's unnatural strength. It was there now, but controlled. I could feel the compelling force even though he handled me gently.

The colonel wasn't alone when he returned. I recognised Dr. Frome and tried to protest when he insisted on examining my back. The colonel retired discreetly to the far end of the room while he did so, talking over his shoulder.

"Mrs. Grayson fell down the stairs. Probably caught her back on one of the steps. Not serious, I hope?"

The elderly doctor accepted his explanation without demur, whatever he may have been privately thinking.

"Very badly bruised, that's all. You're going to have a very stiff back for several days, Mrs. Grayson, but there's no serious damage. Just take things easy for a time."

On his way out I heard him murmuring to the colonel, "It must have been a very nasty fall. She's suffering from shock. Keep her quiet and don't let her overdo things. You'll be keeping her here tonight, I suppose . . ."

I didn't catch the answer; the murmuring died away in the hall.

And then the colonel came back once more and I relaxed. The luxurious atmosphere of his home enveloped me in comfort; almost as much as the colonel's presence, bringing a measure of tranquillity and composure. I was drowsy with warmth and a transitory feeling of security. I think I slept.

When I awoke he was sitting in the opposite chair; so still that I thought at first he must be sleeping until I saw that his eyes were not closed. I noticed with surprise that the hands of the carved gilt clock over the fireplace pointed to nearly two o'clock. The fire had died away again to red embers. He had perhaps not replenished it for fear of disturbing me, but the room had retained its warmth owing to the adequate central heating. It was very still and quiet; only the soft ticking of the clock and an occasional rustle from the logs as they settled.

The colonel didn't notice at first that I was awake. He was sunk in some profound contemplation, his face grave, the lines round his mouth and eyes deeply stressed, ageing him. The cluttered ashtray by his side proclaimed that he had been smoking almost incessantly, and the air was still hazy with the smoke, but there was no cigarette between his fingers now. But even as I watched him he reached out absentmindedly for the carved jade box, groping for the table lighter with his mind obviously on some problem with which he grappled and not on what his hand searched for.

In doing so, he glanced up and saw that my eyes were open, and immediately his face lightened with a smile.

"Better now?" he asked.

"Yes, thank you. It's late, I'm keeping you up," I said in compunction.

He shrugged that aside as of no consequence. "Would you like anything? More brandy? Victor is still up, if you would prefer tea? Or a cigarette?"

"I'd better go," I said with reluctance.

"My dear girl, you are not going anywhere tonight, except up to a bed that's waiting for you whenever you're ready. Victor has already collected your nightclothes from Far End. Found the key in your handbag. Hope you don't mind?"

"You think of everything."

"Victor's idea, that. Afraid it wouldn't have occurred to me, my dear. He's very proficient, I'm sure you'll find he's brought all you will need."

"I shouldn't impose on you like this," I said, but it was a half-hearted protest. I was grateful that he had taken the decision entirely out of my hands.

"Nonsense!" the colonel retorted briskly. "Who else should you impose on, as you call it? Damned glad you had the sense to come to me. Now, what about bed? You look tired."

I was, but it was a tiredness that sleep would not remedy. I sensed, also, that the colonel's mind seethed with a natural curiosity that his consideration had not allowed him to satisfy. He had half risen but when I made no offer to move he sank back again.

"Feel like talking?" he asked.

I nodded.

"Old Frome said you should rest." He looked dubious, and then, with a perfunctory dismissal of the advice, "Rest isn't always the answer. All right, then," he said.

But I just sat there. He waited, helping himself to the cigarette he had been interrupted from lighting previously, watching me expectantly through the cloud of smoke he exhaled. I was composed now. Still shocked, but with the remembered distress of a nightmare that is still retained with consciousness. I wanted to tell him. There was the wish now that I had confided fully in him earlier. I couldn't start. No sentence seemed the right one. Even yet, there was no full coherency in my mind, only a jumbled conflict of emotions.

The colonel studied me for a long time, with the questions building up inside him, the perplexity deepening in his face. When he spoke at last it was in utter incredulity.

"Palmer said you were meeting Robert. The man's mistaken, surely? You couldn't have been."

He was expecting me to deny it. He looked even more astounded when I moved my head in agreement.

"You mean you actually saw him? Spoke to him?"

"I saw him. At least . . ."

"But you couldn't have!" he said. He was brusque in his bewilderment. More evenly, he went on, "Palmer said it was arranged; you were followed and Robert was nearly apprehended. It isn't possible." He paused, shaking his head in a slow motion as though to clarify his mind, framing the words with care. "Forgive me if I seem obtuse. Am I to understand that you've known all along where Robert is? That you've been in touch with him? It isn't possible!" he repeated, adding after a moment, "You would surely have told me."

"I don't know where he is. The police won't believe me but I don't."

"Then if you've had no contact with him, what led you to believe that Robert would meet you tonight?" he wanted to know in some mystification.

"I don't know where he is—but I know someone who does."

He started to say something and checked. "You know someone who does?" he said carefully. "Who might that be?"

"His wife," I told him simply.

The colonel stared at me long and thoughtfully, the cigarette arrested halfway to his mouth. He held my gaze for some time, his face very grave and still. When he spoke at last it was with infinite patience, as though he humoured an over-imaginative child.

"That's a very ambiguous remark, Rosanne. Could you explain it more concisely to me? Afraid my wits are rather scattered tonight."

"I'm not married to Robert," I said. "I never have been." Something in the politeness of his expression prompted me hastily to explain. "I didn't know until recently. Robert was first married years ago—to a Hungarian girl. Did you know that?"

"I had heard something of the kind," he admitted cautiously.

"I thought she was dead—Robert thought so too." Misery overwhelmed me. In a burst of uncontrolled passion I said, "I wish she had died! I wish she *had* been killed! Why did she have to come back? She doesn't love Robert, she only used him. He was happy with me—he *was* . . ."

I began suddenly to cry, the tears flooding up and spilling down my cheeks as I shook with deep, rending sobs.

The colonel didn't offer any sympathy; neither did he attempt to restrain the heart-broken outburst. He didn't even offer me a handkerchief when I fumbled helplessly for my own and failed to find it. He sat impassively until the spasm had spent itself and I was calmer.

"I think," he said then, "you should tell me how you came to discover that Robert's wife is still alive—and in what way she has used him."

So I told him, still hiccoughing a little. In the midst of it, I started searching for my handkerchief again and this time he leaned over silently to tender his own, the gesture in no way distracting him from his complete absorption. He uttered not a single word of interruption, not even to prompt me back when I strayed from the direct narrative. I was probably not too coherent, but he let me tell it my own way.

His calm, controlled patience was all the more remarkable in contrast to the inward rage which slowly accumulated. The quietness in him was of a dangerous quality, a calmly deceptive veneer repressing the surging depths of an immense fury. The extent of that latent anger took me by surprise; at times the cause, as much as my own distress, of making me falter uncertainly. I expected any moment the fermenting storm to erupt. I think I was even a little afraid of the enormous volume of violence suggested by the tightness of the darkening face and the grey, glinting steel of the blue eyes.

The anger, when it came, was directed at me. But there still wasn't the violence I feared, only a cold, biting hardness.

"I thought you trusted me!"

"I do . . ."

"And yet you gave no intimation, you said not a word to me . . ." A thought struck him. "Did you know about this meeting when you were with me last night?"

"Not exactly when it would be . . ."

"I should have guessed! I just didn't believe it possible, even though you puzzled me. You didn't see fit to confide in me?"

"I didn't want to involve you," I said.

"Involve?" He gave a sharp bark of unamused laughter. The anger had not lessened. Although he softened his voice it was with a visible effort. "I am involved. Whatever concerns you, concerns me. I thought you knew that, Rosanne."

I hadn't realised he would feel so intensely. It confused me, making me drop my eyes, to begin pleating the corner of the blanket into symmetrical folds. When I glanced up later he was watching me in dark, brooding thoughtfulness.

"Did you tell Palmer about this woman—Lya Logasi?"

"Of course not."

"They'll find out, you know, in time. I'm surprised they haven't already done so. But maybe they have."

In alarm I said, "Palmer didn't mention it."

"He wouldn't."

"But why wouldn't he, if he knew?"

"The police are reticent, my dear girl. They don't broadcast all they know. He could have been giving you the opportunity to tell him." Musingly, he went on, talking rather to himself than to me, "It is unlikely they don't know. You visited her twice, you would undoubtedly be followed. It is also unlikely they will as yet have questioned her, if they hope to get a lead on Robert without her suspecting."

"I don't think she would tell them where Robert is."

"I don't, either," he said with some grimness. "If she is wise—which is debatable—she would strenuously deny all knowledge of him, at least in recent years. She will not be able to deny her marriage to Robert, once her background is investigated. This man—Merrick," he said suddenly. "Does he know who Lya Logasi is in relation to Robert?"

"I don't think so."

"But you're not sure?"

"Yes, I'm sure," I amended with conviction. "There's no reason why he shouldn't have said so, if he did. Does it matter?"

"Not if the police already know. In fact, not really at all. I think my advice to you, Rosanne, is that you should tell Palmer yourself."

"No!" I said forcefully.

"I've told Palmer you will be at your flat tomorrow afternoon. He wants to question you again, naturally. I said I would let him know if you decided to remain here. In your own interests it would be wiser for you to make a clean breast to him."

"I shan't tell him! I won't help him to find Robert!"

One eyebrow was elevated slightly at my defiance, giving him a rueful expression, but his voice still held the cold hardness.

"I didn't think you would."

I asked fearfully, "Do you think they will catch him now—through Lya?"

"I doubt it. Robert appears to be both wily and cautious. He is not likely to go near her now, if he suspects you have been seen going there." He waited before saying, with a touch of sadness now, "Still this concern, Rosanne? Still this passionate faith in Robert's integrity, even after he tried to kill you tonight?"

I flinched, shrinking back into the depths of the chair as though from a physical blow. It was several moments, with the colonel watching me in compassion, before I managed to articulate, "They could have been mistaken . . . they couldn't really know. How could they when it was so dark . . . ?"

"They would not make such a serious accusation, my dear, if there had been any shadow of doubt."

"But Robert has no reason to—kill me," I pleaded piteously. I wanted affirmation from him for the preposterousness of such an attempt. He didn't give it.

"He could have reason enough, Rosanne, if you constituted a menace not only to his own freedom but also that of his wife."

The last words hurt, although I think he had meant them only to emphasise the position.

"He would know I wouldn't do anything to harm him . . ." I faltered.

"You had already harmed him. You had made too many inquiries; you had connected him with a woman he would wish to safeguard. You had compelled him into agreeing to meet you." He was inexorable in his persistence.

"But Robert wanted to see me. Why else would he have waited in the square near our flat? He *wanted* to see me," I reiterated.

The colonel hesitated, momentarily uncertain. "You are sure it was Robert?"

"Who else would it be? Anyone waiting innocently would not have run off like that," I argued with reason. "And have been waiting there the previous evening."

He moved his head non-committally. "Perhaps not," he conceded finally.

"And Lya was lying when she said he had been with her both those evenings. I know she was!"

There was very nearly a spark of amusement in the glance he shot at me. "Feminine intuition?" he queried. "Not always too dependable, but in this case it could probably be right. I wonder," he said after a moment, "why that same intuition fails you so abysmally in your estimation of Robert?"

"I lived with him for three years—I knew him . . ."

"You were blinded by love. Would you be interested in an insight of Robert as I saw him?" When I didn't answer he went on just the same. "I saw him as an ambitious man, with an eye to opportunity. Good natured, but a little selfish, egocentric. He liked to be admired, applauded; he would exert every ounce of congeniality to obtain these ends. Still, he was likeable. He had charm, I grant you. I can understand how you were bemused by it. Some of the biggest rogues in history have been plausible and endearing to those who loved them, and even to some who didn't. How could you, with your naiveté, be expected to realise that the charm was superficial, concealing a shallow nature?"

It was unpalatable. All I could say was, "Robert loved me . . . he *did!*"

"I think he did," the colonel agreed. "In his own way. Why should he not? He had a delightful and lovely young wife whom it pleased him to indulge and pamper. He was flattered by your obvious devotion, it inflated his ego."

"There was more to it than that," I said in a whisper. "You couldn't know. He was gentle and kind—thoughtful . . ."

"Why not? He had no cause to be otherwise. One doesn't beat a pet dog that is tractable and adoring." I gave a small smothered exclamation of hurt and more gently he said, "I am not being deliberately cruel, Rosanne. Only realistic, which you will not attempt to be." The hardness was creeping back into his voice, the words clipped and cold as he went on, "Previously, I thought Robert to be no more than self-centred and shallow beneath the outward charm. Now I know him to be utterly callous and ruthless. Whatever extenuating excuses could be found for his earlier conduct towards you, execrable though it was, even you, surely, can not forgive such a heinous attempt on your own life."

"I'm not sure it was Robert . . ."

The colonel took a deep breath. "If you saw him—"

"It was dark. I thought it was . . . But it couldn't have been!"

"You thought it was Robert until you were told he had tried to kill you." He was remorseless. "It was only refusing to believe that of him that put the doubt in your mind."

"No," I said in despair. "No—there was something . . ." It was all too confused. I didn't know now whether I had sensed that difference at the time, or only after. I started suddenly to cry again, but in quiet anguish now, not with the overwrought paroxysm of the previous outburst.

This time the colonel crossed over to me and held me close, cradling my head on his shoulder while he smoothed the hair gently back from my face. Even in the midst of my grief I was aware of the comforting strength of his arms, and of the smell of tobacco and the faintest trace of what could have been after shave lotion, that clung to him. The tweed of his jacket was rough against my cheek but I didn't move. It was the colonel who stirred at last, cupping my face gently between his hands.

"The light still shines very brightly, Rosanne," he said, with something that could have been regretful resignation in his voice. When I looked at him uncomprehendingly through drowned eyes he explained quietly, "The light you burn in the window to guide Robert home. But he doesn't need it, my dear. He has deliberately turned his back on it. Sooner or later, you are going to have to extinguish it."

"I know," I said sadly. "I know he won't come back to me. At first I hoped—I thought that if I could only see him again . . . But not when I knew it was Lya. But I just can't believe Robert would harm me."

"Robert is involved with people who are playing a dangerous game. They risk exposure and imprisonment, the ruination of a complex system of network if there is a weak link. Those they serve are hard task masters; mistakes are not easily forgiven. Robert would have to play it their way once he had chosen to become one of them."

"But it might not have been Robert tonight—"

"Whether it was or not, technically he is as guilty as whoever tried to commit the act. Will you promise me you will not keep any more assignations with him?"

"I can't do that . . . I would only break it, if the opportunity arose. I know I would."

There were signs of exasperation in his face. "Then you will let me know first?"

"If I could," I said hesitantly.

The exasperation was plain now, even though it mingled with deep concern. "Rosanne, you are in danger! I didn't tell you last night because I didn't wish to alarm you unnecessarily, but that graze on your arm could have been caused by a bullet. The tear in your sleeve was consistent with the damage a bullet would have done. It was only a suspicion I had, I dismissed it as being preposterous. The whole incident of those motor cycles struck me at the time as being damned odd behaviour, even for hooligans, but I had no cause to believe there was any reason why you should be personally victimised. Now I know differently! That was as much an attempt on your life as was tonight's episode. There would perhaps have been no occasion to arrange this meeting if Victor had not been at hand to pull you on one side at a crucial moment."

"We should have heard the shot," I objected faintly.

"Over that infernal racket? We should scarcely have heard if an atom bomb had been detonated! You are in danger, Rosanne! Last night I was merely uneasy over a ridiculous notion; now, frankly, I am afraid for you. You can't continue to be so repeatedly lucky." The anger was predominant again. It had never fully subsided; it had smouldered coldly behind every other emotion, but now there was only the anger consuming him.

He spoke harshly. "You have told me in confidence. I should

deeply regret to break it, but I shall have no compunction in doing so unless you agree to one of two things. Either you will place the whole facts fully before Palmer tomorrow or you will leave immediately for—Johannesburg, I think you said your sister lived."

"I couldn't do that to Robert," I said in distress. "Whatever he's done, I couldn't be the means of his being arrested."

"Then you will leave for Johannesburg on the first available flight, because otherwise I could, and will," he said inflexibly. "You will stay there until either Robert has been arrested, or any immediate danger to yourself is resolved."

Clearly, he expected no contradiction. He had meant what he said, leaving me no choice. He knew I would go, willingly or otherwise. What I was not sure about was whether or not I was sorry he had made the decision for me.

"And now," he concluded with a brief glimmer of a smile, having delivered his ultimatum, "it's time you were in bed. Frome left a sedative, you'd better take it."

He pulled me to my feet, steadying me as I swayed. As he stood with his arm round me I thought he would kiss me. I hoped he wouldn't, in that moment, but I would not have refused him. It would not have been anything other than a paternal benediction; I was certain of that. But, finally, he didn't even bestow that. He just stood looking down at me, his face very close to mine but I couldn't read the expression that was on it.

And then he said, in complaining exasperation, "Your eyes are so damned *candid*, Rosanne."

Twice, during what remained of the night, I roused sleepily to awareness that he had come in to see that all was well with me. He may have come oftener, for all I knew. He just stood there, quietly gazing down at me, the shaft of light from the open doorway outlining the breadth and height of him. He looked bigger than ever, silhouetted like that. Somehow immensely protective and comforting.

He had on a dark red silk dressing-gown. I remembered that later. I also remembered that his hair was untousled, as neatly brushed as always. I don't think he had been to bed.

He didn't speak. Once, I had felt the movement of bed-clothes as he pulled them up to cover my shoulder, the slight disturbance evoking the drowsy murmur of his name from me. But he didn't answer, and I had drifted back into drugged sleep, feeling oddly content and secure in the knowledge that he was watching over me.

13

It was late when I woke. When I pulled back the curtains the sun was already slanting obliquely through the south-facing window. Through another window on the side of the room I saw Victor washing the Mini. I think it was the soft hiss of the hose that had finally penetrated into my sleep, rousing me. It was a domestic scene, the very prosaicness of it making the events of last night seem remote and unreal on that peaceful spring morning.

I stood for a few minutes before turning reluctantly away from it. I saw that Victor had thoughtfully brought a change of clothes for me. The suit was laid out ready for wearing, fresh underclothes folded neatly by the side. There was no sign of those I had worn yesterday. It wasn't difficult to guess that they had been removed for laundering. My toilet requisites were arranged on the dressing-table. Victor had even known which shoes I would wear to the suit he had chosen to bring.

I felt a rush of gratitude for such care and consideration. They thought of everything.

I dressed slowly, my bruised back causing me to wince painfully with every movement. The suit was one I kept at Far End. I hadn't worn it for some time and I was surprised to see how loosely it hung on me now. I hadn't realised how much weight I had lost, although the hollowness of the face reflected back at me in the mirror should have told me.

Apart from a faint stirring of activity from the kitchen in the rear quarters the house was quiet when I descended the wide staircase. There was no sign of the colonel. I ventured glancing into the lounge and the dining-room, even the small breakfast-room; all rooms which were socially admissible to any guests. When I drew a blank I hesitated outside the only door left, which led to his study. I had never previously been invited into this sanctum. I doubted anyone had, and I was unwilling to take the liberty of intruding beyond the limits he imposed on the extent of his hospitality.

But I need not have worried. When I finally knocked timidly, only opening the door in response to his curtly abrupt "Come!", he jumped up immediately, smiling in pleasure.

"It's you, Rosanne. Come along in, my dear."

Unlike the rest of his luxurious home, his study was austerely masculine, almost bare. Apart from the mahogany desk, which was orderly even though he had been working at it, the only other furniture in the room were two deep leather armchairs by the fireplace. There were none of his priceless *objets d'art* in here, no treasures of antiquity which filled the rest of the house, no delicate blendng of colours to delight his connoisseur's eye. The carpet, though expensive, was of nondescript shades of brown and fawn, the dark brown velvet curtains were rich but sombre. Book-lined walls added to the heavy drabness of the room. The contents of the shelves may have been valuable editions but they did nothing to enliven the gloom. It was not at all what I would have imagined.

"Disappointed in my holy of holies?" the colonel asked. He hadn't missed my appraisal of the room; equally obvious, he hadn't failed to detect my reaction to it. I flushed uncomfortably to think that my expression had conveyed too clearly my candid opinion. "This is a working room," he explained. "The rest of the house is for my pleasure. If you don't like it, we'll go into the lounge."

"I ought to be going," I demurred.

"Not until you've had breakfast. Nonsense! I insist you have something. It's time for my coffee, anyway. Join me in that and Mrs. Cooper shall make you some toast, at least."

As we waited for the arrival of the coffee he said bluntly, "Pointless to ask how you are. That haunting sadness gives you an ethereal appeal which is enchanting in its way, but I prefer you as you used to be, vivaciously sparkling with life. However, you slept well."

He showed no signs himself of a sleepless night. His eyes were as keenly alert as ever, his face a little less grim this morning, but still purposeful. I guessed it would be useless to ask if he had had a change of mind. Last night I had been dismayed that his ultimatum had compelled me into accepting the proposed exile to Johannesburg. Now I was not so sure.

"You came in, I know," I murmured.

"Little anxious about you," he said gruffly, but he didn't enlarge on what was plainly an understatement, and he made no reference to the cause of his anxiety, beyond as I was leaving, the still gruff reminder, "You gave me a promise, don't forget!"

I had expected him to try to detain me, but he made no such attempt. As I climbed into the Mini which had been brought round to the front door, he asked, "Would you like Victor to drive you?"

When I declined he slammed the car door firmly before stepping back. I looked round as I braked for the turn into the road to give a last wave to him, but I saw, a little ruefully but without surprise, that he had already gone back into the house.

He had done what was necessary—more than necessary, I reflected in gratitude; having done it, he was not the man to waste time on over-prolonged courtesies of speeding a departing guest. Even me.

I had not been at the flat many minutes when Superintendent Palmer phoned to see if I had returned. He said he would be round to see me shortly and arrived less than half an hour later.

He was no more satisfied with the results of the interview than he had been previously. The knowledge that I was concealing facts from him made me evasive and unconvincing; plainly he didn't believe me when I insisted truthfully I didn't know where Robert was.

I could see no reason not to tell him frankly when he wanted to know how the meeting had been arranged last night. He had Mrs. Lloyd in and questioned her with equally unsatisfactory results. Her description of the boy who had handed her the note was vague and unhelpful.

"Not that it would make much difference," he commented,

when he had let her return to her duties. "Just anyone, probably. Any boy in the street would do a small task like that for a reward. You say you burnt the note, Mrs. Grayson? You know it was your duty to inform us when you received that message?" he said on a heavy note of censure.

"Would you really have expected me to?" I asked.

"I shall, if there is another," he retorted with grimness. "I warned you last night, you're dealing with a dangerous man. I had hoped Colonel Haldane would make you see reason. He seems a sensible man."

I told him that the colonel had persuaded me to join my sister in Johannesburg, wondering if he would raise some objection about my leaving the country. He seemed, on the contrary, to regard it as wise procedure.

Before he left, he warned me as the colonel had done, about the danger of another meeting if Robert should attempt to arrange one.

"It's hardly likely he would expect you to risk it, not after last night. If he should have the audacity, for your own safety alone, Mrs. Grayson, I advise you to notify me."

Dale Merrick was on the point of ringing the door bell as the superintendent left. The two men eyed each other without speaking. Palmer had seemed about to administer another injunction of caution to me but he refrained in Dale's presence, merely leaving with a curt nod.

Dale barely waited until the door had closed behind him.

"I've been ringing up all morning," he said. "Mrs. Lloyd said she'd have you phone as soon as you came in."

"I intended to. There wasn't time . . ."

"Where have you been, Rosanne?" I told him. "Ah, the colonel, yes," he said. "I should have thought of him. To tell the truth, I haven't been thinking very clearly. Are you all right, that's the main thing? My God, when I think . . . You could have been killed, Rosanne!"

He looked distraught, even a little dishevelled. His hair was unruly, as though distracted fingers had repeatedly disturbed it, and his usual neat appearance was marred by a crooked tie and an unfastened shirt button.

He had taken my hands, holding them forcibly, even shaking them in his urgency as he asked, "What happened?"

Even that slight jerking of my body pained my back, but not until he saw the grimace which I couldn't control would he allow me to withdraw them from his hold.

"Sorry," he muttered. "I've been so damned worried, you know. Is it very painful?"

"Mainly only when I'm shaken," I said, and a small rueful smile flitted across his face.

"Sorry," he repeated. "I'm a clumsy idiot." But his main concern was hearing about last night. "What happened?" he asked again. "What went wrong?"

"Everything," I said.

"Whatever possessed Robert? He must be mad! For God's sake, why should he try to kill you?"

"If it *was* Robert . . ."

"If it . . . ?" He stared incredulously. "Is there a doubt?"

"Only in my mind, it seems," I said rather bitterly.

"If it was Robert you were meeting, surely it was Robert who turned up?"

I gave a small, weary sigh. "I don't know. It's all so mixed up . . ."

Something was fretting at the back of my mind. Just an irritating sensing of something wrong; so vague, as barely discernible as when one instrument of a large orchestra is so slightly out of tune that it is perceptible only to the hypersensitive ear. Something, perhaps, that I should have remembered, but my mind wouldn't bring clearly into focus.

Dale was saying, "I wish I had never told you about Robert," and I dragged my mind away from trying to clarify the cause of that obscure uneasiness, turning to look uncomprehendingly at him, and he explained, "I feel it's my fault, by drawing your attention to him hanging about round here. You might never have had any contact with him, but for that." After a moment he added casually, "But I thought you told me you didn't speak to Robert that night?"

He was seeking an explanation; trying not to appear too obvious and failing dismally.

It wasn't that I didn't trust him. I was, in fact, surprised to find how much I felt I could. There was no doubting his genuine concern. His face, despite the stress of anxiety, had an unexpectedly ingenuous boyishness and his hazel eyes had a depth of warmth I had never seen previously. I was sure that if he should smile they would not remain cool and aloof from the curving of his mouth, the smile would be reflected wholeheartedly in them.

It was perhaps that it seemed pointless to go over the same ground with him that had been thrashed out so fully with the colonel.

"It wasn't your fault," was all I said.

He didn't press it, as he would probably once have done, with disarming obliviousness of unwelcome intrusion. There was no trace today of the brashness I had earlier deplored; he was a serious, troubled man, whom worry made appear oddly youthful. I had a feeling that, of his guises, this one was the more authentic.

He was not to be fully consoled, although this time I didn't think it was an angling after information as much as a reproach to himself.

He sounded humble. "I wouldn't like to feel I had been the cause of any harm befalling you. I should have left well alone."

"It wasn't your fault," I repeated a little irritably; abstracted, because realisation of the evasive memory that teased at my mind was very nearly there. If he had not diverted me, I should have remembered then. He had fallen silent, as though crestfallen by the impatience, leaving me for those few brief moments with that suppressed knowledge almost germinating into elucidation.

And then Dale said, "Could I trouble you for a cigarette? Mine seem to have got mislaid."

I think the words were identical; but more than the actual words it was the request, uttered in a tone so similar as to almost be the same voice, bringing remembrance flooding in of a nearly forgotten episode on a never to be forgotten night. A voice that had hardly registered at the time in the turmoil that had been my mind that night, but I knew now what it was that from the beginning had made Dale seem familiar to me. Not his appearance, not the very ordinariness of him, but that timbre of his voice which had touched a dim chord of memory. If he had not made that exact request I should perhaps never have placed the feeling of familiarity, touching off that other recollection.

I jerked round, holding the cigarette box, my hand arrested in the act of passing it to him; incredulous, still not quite believing it myself and yet knowing it was true.

"That's where I lost my lighter," I said in a small, wondrous voice.

He didn't understand. He said "Uh?" inquiringly, as he relieved me of the box and extracted a cigarette from it. I didn't even notice that he had offered it to me first before helping himself.

"That's where I lost my lighter," I said again. "I gave it to that man—the man who crashed his car . . ."

I was still not making sense to him.

"I thought," he said cautiously, "you claimed the lighter that was found in Keith Forrester's pocket was yours?"

"It was. But it couldn't have been." I was contradicting myself in excitement. I tried to be more explicit. "It *was* mine. But it couldn't have been found in *his* pocket. How could it, when—"

"The police would not make a false statement like that," he pointed out reasonably. "If they said that's where they found it, you can accept the veracity of their word."

"It *couldn't* have been on him!" I was becoming impatient of his obtuseness. "I left it with the man who crashed his car."

"What man was this?"

"I don't know. I don't think the police know—or at least they hadn't identified him at the time of the inquest. I had to attend it, I was the only witness—"

"I didn't know you'd been involved in a car accident."

"I wasn't involved. I just saw it happen."

"When was this?"

"The night Robert left me."

"The night Forrester was killed?"

"If he *was* killed that night. There's no certainty about that."

"It's a safe assumption," he said. "But go on about this accident. Where did it happen, and how?"

"Near Rillerby. I was on my way to Far End. He was driving like a lunatic, much too fast; he couldn't take the narrow bridge."

"You mentioned inquest, but he couldn't have been killed outright," Dale said. "You claim you gave him the lighter."

"He asked for a cigarette. It was easier to give him my own than search for his in the darkness."

"Did you tell Palmer this?" he wanted to know.

"I've only just remembered. I haven't really thought about the accident since. That night . . . I wasn't thinking about anything except what Robert had told me on the phone. I was nearly out of my mind. Even when I heard later the man was dead I scarcely thought about him beyond feeling resentful towards him because his sheer folly had detained me—if the accident hadn't occurred I might have reached Far End before Robert left. And then now —when you asked for a cigarette, your voice was so like his . . . he used almost the same words."

"You left your lighter with him—just like that?" The consternation in his voice was out of all proportion, even for an expensive gold lighter.

"I told you, I wasn't thinking clearly. I was in a frantic hurry. If I thought about it at all, I suppose I expected to go back, but when I had reported the accident it seemed unnecessary. I didn't realise he was so seriously injured—but the police were going, and an ambulance. I couldn't have done anything."

"It seems—odd," he said slowly, "you should remember now; be reminded by a voice . . ."

"You have the same upward inflection at the end of certain words—"

"I've been told that." He had been holding the unlighted cigarette in his hand, studying it thoughtfully. He threw it away, now, almost with repugnance. "This man," he said.

"The man isn't important," I stated irritably. "Not really. Only in regard to the fact that that's where I lost my lighter."

"You must be mistaken. You said you were confused that night." His eyes were veiled as he watched me. "You're sure you are not still confused?"

"Of course I'm not!"

"Palmer thought you were lying when you said it was yours," he reminded me. "He thought you were trying to protect Robert. He could possibly still think you are lying."

"It was my lighter," I said fiercely, "and whatever he says, it could not have been discovered on Keith Forrester's body."

"Then how did Palmer come by it?"

"He must have got it from the things that were found on the other man, the one I gave it to."

Dale shook his head. "I doubt he would know anything about that. A local road accident, even a fatal one, doesn't normally come under the jurisdiction of Scotland Yard."

"But if he knew I had been connected with it, even innocently . . ."

He shook his head again. "Rosanne, Palmer is a highly respected member of the police."

"He thinks Robert murdered Keith Forrester—"

"Whatever he thinks, he would not perjurously confuse the issue by deliberately transplanting evidence. Trust Palmer, Rosanne, even if you trust no one else." He spoke very seriously, very earnestly, his face no longer ingenuously youthful but grave. He had turned to gaze out of the window but it was improbable he saw the scene in the square on which his eyes dwelt. From there he asked, after a little pause, "I suppose there is no possibility of two identical lighters?"

I scoffed at that. "Do you think I don't know my own property? It was one Robert had specially made for me, my initials engraved on it, too."

"And you're still convinced you're not mistaken where you lost it?"

"I'm not mistaken!" I declared positively.

He was silent so long now, still gazing unseeingly out of the window, that I said at last, uncertainly, "Dale?"

He turned then, squaring his shoulders which had drooped wearily as he stood there in contemplation; his eyes unfathomable beneath the sombreness lurking in them.

"I'm beginning to wonder," he said, "whether you might not wish that you were."

He wouldn't explain the remark. He had left soon after but somehow, today, he was not to be dismissed so easily from my mind. It amazed me, in fact, that I had hitherto regarded him as of so little significance. Whatever else he was, Dale Merrick was not an insignificant man.

He loomed largely in my thoughts, intruding persistently, when I wanted to concentrate on more pressing problems. There was no reason why he should, except, perhaps, that the sombre intensity in his eyes had disturbed me irrationally.

Superintendent Palmer was out, I was informed when I tried to reach him on the telephone. I gave my name, refusing to leave any message beyond that I should like to see him as soon as possible. He would probably jump to the wrong conclusions when he heard that, I reflected, but I guessed that he would come running.

I waited a while. It was a situation I wanted clarified without delay, but I was impatient; inclining once more to the notion that had obsessed me ever since waking. An even more urgent point that needed resolving was the truth about last night.

There was no certainty I would get the truth from Lya. She would lie; she was clever, much more experienced than I. She could hardly be less, but even someone as worldly wise as Lya was not continuously proof against that unguarded glance or word. There was always the odd moment when the defence was vulnerable. She might even be devastatingly candid if I told her I was going away.

My conscience troubled me more than a little. The promise I had made the colonel about not seeing Robert had not been verbally extended to embrace Lya, but the inclusion had been in his mind when he extracted it, as he had assumed it was in mine. It was a partial violation of my word, no matter how I reasoned round it. If I told him, later, he would be justifiably angry; worse than that, he would be hurt and disillusioned.

I thought that whereas I might possibly be a little afraid of his anger, I should be grieved to have debased myself in his estimation. I valued his opinion quite disproportionately.

It would be more honest to give him warning of my intention, but when I phoned through to Coplands Victor told me that the colonel, also, was out. I couldn't wait until another day; I had no means of knowing how soon he would be able to arrange an air passage for me. I knew I couldn't go with that cankerous doubt forever in my mind.

I wouldn't allow myself to wonder if I could bear the truth. Deep inside me I acknowledged that the colonel's assessment of Robert's character had shaken me; at the time, although I wouldn't admit it, planting the first seeds of indecision about my own omniscience.

Palmer's opinion of the identity of the man on the bridge was incontrovertible, as was the colonel's. Even Dale . . .

Even Dale . . .

There was realisation then of what it was that earlier had fretted vaguely at my mind. Now it was so glaringly apparent I could marvel that it had only gently teased at me rather than shouted the inconsistency aloud.

He had been greatly concerned by the near-catastrophe of last night. He had been consumed with anxiety at how narrowly I had escaped disaster.

But how could Dale Merrick possibly have known about it?

There would be a perfectly plausible explanation, of course; one that I was too muddled at the moment to reason out for myself.

I was surprised to find how much I had grown to like him. At first I had just barely tolerated him for the sake of old boyhood association with Robert. Later, I had become more tolerant, partly because he had been so kindly anxious to give aid, but mainly because I had thought the regrettable brashness was an attempt to conceal an ingrained reserve. Some people were affected that way; in an endeavour to overcome an innate shyness they went too much to the extreme. The other day at Merrick— only yesterday? I recollected disbelievingly—I had had glimpses of what I had believed to be the real Dale Merrick behind that trait in him to overdo the efforts of friendliness. And again, today, I had been drawn to him as I never had been before.

Previously, even apart from the brashness, there had been an— oddness—about him that, even while it had not actually repelled, had held me aloof from the wish of any closer intimacy of friendship. There had been no sign of it today and there had been times, yesterday, when it had been lacking. But I knew now, with a sudden flash of insight, what the oddness was that I had only vaguely sensed.

It was as though he had been playing a part. A well rehearsed role in which half of his attention had been engrossed in the remembrance of his lines. But he had not been a sufficiently experienced actor, except on rare occasions, to make that too ingratiating smile penetrate to his eyes.

I had deplored that smile, but I had not previously distrusted it.

Previously? I was being stupidly unfair. He had gone out of his way to help me. In the short space of time in which I had known him, how much of that time had he devoted to my interests when there must have been other, prior, claims. For all his glib explanation about latitude, he must have neglected his own business to spare so much of it for me.

That, in itself, seemed strange. I would have imagined him to be plodding, methodical, in his work; it was out of keeping that he should not also be conscientious.

I was over-imaginative, I reflected a little disgustedly, to start entertaining misgivings about a man who had befriended me, simply because he had been deeply concerned over something I thought he should know nothing about. All I had to do was to ring the insurance firm where he was employed, and ask him. If he was not there, I could either leave a message or they would give me his London address.

I was ashamed of my doubts as I looked up the number and dialled it, almost on the point of hanging up. Robert had disliked personal calls interfering with business; unless of the utmost importance, he had firmly discouraged them. Probably most firms discouraged them, too.

Dale had wanted to know if I would still be at the flat that evening. He hadn't said so outright, but the query had implied that I might expect to see him then. I had already decided to wait when a bright young voice at the other end proclaimed that the call was through.

I need not have worried about importuning Dale's employers by intruding personal affairs into business hours. That particular firm had not, nor had they ever had, Dale Merrick on their list of employees. They had, in fact, never heard of him.

14

I sat puzzling over it a long time after the bright young voice had rung off. At my insistence she had made intensive inquiries, but finally having to express regret that she could give me no other information.

I had not mistaken the firm. I knew I had not. Dale had mentioned it once, and only casually, after I had pressed. At the time it had been only polite interest on my part, but I had remembered the name.

What then—and who—was Dale Merrick? If he was not an insurance investigator, why had he presented himself at Far End under that guise? Why had he lied, and so deliberately, that first morning, and later, when I had been idly questioning him about his work? And if he had not been following the pursuits of his employment, what had he been doing there in the first place?

I wondered if, after all, he had been merely another morbid sightseer as I had thought, and then had had to continue with the pretence. But the deception could have ended there and then, that morning. That need have been the one and only encounter.

Instead, he had chosen to befriend me. He had, I realised, determinedly and persistently befriended me, despite my all too obvious indifference.

Was I being unfair again? There was no reason to suppose that he would have sought to inflict himself on me further if he had not seen Robert that evening and reported the fact. Perhaps, even then, he would not have persisted if we had not met by chance the day we had lunched together.

The thought came, unbidden, that he had been a very ubiquitous young man. He had cropped up in exactly the right place at the right moment. There had been no genuine reason for his appearance at Far End that morning; he had been *passing* the square when he saw Robert; out of all London, by *chance* he and I had happened to be in the same street. Surely it was all a little too fortuitous. The limits of coincidence could extend only so far and still remain credible.

For the rest, he had been insistent, overruling objections; if the brashness had been only a façade, he had ignored snubs which should surely have deterred a reserved man. But not, perhaps, a man with a legitimate desire to be of assistance.

It was natural he should have felt interest and concern in the whole affair; he had known Robert in his younger days, he had been at school with him.

So had several hundred other boys, none of whom had thought fit to offer false credentials as a means of becoming acquainted with me!

If I were to inquire, would I find that statement as false as the other; would there be no such name on the roll of old scholars? I was suddenly so confident I was not even tempted to seek that proof. That, too, had been a lie.

But why had it been necessary for him to resort to those lies? If he hadn't known Robert and had no authentic interest through his employment in the affair, why had he interested himself at all by so determinedly cultivating my friendship. I couldn't deny he had sincerely tried to help. When he had seen Robert in this vicinity he could have given that information to the police instead of to me. And it was he who had told me, however unwittingly, of Lya's real identity.

Lya . . . Only Lya and Robert, besides myself, could have known of that arranged meeting for last night. But Dale Merrick had also known. Not from Robert, surely. But Lya . . .

Dale had known of her real name but he had given no intimation of knowing her personally; even if he did, it was absurd to think that Lya, with all the covert secrecy of her profession, would ever have divulged such information to anyone.

I pushed the riddle irritably on one side. When I tried ringing

Superintendent Palmer again, it was with the same result, and I decided not to wait any longer.

A light rain was starting to fall, dampening my hair as I crossed the yard at the back of the house to the garage, clinging finely to the old suit I was still wearing. Lya would be impeccably groomed, beautifully gowned, but I no longer cared about comparisons in appearance. I couldn't hope to rival Lya, even if I had troubled to make the attempt. There was no chance that I should encounter Robert at her apartment now, as the colonel had pointed out. I found that I no longer cared, even if he should be, that he should see me looking dishevelled and drab.

Reaction had set in from the shock of last night. The culmination, after weeks of sustained stress, had resulted in an unutterable weariness. Even the flare of excitement over the lighter had dissipated. It was just that one factor that I had to know now. After that . . .

It continued to drizzle as I drove through the streets, falling in a fine mist as I approached Elbury Court. The forecourt was unusually busy, even the entrance jammed with vehicles. If it hadn't been, making it impossible for me to drive in, I should not have seen Dale.

I had to go farther on to find a place to park. It was as I walked back that I noted first the faintly familiar outline of the green Alvis parked in the side street facing Elbury Court, and then, with a flicker of surprise, I recognised Dale sitting behind the wheel.

I would have asked him then about what had puzzled me. I was crossing the road with that intention when something in his attitude stopped me, making me stand in uncertainty. Although he watched the entrance opposite, he was a man totally absorbed in some inner contemplation.

It was that profound meditation that prevented him from noticing me, even though I was only a few yards away. So close that I could discern every detail of that face graven into immobility, the darkly brooding eyes fixed intently ahead; but I was sure that what he watched was not reflected in his mind.

I stood there, not knowing why the intense stillness of spirit in which he was wrapped disquieted me so much; even less being able to reason why suddenly I didn't want him to know I had been a witness to it.

I edged cautiously away, wondering if there was a back entrance to Elbury Court. I hadn't previously given a thought that by coming here I could be leading the police to Lya. If I had been followed now, I had been followed before. Even if it had occurred to me, I should not have made any attempt at evasion. My desire now to go in unnoticed was not an effort to deceive the police but because, inexplicably, I knew I didn't want Dale Merrick to see me.

I found a tradesman's entrance round the back and let myself in. A staircase immediately on my right reached to the upper floors. Several doors gave access to what I guessed would be kitchen quarters of the ground floor flats, one of which would be Lya's; but I would not sneak in by that back door. I had evaded being seen by Dale, which was all I wished.

I did have the wonder now what he should be doing there at all, but it became lost almost at once. The door immediately in front of me was obviously the one that led through into the main front entrance. I opened it, to be confronted by a scene of unusual activity.

There was no reverent hush in Elbury Court today. The warm, elegant foyer was packed with people, the customary quiet displaced by a bedlam of excitedly chattering voices. I stood in bewilderment, but guessing already, even before I noticed that one of the policemen present was on guard at that door, that the activity centred on Lya's apartment. Even as I watched, the door opened and Superintendent Palmer appeared at it, to speak a few brief words to the man stationed there. Before he had a chance to withdraw he was besieged by men of the waiting group who surged forward, urgently clamouring, many of them armed with flash cameras. I had a vague recognition of some of those men as belonging to the bevy of reporters who had harried me after Keith Forrester's murder had been discovered.

I shrank back, not wanting to draw either their attention or that of Palmer's, but not before I had seen the superintendent shake his head; even, in a momentary lull in the hubbub, heard him say, "Not now. Later."

In the increased outcry of disappointment which greeted his words, I withdrew unnoticed into the calm of the rear quarters, my mind racing in chaotic tumult. Was Lya being arrested? Had

Robert been discovered there? Was it Robert who was being arrested?

At that last thought I almost flung myself back through the crowd, demanding entrance. Only the thought of attracting the attention of that crowd of reporters by doing so deterred me. They were only doing their work, but they had terrified me with their importunities. Not until I knew for sure would I risk that barrage again.

To reach the lift, or any other apartments on that floor, I should have had to push through that gathered throng. Instead, I chose the back staircase to the floor above.

It was quiet up here, all the excitement concentrated on the ground floor, but it was unlikely that any occupants of the building could have remained unaware that something untoward was happening in their expensive, exclusive precincts.

I made a bad choice in my quest for information. The ringing of the bell at the first door I tried elicited no response. At the second, the white jacketed Filipino manservant who greeted me was charmingly courteous. His smile practically split his face in two, displaying an array of strong, perfect white teeth. His effort to sustain that wide smile while he spoke gave the words a faint sibilance.

"Yes, please?"

"I was wondering," I said haltingly, "if you could tell me what is happening downstairs?"

Clearly, he didn't understand me. He managed to frown and smile all at the same time.

"Name, please?" he requested.

I shook my head. "My name doesn't matter. It's just that I saw the police below and wanted to know why?" He didn't understand that either. "Police," I said. "Below," pointing downwards.

"Who calling?" he asked. His knowledge of the language was confined to the necessities of servitude only.

"Are your employers at home?" I remembered that there would probably be a name plate, and read it. "Mr. and Mrs. Bradwell? Are they at home?"

That registered. His face expressed suitable regret. "Sorry, no. Not at home this time."

I was turning away, giving it up as hopeless.

"Message, please?" the man said. "Who say calling?"

"It doesn't matter . . ." Names, he understood. I tried again. "Mrs. Logan," I phrased carefully. "Mrs. Julya Logan. Below," pointing down. "Something wrong?"

He had been smiling again; it was wiped away suddenly. I thought it was because he had failed once more to get the gist of what I was saying. I was moving away again when he said, "Lady dead."

I swung round, not believing what I had heard.

"Dead?" I said stupidly.

"Bad dead!" He was delighted at last to be able to be of assistance; anxious to please. Too anxious. He struggled for a word and failed to find it. When it eluded him completely, he put his hands round his own neck and squeezed realistically. He meant only to be explicitly helpful, but the crudely explanatory action, coupled with the dramatically rolling eyes, was horrific. "Bad dead," he said again and this time, in horror, I knew what he meant.

I turned, once more, blindly, instinctively, to the colonel.

15

I think, now, that in my heart I was finally acknowledging that Robert could be guilty.

It wasn't something I could face openly. Not yet. But if I had been honest with myself I would have admitted that those first seeds of doubt were there.

I tried to keep from exploring the possibility. It didn't prove too difficult, because my mind had an automatic aversion to thinking on those lines. It sheered violently away from even the first tentative probing down that avenue.

Lya, I found I couldn't dismiss. The Filipino's demonstration had been too realistic, conjuring up in ghastly detail the darkening of those perfect features as the life choked out of her, the lovely eyes protruding from her head in that last agony. I saw the limp, lifeless body thrown uselessly aside; the slim, curving body that I had expected to find so exquisitely dressed that in comparison I would appear unpresentable and dowdy. I wondered if she had screamed before the cruel pressure had crushed all sound forever out of her, or whether she had died silently, in mute horror but with the elegant grace with which she had lived.

It was even better to dwell on those gruesome details than to speculate on who had been responsible. I concentrated, also, on the roads, being over-meticulously observant. I drove cautiously, with exaggerated care, warning myself needlessly, well in advance, that there was a notoriously dangerous cross roads which had to be approached warily; that there were road repairs with single line traffic ahead, long before I came to the cautionary signs. My courtesy towards pedestrians and other drivers was too punctilious, too regardful of their needs. I gave way unnecessarily when the right of way was mine, to the fury of those I held up behind. It was no fault of mine if the rate of rising blood pressure failed to take a sharp upward trend.

My mind was two-dimensional. While one half of it recalled ahead, as though I planned a map in my head, every feature and junction of the road that was so familiar to me I could have taken each turning unconsciously, the other half was engrossed in a fascinated hypothesis of every last detail of Lya's death. I passed the place where the accident had occurred. Although there was no other traffic about on the quieter roads I was still exercising that extreme caution as I negotiated the bridge, but I gave scarcely more than a thought to my remembrance about the loss of the lighter. A few miles farther on, as I drove past the junction of the lane leading down to Oxton bridge, there was once more the wonder how Dale Merrick had known what took place there last night. But that, too, was only a transient reflection, submerged under the deluge of ghoulish horror which engulfed me and the desire, growing ever stronger now as I drew nearer, to be with the colonel.

But the colonel was still out.

Victor could give me no assurance of how soon he would return. He urged me inside to wait, and for a while I did; but in the colonel's absence the house held no alleviation of the turmoil in my mind. I was too restless to sit still; I had no interest in the magazines Victor had thoughtfully provided; and Victor seemed alert to every movement. Each time I paced the floor he came in, ostensibly to inquire if there was anything I needed, but mainly because he could not have remained unaware of the restlessness and was perhaps rendered uneasy on my account.

Eventually I told him I would go to Far End. He handed me my gloves and bag in silence; eyeing me, but unobtrusively.

"Will you ask the colonel to let me know immediately he gets back?"

"I'm sure the colonel would prefer you to wait here." He hesitated before saying, "You seem disturbed, Mrs. Grayson."

It was an understatement. I was agitated, unable to marshal

my confused thoughts into any coherency. It was so obvious I didn't trouble to either confirm or deny it.

"Is there anything I can do?" he wanted to know. He added, deferentially, "I have a good measure of the colonel's confidence. If it is something urgent, perhaps I could give you some assistance in his absence?"

"It will wait," I said. "But thank you, Victor."

"Let me bring you some tea," he suggested. "The colonel will not forgive me for allowing you to leave without insisting upon it. Perhaps by the time you have had it, he will have returned. I am sure he could not have been expecting you back so soon, Mrs. Grayson, or he would not have gone out without leaving word where he was to be found."

"No. Something came up . . ." He didn't press me on that point. There was no curiosity in him, his eyes were politely impersonal; although if there had been, he was too well trained to parade it. "I'll make tea when I get to the cottage," I said, to satisfy him.

"Then allow me to come with you to get the stove going. They can be a little difficult, and the cottage will be cold."

I fancied he feared the colonel's wrath if it was felt he had not taken suitable care of me. I managed a wan smile in gratitude for such solicitude but rejected the offer. I wondered, a little bleakly, what I would have done had I not had the colonel, and Victor, to run to.

Far End was cold, as Victor had predicted it would be. I switched on the electric heater, not bothering with the intricacies of the out-moded stove. I didn't expect, I hoped I wouldn't, be here for any length of time.

My friendly little cottage held the appearance of being unwanted, neglected. The neglect was not visual; the woman from the village was obviously still giving her attention to it; she would, until she was given word. I should have to make arrangements about paying her off, but I didn't doubt that the colonel would undertake such tasks for me.

The neglect was in my mind. Already I was discarding it, and what it had stood for. I no longer minded parting with it, but the sight of the fading daffodils in the garden saddened me a little. They were too densely overcrowded; they needed thinning out. Last year, we—Robert and I—had planned that *next* spring, after flowering, we should attend to them. I spared only a fleeting wistfulness that someone else would do that now.

But the pervading tranquil atmosphere of the building which had always been its main charm still held its power to instil a calm repose. I sat for a while, letting that atmosphere seep into me, quieting jangled, too-highly strung nerves. At Coplands, I had been too muddled to reason. Alone and undisturbed at Far End I found I could make some semblance of order out of my chaotic thoughts. I was no longer dwelling too vividly on the gruesome details of Lya's death. With the horror of it temporarily numbed I could bring the question of Robert's guilt into the open and face it squarely, without bias.

Was Robert really capable of such an act? Either in cold anger, inflamed heat, or in fear? I tried to see him as the colonel had seen him, but I still could not entirely disorientate my own knowledge of him. In three years of constant companionship there are traits in character that can not remain concealed even from a doting and bemused wife.

Generally, his had been a placid nature. I had known him on occasion give way to quick bursts of annoyance. On rarer occasions, when more deeply stirred, he had resorted to a cold, disapproving withdrawal. Neither type of display of anger had been long-lived, holding no after rancour against whom it had been directed. I could not imagine him, in either extreme, being so strongly provoked into drastic violence.

Fear was a commodity I had never encountered in him. I had no means of knowing how he would react to it. But there was no conceivable reason why he should kill Lya in fear.

Me, perhaps—and I felt pain for that now only in a small detached part of my mind. I knew now he had never loved me. Affection, yes, and indulgence; he had accorded me those. The colonel had said he would be unlikely to kick a pet dog. But what if he was afraid of the dog turning on him? The instinct of preservation was strongly developed in everyone, and even stronger when it is a loved one who is threatened. But what possible motive could he have had for killing the woman he had loved so devotedly he had sacrificed everything for her?

If I had left well alone, would Lya still be alive? Was it my interference that had precipitated her death?

I could wish now that I had let Robert go out of my life as completely as he had tried to do; that Dale Merrick had never told me of the waiting man in the square. It was improbable I should ever have known of Robert's presence there otherwise.

Had I started a train of action because I had discovered Lya's identity? But what sense was there in Robert attempting to kill me to protect Lya from implication in his subversive activities, if there had been the need to kill Lya herself?

Had it really been Robert at Oxton bridge last night? I was no longer seeking extenuation, but floundering bewilderedly for reason. I tried to recall faithfully every detail, to remember in sequence the event as it had taken place, but the confusion caused first by the excitement and later by the desolated loss in that moment of fulfilment still clouded my memory. I did not even know now whether he had actually spoken, to recollect anything of familiarity in the voice. In the enveloping darkness the outline had been blurred, but the man had been of Robert's height and build. Of that I was sure. But there were many men who belonged to that average conformity of height and build. Many, even amongst the circle of my own acquaintanceship.

The ringing of the telephone cut shrilly through my thoughts, unnaturally loud in the stillness of the isolated cottage.

Some intuition told me it was Dale. With my hand outstretched to lift the receiver I stopped. I had a vividly clear image of his face as I had last seen it, outside Elbury Court; that withdrawn communing of spirit that had held him in such oblivious pensiveness. The disquietude it had caused me at the time returned. It was more than disquietude. That loud, imperative summons of the telephone filled me suddenly with a ridiculous apprehension. To my jangled nerves, the sound of the bell was magnified, holding me in complete subjugation to its strident reverberations. It continued so long I thought it would never cease. When at last it did, releasing me in some measure from that pent up tension, the former silence was even more pronounced, as though everything had stopped, suspended in space. I couldn't move. The telephone, silent now, inanimate, assumed more than life size proportions, an instrument holding unnameable fear.

I should not have jumped so nervously when the ringing commenced again. Whoever was trying to get through was insistent, had probably redialled to ensure of no error in the first attempt.

I had been expecting it, waiting breathlessly. There was urgency in its demands; it was absurd, but I sensed it.

Common-sense asserted itself. It would be the colonel; only he knew I was here. If I didn't answer he would assume I had gone back to London. I gave a huge sigh of relief, anxious now to make the connexion before he should ring off again.

But the intuition had been right. He said only the one word "Rosanne?", in inquiry, but I recognised the voice immediately by that slight upward intonation at the end of the name.

Some instinct told me not to respond. It would have been sensible to do so; it was foolish to be so filled with misgiving; but I couldn't bring myself to speak to him.

He said, "Rosanne, is that you?", and he seemed so close he could have been standing next to me. I could hear the sound of his breathing and wondered if he could hear mine. I held my breath but nothing could subdue the apprehensive thudding of my heart, and I put my hand over the mouthpiece. Suddenly it seemed imperative that he shouldn't know I was here.

He spoke again, "Rosanne?", and now there was a cautiousness in the voicing of the name that brought an inexplicable confusion of fear.

I didn't replace the receiver until I heard the click at the other end. There was nothing to be gained by that futile attempt at deception except the odd feeling of security it gave me. He would know perfectly well that someone had answered the call, and that it would be unlikely to be anyone other than myself. He would know I was here; and somehow that filled me with alarm.

I lit a cigarette, annoyed because my fingers were so unsteady I could hardly apply the flame. It was senseless to feel like this about him, even if he had lied to me; but he had seemed so close on the telephone that I couldn't rid myself of the notion of not being alone, making me glance round uneasily.

The room was warm now but I shivered. I was overburdened with a suggestion of foreboding, no matter how I ridiculed myself.

Why didn't the colonel come? If he was not here soon I knew I would be unable to wait here with that eerie, apprehensive sensation of imminent evil oppressing me. I was afraid, even more with that weird feeling of not being alone, than of being alone. When a board creaked I was so nervously tensed I leapt right out of the chair. There had always been faintly protesting sounds like that from the old building; I had lain often, half way between wakefulness and sleep, listening contentedly to those grumblings. They had been reassuring noises, as though the whole structure of the cottage was also settling down comfortably for the night.

Now they, too, alarmed me; suggesting an unwelcome intrusion caused them. Imagination started to run riot, making me glance timorously over my shoulder until I couldn't stand the suspense any longer.

I grabbed my handbag, fumbling in it for the ignition key as I ran out. When I reached the Mini I still had not found it and I couldn't remember what I had done with it. I was becoming keyed up to such a pitch I was practically in a state of panic when a fevered search through the contents of the bag by the car's lights failed to uncover the recalcitrant key. Most likely I had put it down somewhere in the cottage but I didn't want to have to go back inside to look.

I should have to. The decision to walk to Coplands suddenly held as little appeal as returning to look for the key. It was dark now; the drizzle of rain had ceased but the skies were heavy and overcast. The lights I had left burning in the cottage should have been warm and inviting; instead, in contrast, they served only to emphasise the darkness. I was afraid of the loneliness of the friendly country lanes down which I had always enjoyed rambling. As I stood torn in indecision the clouds parted momentarily to reveal a fleeting glimpse of the moon. I thought I caught a faint reflection of light down the lane, as though from the polished surface of a car. The Alvis?

Why should that thought come into my mind? This was absurd; I knew it. Dale Merrick was in London. Even if he wasn't, there was no reason why he should be skulking down the lane. There was even less reason why the idea of his presence should cause such trepidation in me.

And it had been only a trick of the moonlight, after all; it still sent me scurrying back into the cottage like a frightened rabbit.

But I couldn't find the key. The failure to do so seized me with senseless rage against the colonel because he hadn't come. I was ashamed of both the unjust anger and the panic when I rang Coplands. Victor answered, his voice calm and reassuring, steadying me. I had intended asking him to fetch me, but he told me that the colonel had just returned and was on the point of leaving again for Far End.

"Would you like a word with him, Mrs. Grayson?" he asked. "I could catch him."

"No," I said. "No—it doesn't matter . . ."

Everything had settled into perspective once more. The colonel could not be more than a few minutes at most. Even to talk to Victor had dispelled the absurd cowardice.

I relaxed, almost ready to laugh at my panic. I concentrated on Robert, and what it would mean if only he could be exonerated of the suspicion of murder. Surely he would give himself up and face the lesser charge against him. His career was finished, but later he could start again in something else.

I couldn't help it; her death had been horrific, but I couldn't prevent my mind dwelling on the fact that there was no Lya now. What difference would it make—to us?

To us? Could I dare to once more couple Robert and myself together like that? Would he want me again, in time?

It never occurred to me to question whether I would want him. All at once, for the first time in weeks, Far End was *my* cottage again; a retreat of tranquil security. I wandered round, my eyes clouded with memory, touching treasured things that during those weeks had lost all meaning for me. Handling my precious Tudor lady with loving care, running my fingers down the delicate green porcelain of her dress. Eager now to hear the haunting little refrain I had thought I could never bear to listen to again.

But the mechanism of my Tudor lady was broken. When I pressed the switch there was a faint, burring sound, but no tinkling notes to delight my ear.

I was overcome with a quite disproportionate dismay. I told myself it could be only a small mechanical fault, it could be repaired, but nothing could dissipate the heavy oppression with which that fault burdened me. It seemed an omen of disaster that my Tudor lady should fail me now, at this moment.

I think I knew then, as I stood with the damaged figure in my hand, that my optimism of the past few minutes had been premature. Deep down inside me, a perception of fatalism was already numbing me. I was annoyed at being so foolishly superstitious, but even the discovery that it was not a mechanical fault could not dispel it.

The mechanism was under the wide crinoline skirt. When I turned the figure over it was obvious why the touching of the switch had failed to evoke any response. Wedged inside the workings, preventing contact between the switch and the musical apparatus, was a small, neatly folded piece of paper. Immediately I released it the melodious little tune tinkled forth. But I wasn't listening to it.

The small scrap of paper was wrapped round a ticket of some stiffer substance that looked as though it had been subjected to many bending manipulations to render it sufficiently pliable to push into that minute aperture. The ticket fluttered to the ground, but I didn't really notice that any longer, either. Only the crumpled piece of paper I was smoothing out claimed my attention.

There was writing on it. Cramped, to fit many words on to a confined space; abbreviated, for the same purpose; some of it almost illegible as though the writer had been pressed for time.

Cramped, abbreviated, almost illegible—the writing was unmistakably Robert's.

I was still reading it, still trying to make sense of the utterly incomprehensible sentences; still floundering in complete incredulity, when, right beside me, someone quietly spoke my name.

16

I gave a little scream of terror. I had heard nothing. If there had been any sound to warn me I had been too engrossed in those scribbled words to notice it. I had forgotten my previous fears. I had forgotten everything but the message Robert had written on that scrap of paper.

It came rushing back to me as I swerved away in fear from the closeness of that voice. I stumbled, half falling across a low table in my haste for the safety of distance, violently flinging aside the hand that was extended to steady me.

"Sorry," the colonel said. "I startled you. Didn't you hear me? I knocked."

He loomed large, reassuring, a bulwark of strength; his face expressing faint surprise for the extent of such nervousness.

I was conscious of such relief I lost my balance again but this time I didn't repudiate the helping hand. On a sharp intake of breath I said, "It's you, Gregory," and it came out in a wavering tremor.

He pushed me gently into a chair. "But of course. Surely you were expecting me?" In concern he said, "My dear girl, don't tremble so. You should have waited for me at Coplands. I was furious with Victor for allowing you to come here alone." He sat on the chair arm, his arm resting lightly but comfortingly round my shoulders. "There's no need to be afraid. You're all right now. Sorry I took so long in getting here."

I let my head fall back against the support he offered, closing my eyes. The colonel let me remain like that for several minutes before asking curiously, "What's that?"

I was still clutching the scrap of paper. When he gently took it from me, I yielded without demur. Even if I had absorbed the full implication of that accusation I would still have been too disbelievingly dumbfounded not to give it to him.

The colonel read it aloud. He was not as familiar with Robert's handwriting as I was, and even to me some of it had been difficult to decipher. Read out slowly, haltingly, it was as completely senseless as when I had scanned it myself. " 'Rosanne, darling. Hiding this where know you will find it. If you don't hear from me—have feeling you may not—ticket to Paddington left lugg. Full explan. Robert.' " He read the additional part stressed, as heavily scored as it had been in the writing. " '*Have police investigate the colonel. Comm. agent!*' "

In the silence that followed the colonel removed his arm from my shoulders and got up, to stand in his favourite position with his back to the fireplace, even though it was an empty grate. From there he continued to hold my bewildered gaze for a long time, with something that could have been almost comical regret in his own expression.

"Well, well," he said at last. "What a very dramatic denunciation. It seems that, after all, I underestimated Robert. A fatal mistake. I should have been more careful."

I couldn't believe what he was saying. I felt to be floundering helplessly at cross purposes with him.

"I don't understand you," I complained.

He looked completely nonplussed; strangely unsure of himself. After a moment he said in some wonderment, "You didn't believe it, did you? Not even though Robert wrote it?"

"No . . ." I drew the word out, trailing it plaintively.

"It appears," he said ruefully, "that I was a little premature in admitting it." He seemed to be ruminating; even yet marvelling at my disbelief. Then, more briskly, "Still, it would only have been a matter of time before you began wondering about it, once the idea had been put into your mind. You would have started speculating, having doubts . . ."

"I don't believe it," I said, and I didn't. It wasn't possible. Still, I waited for the denial of such a preposterous accusation.

"You should." He was calm now, quite matter of fact. "It happens to be true."

I sank deeper into the morass of perplexity. My mind was whirling, too utterly confused to accept such a fantastically ridiculous statement.

"You mean—" I phrased the words carefully, more for my benefit than his, so there should be no possibility of misunderstanding in my addled brain, "—you mean, that you are a—Communist agent?"

The colonel looked slightly amused. "That is not exactly how I would describe myself but it is an expression that you would understand, I suppose. Yes, I am."

"You can't be . . ."

"My dear, I don't know whether to be flattered or annoyed by such incredulity. I expect it depends on the viewpoint. In your eyes, I gather that the disbelief is intended flatteringly. For myself, I am neither proud nor ashamed of my profession. I just accept it as a remunerative means of earning a living."

Even yet I wasn't prepared to believe it. I continued to choose my words very carefully. "You sell—information, secret information—to another country, for money? Like—Robert did?"

"Like Robert did." He was prompting me along to understanding with the patient gravity he would have accorded a child who had difficulty with its lessons. "Yes, that's right."

I shook my head slowly. "Not you . . ."

"I see," the colonel remarked regretfully, "that it would have taken very little denial on my part to convince you. Too late now, of course."

"But how could you? I thought you were British . . ."

"What has that to do with it?" He looked genuinely perplexed; then his face cleared. "You mean patriotism? You really are rather naive, Rosanne," he said, with musing indulgence. "Though oddly enough, that has been your greatest attraction to me. Your naiveté and the fact that you are just a little—scatterbrained. Delightfully so, my dear. We are the complete antithesis of each other. I have found you quite charmingly relaxing. I am sorry that our friendship has to be ended, and particularly through the lack of my own vigilance. It was rather stupid of me to so lightly overlook such resourcefulness on Robert's part."

"Did Robert work for you?"

"Indirectly, yes. His immediate contact was Lya, of course."

"Lya?" I said in stupefaction. "You knew Lya . . . ?"

He seemed faintly amused by my utter astonishment. "Oh, yes."

"Even before I told you about her last night? You couldn't have—you didn't tell me . . ."

"Well, naturally not, my dear. But she has worked with me for some time. She is one of the best operatives I have."

"Did you know she was Robert's wife?" I could hear my voice squeaking with incredulity.

"But of course," the colonel said. "I used her in this case solely because of the pressure she could put on him. Robert's position in the Foreign Office was a useful one for me. It needed a means of persuasion to enlist his co-operation. Lya was an excellent means of doing so."

I gazed at him in an abhorrence that was slow to gain full strength owing to the whirling confusion of my brain. My mind was such a conflict of mixed feelings that it was difficult to distinguish one from the other. Primarily, I think, superseding even the aversion for his professed occupation, was the disillusionment for the deceptive betrayal of my trust. He had accepted my confidences, comforted me, sympathised with my bewildered incomprehension of Robert's actions, and all the time he had been fully cognisant of facts of which I was ignorant. Not only had he known, he had been responsible for the heart-breaking upheaval of my life. He had set about the furtherance of his schemes with cold deliberation to wreck both my life and Robert's.

It seemed of little importance in that moment that Robert had proved a willing victim. What did matter was that this man, under the masquerade of friendship, could have so debased the meaning of trust. I could never have loved him as I had thought he could wish me to, but I had admired and respected him. I had had such faith in his integrity I would blindly have entrusted my life to him; even Robert's.

"You're monstrous!" I burst out.

"No histrionics, please," the colonel said calmly. "You've behaved quite admirably during the past weeks. Don't spoil the record by going to pieces now." More sharply, he added, "And there is no need to be so outraged, Rosanne! You were not too disgusted with Robert."

That had not been the cause of my outburst. I was too emotionally involved yet to see any other than a personal view, but momentarily he sidetracked me.

"Robert did what he did because he loved Lya. Not for money."

"There is a difference?" His mouth twisted cynically. "A man who betrays his country is a traitor, no matter what his excuse."

"And what," I asked him, "is a man who betrays a trust. All this time . . . Even last night, when I told you about Lya, you acted as though it was all news to you. You let me go on, when all the time you knew . . ."

"If I had told you, you would have wanted to know *how* I knew: I would have automatically identified myself. I regretted you had learnt of Lya's existence. I had no intention you should ever know of her, for your own sake—"

"For my own sake!" I repeated after him bitterly. "When I was distracted with worry! When I didn't know where Robert was . . ." I stopped, meeting his calm gaze with sudden wariness. "*You* know where Robert is, don't you? It stands to reason . . ."

I held my breath, seeing the guarded look that veiled his eyes.

He hesitated, but only briefly, before he nodded. "It stands to reason, as you say. But I fear I am not disposed to tell you at this moment, my dear. It would do you no good if I did. Robert would not return to you, even were he at liberty to do so."

"At liberty?" I fastened sharply on the words, to the colonel's amusement.

"You are melodramatic, Rosanne. Do you imagine I have Robert tied by the heels in my cellar? I assure you I have not. By at liberty I meant merely that he is not a free man to come and go as he pleases, to take up his old life again with you. I think, also, you are forgetting that he left you, he chose to return to his wife—"

"Lya is dead," I stated baldly. If I had thought to surprise him I would have been disappointed.

"Oh, you know that, do you? Palmer would tell you, I suppose?"

"I went to see her."

His eyebrows raised very slightly. "I thought we had agreed you would not do that again."

"*You* remind me of promises!"

"I suppose," he said, "it was too much to expect you to abide by it. No matter." He shrugged. "The damage was done, anyway, the first time you went there. Lya's usefulness was over."

"Robert didn't kill her!"

"I'm sure he didn't," the colonel agreed blandly. "I wonder, however, whether he will be able to prove it?"

My breath caught in my throat, almost suffocating me. The room spun dizzily round and I had to wait until it steadied. Then I said very slowly, "You killed her, didn't you?"

I had expected anger at the accusation, not the expression of distaste that crossed his face. "My dear girl, I have never killed anyone in my life. What on earth do you take me for, some knuckle-duster, street corner thug?"

For some reason I had touched his pride. I wondered why, until the reason came to me.

"You wouldn't soil your fingers. But you wouldn't be above ordering someone to do the foul work for you."

He waited, watching me speculatively.

"It was Victor," I said. I would not have believed a denial if he had offered one, but he didn't.

He hesitated only very briefly. "You're really becoming quite astute, Rosanne. Still, no harm in your knowing, I suppose."

"But why?"

"Why did I have her killed?" His face hardened. "Because I don't forgive incompetent bungling. Nor the concealment of vital facts that should have been immediately submitted to me. Lya's duty was to inform me when you called upon her. At the first suspicion that a connexion had been made between her and Robert she should have alerted me. Instead, knowing she would have incurred my wrath for not having been sufficiently circumspect in her dealings with Robert, she took matters into her own hands. Lya could not, of course, know that I had a personal interest in you. Whether she knew or not is beside the point. She has always been a very efficient operative; I would not have believed her capable of such ineffable blundering. When you told me last night . . ." Words failed him. He got out a cigarette and lit it, with stiffly disjointed actions that proclaimed a smouldering, barely contained fury.

I found myself disgusted at my own naiveté. "And I thought you were so angry because I had nearly been killed." It was almost laughable; but the colonel was not laughing.

Through a cloud of smoke he regarded me very seriously, saying with an undeniable sincerity, "Indeed I was, Rosanne! I have a great affection for you, as you know. It would grieve me deeply . . . For that alone, I believe that this once I would have been capable of killing her with my own hands."

"That wasn't the reason . . . ? Oh, no!" I couldn't endure the thought.

"I do nothing purely for vengeance. I have an organisation that has taken years to perfect. I would not endanger it by an unnecessary murder solely for personal motives. But the police could not have failed to be aware of her existence. The fact that she had not already been apprehended meant only that through her they hoped to get a lead on Robert and, of primary concern to myself, someone higher in the network than Lya herself. If she could be panicked into such ill-considered action as the two badly conceived attempts on your life, I could not take the risk of her not revealing my identity if she thought co-operation would serve to help her own position."

"It wasn't Robert last night, was it?"

He appeared faintly annoyed that I should introduce such a triviality. "Still the touching faith!" he said and then with indifference, "I really wouldn't know, my dear. I told you Lya acted entirely on her own initiative."

"But you *know* it wasn't," I insisted.

He hesitated again before making the concession. "I should think it very improbable. I doubt Robert would take that chance himself, knowing that you would undoubtedly be followed. Lya herself should have realised you were a novice at the game, too inexperienced to successfully evade being shadowed." He studied the tip of his cigarette reflectively, adding with the same indifference, "I have no first hand knowledge of everyone whom my main operatives employ for different purposes. They are allowed to use their own discretion—to a certain extent and in certain matters. But it is of no real concern. Whoever it was, he would not know me, either. No one in the organisation knows anyone higher up than his immediate superior. That way, in the event of discovery of one man, the entire network is not imperilled."

I asked him, but I didn't really expect an answer. "Who killed Keith Forrester? Victor?"

He looked annoyed again and even a little bored . . . I realised that he had an obsession about his infamous organisation. He was proud of it, but by nature of its essential secrecy he was not usually in the position of being able openly to discuss it. Now that he had a rare audience, he disliked being diverted. But he gave me an answer after only a second of indecision.

"Yes. It was all very regrettable, I'm afraid." He heard the breath go from me in a long, slow sigh and paused, to say sardonically, "Your profound faith in Robert was justified after all, you see." But he couldn't resist the taunt. "But only in regard to his capability of committing murder, my dear. Don't hope for miracles in any other respect. Robert used his position in the Foreign Office to act as a spy for Lya, and he discarded you for her."

I ignored that. "What happened here that night? The night Keith Forrester was killed?"

"It was rather unfortunate, as I said. I dislike having to resort to the taking of life. My contacts erred by failing to notify me that Robert was already under surveillance. Had I known that I should not have come here that night. As it was, I foresaw no risk when Lya rang up to say she was having some difficulty with Robert. He was proving awkward over carrying out a point I had insisted upon. Robert, you see, wanted to disappear without a word to you. I regret I can't say whether it was from a desire to spare you as much as possible, or from sheer cowardice." From the contemplation of the glowing cigarette tip he shot a sideways glance at me, but I wouldn't give him the satisfaction of wincing. I met his gaze serenely and he was the first to look away.

"However," he continued, "I couldn't allow him to leave you that way. You would have moved heaven and earth to find him, started a chain of investigations that could have proved undesirable. As I said, I didn't know at that time that Robert was already under suspicion. There was no sense in starting a hue and cry for him that could lead to the unearthing of facts that I preferred to remain undisclosed. I thought that if you knew part of the truth, that he was leaving you for another woman, you would accept that and let him go without undue fuss. Also, although the other reason was my main concern, I preferred you to know he had discarded you. If you were angry with hurt pride and disillusionment I expected you to forget him the sooner. I thought it would make relations easier between us."

He waited, seeming to anticipate that I would make some remark, but although I let the loathing show plainly I sat quietly.

"When Robert refused to co-operate in fulfilling this condition, Lya rang me for instructions and I came over. After a little persuasion Robert yielded, as you know—"

"Persuasion? What kind of persuasion?" I demanded.

The colonel gave a short bark of laughter but he sounded bored again. "My dear Rosanne, how you do jump to conclusions. You are imagining all the gory aspects of torture, aren't you? But it needed only a little reasonable argument, no tearing out of finger nails or any such ghastly methods, to make Robert see the wisdom of complying with my wishes. Everything went quite smoothly until it was discovered that this man, Forrester, had overheard all that had been said here. It was regrettable, but I had no alternative. The man was only doing his job in trailing Robert, it was unfortunate that he stumbled on my identity. For my own safety, I couldn't allow him to live to pass on that knowledge."

"Your own safety!" I said bitterly. "Everyone else is expendable! You allow Robert to be suspected of a murder he didn't commit, you let him be hunted like an animal—"

"He was already wanted on other charges," the colonel said imperturbably. "So long as he is not arrested, it can't make any difference to him. And while the police concentrate on him, they are not looking elsewhere."

"And what if he *had* been arrested?"

"That problem hasn't arisen."

"But when it does?" I realised I was becoming a little hysterical and forced myself to speak quietly. "What then?"

"I refuse to discuss a purely theoretical possibility. I have already wasted too much time when there are more pressing problems." The curt briskness was shed, leaving him in an attitude of indecision, his face looking drawn and older. "I can't tell you how much I regret you should have found that note, Rosanne. I would have given much for you not to have done so. I have valued our friendship, I had hoped in time for more—much more. Even now—" he spoke musingly, wistfully, "—even now, if I thought you had any love, any feeling of loyalty towards me—"

I seized on the word and spat it back at him. "Loyalty? *You* speak of loyalty? I wouldn't marry you . . ." Words failed me.

There was the faintest of whimsical amusement in his eyes. "It wasn't marriage I had in mind, my dear. I told you I wasn't a marrying man. But we could have enjoyed a very pleasant relationship—"

"Or anything else!" I said contemptuously.

"Yes—well . . . It was only a momentary weakness . . ." And then abruptly he changed once more, throwing off the wistfulness as he would a coat, squaring his shoulders. Employing his curt, clipped manner of speech. "Couldn't be any other way, of course. Allowing myself to be swayed by sentiment. Fatal mistake. Have already allowed my feelings for you to bring me too much to the notice of the police, by involving myself too closely in your affairs."

He crossed over to the window and stood peering out into the darkness, stepping back finally to draw the curtains; saying in some dissatisfaction, "I dislike having to make plans on the spur of the moment." He turned sharply as he heard me move. "Where are you going?"

I had risen, too. "Back to London."

"I'm afraid," he said slowly, "I can't permit you to leave just yet, my dear. There are a few things to be settled first. It would be very inconvenient for me at this moment were you to rush headlong to Superintendent Palmer to unburden yourself. Which I presume is your intention? I hope I shall not have to use force to restrain you, Rosanne."

I paused in my search for the ignition key to glance uncertainly at him.

"I assure you I shouldn't hesitate to use any means to prevent you," the colonel said and I believed him. "I need a little time before you do your utmost to expose me. Now be sensible, my dear, and don't make me have to resort to force. There are more important matters at stake than my reluctance to inflict physical harm on you. I advise you to sit down and be quiet."

I capitulated, fuming impotently. I wouldn't submit myself to the humiliation of indisputable defeat if it came to a contest of strength.

The colonel stood meditating, talking more to himself than me.

"This is rendered more difficult by your being under surveillance. One of your faithful watchdogs is out there somewhere. I didn't actually see him but I passed a car parked up the lane. No—no!" He forestalled me hastily. "If you attempt to attract his attention in any way, I promise that I will make sure you never see Robert again." When I wavered in indecision he added gravely, "And if that is not sufficient incentive, I warn you that to draw his notice to anything untoward would almost certainly be the cause of that man's death."

I recoiled in horror. I couldn't doubt he meant what he said; the cold ruthlessness in his voice was an even graver warning than the words.

After subjecting me to a keen scrutiny to ensure that the threat had effectively subdued me, the colonel turned to the telephone, not troubling to keep a watchful eye on me. He was confident now I wouldn't take advantage of any negligence on his part.

I heard him dialling and then, a few seconds later, "Victor? The colonel here. 'Fraid I've been delayed longer than I intended. Mrs. Grayson is still rather upset but I should be able to leave her soon. I can't persuade her to return with me. What seems to be particularly distressing her at the moment is being constantly under the eye of the police. Understandable, of course." He paused and then continued, "My apologies to Mrs. Cooper for being late for dinner. Tell her I'll probably be home within half an hour. And Victor? I know you have an urgent engagement. You needn't wait, you understand? Mrs. Cooper can attend to me."

He replaced the receiver, regarding it pensively for some time before turning to face me.

"And what now?" I asked.

The colonel made himself comfortable in the chair opposite. "Now," he said, "we wait for Victor."

17

I was surprised to note a nervousness in him. He was not as calmly composed as he would have appear. When he caught himself beating an irritable tattoo on the chair arm he checked immediately, reaching into his pocket for yet another cigarette. His movements were slow; he took so long extracting one from the case and lighting it, I felt he prolonged the actions in an effort to keep his fingers occupied.

I was sure of it when, a moment later, he asked, "Do you mind if I have a drink while we are waiting?"

Normally he was very punctilious about such things; he would never have dreamed of inviting himself to the hospitalities of someone else's home.

I wouldn't concede to the pettiness of wishing to refuse him. I maintained a stony silence and after a slight indecision he got up and helped himself. It gave me a great deal of satisfaction to see him toss the first one down at one gulp, as though it was something he was very much in need of. When he had liberally refilled the glass he brought it back, settling himself down once more.

This, I reflected bitterly, was the man I had turned to in trust and affection. This cold, hard, calculating creature who, even while he had listened to my troubles in sympathy, had been fully cognisant of facts of which I had been totally and confusedly ignorant. He had let me continue to flounder in the mass of bewilderment and distress; worse than that, he had deliberately

contrived to enmesh Robert even deeper than his own actions
had involved him.

I knew now why Robert had wanted to see me so desperately
that he had risked arrest by waiting outside my flat. He had hidden the note in my Tudor lady, confidently expecting that I
should do the first thing I had always done on entering the cottage, set the tinkling melody into action. He couldn't know that
I wouldn't follow the customary habit because I couldn't bear
such a reminder. When I had done nothing about the note he had
expected me to discover he had had to try to contact me personally. He could not himself openly denounce the colonel without
being arrested for a murder he had not committed but would have
difficulty in proving otherwise.

And all the time this man . . .

I would have liked to maintain the stony silence but the bitterness built up too strongly, compelling me into speech against my
own volition.

"How could you?" I burst out.

I startled him. I think he, too, would have preferred the silence
but he asked politely, "How could I what?"

But there had been no specific question. I lifted my shoulders
in a helpless gesture, and then, on a sudden thought, I said,

"What you said about Robert's character—you deliberately tried
to turn me against him, to mislead me. He's not as you described
him—"

"Whatever I said does not in any way alter the facts. Robert
left you for Lya, he sacrificed everything for her." He studied me
with a cold hardness. "However you try, you will not succeed in
completely vindicating him. You are an incredible girl, my dear.
You are not concerned in the interests of justice at all, are you?
It doesn't really bother you that I am a confessed spy and Victor
a murderer; Robert, however you attempt to whitewash him, is
also a spy even if in a lesser degree. It is only what has been *done*
to Robert that matters to you, isn't it? What about your own
sense of patriotism, Rosanne?"

"Robert is my main concern," I admitted. "I know he is a spy,
but that doesn't mean he should be blamed for what he hasn't
done." I took a deep breath. "As for you and Victor," I added
very distinctly, "I despise everything you both stand for. As for

my feeling towards you, personally, I find you too low to be even despicable. You are beneath contempt!"

The withering scorn angered him. He went white; but he controlled the rage and even managed to muster a tight-lipped smile.

"It would give you satisfaction to see me brought to justice?"

I didn't answer, merely regarding him now with a coldly expressionless stare that reduced him to a complete nothingness in my estimation.

That angered him more than the scorn, but he spoke quite mildly. "It is a pity you will be robbed of that satisfaction."

He stopped, head held alertly listening. If there had been a sound I had not heard it, but his ears had been keener than mine. He had barely time to give a gesture of warning to me before a quiet knock on the door proved the acuteness of his hearing. I was torn between desire for it to be the man who was following me and dread, for his sake, that it should be. The colonel's warning was unnecessary, I would have done nothing to alert the man.

Whoever was there didn't wait for an answer to the knock. The handle turned softly and the door opened.

"Ah, Victor," said the colonel. "You didn't waste much time."

Victor closed the door and stood in an attitude of respectful attention.

"I gathered there was some urgency, Colonel."

The colonel gave a bleak smile. "Thought you'd get the message. Didn't care to be too explicit. Never quite sure with these modern telephones whether our Miss Parkin at the local exchange can still overhear if she's inquisitively inclined. Our friend outside?" he queried.

"Unconscious. Bound and gagged." Victor was matter of fact, taciturn in his replies. "Locked in the garage," he added.

"He didn't recognise you?"

"Never even knew what hit him," Victor said succinctly.

The colonel nodded in satisfaction. "Good! We have run into a snag here, Victor, as you will have guessed."

Victor waited in polite disinterest. He had never once glanced in my direction.

"Mrs. Grayson," the colonel explained, "has discovered a good deal more than it is in her interests to know. It appears we were rather careless with Grayson; he contrived to leave a message— Where is that note, by the way?"

He had placed it on the mantelshelf. I saw it first but he beat me to it, his long legs covering the ground before I was even out of the chair.

"It's mine!" I said.

"Didn't really think I would let you have it, did you? Or the ticket. I'll have that, too, and retrieve whatever Robert left there tomorrow. Should make interesting reading."

He burnt the note, holding the lighter to it and powdering it to fine ashes in the grate. I watched him angrily, knowing it would be useless to attempt to prevent the destruction. It wasn't really important; the ticket was another matter altogether. I didn't know the number, and I wondered if the police would have the power to open up the entire contents of the left luggage office.

The colonel had interrupted my thoughts very successfully.

"They would probably tear the place apart, if they had any inkling. But how will they know about it, my dear?" he asked very quietly.

I started to say that I would give them more than an inkling, and stopped, disturbed more by that quietness than by the fact that he should ask such a seemingly senseless question.

When I looked at him, it was there in his face; all the implacable determination mingled with an inexpressible regret. I should have realised, when he talked so freely; but, stupidly, I hadn't. And I stared at him now in utter disbelief, too completely astounded yet to feel afraid.

"I am sorry, Rosanne," he said, but he wouldn't meet my eyes. Regretful he might be, but it wouldn't alter his decision.

I looked from him to Victor, still standing imperturbably; knowing now why the colonel had sent for him. It was still too totally incredible, I expressed it all in three words of positive dissention. "You just can't!"

"My work is too important; the organisation is far reaching, it has taken many years to perfect. . . . . I couldn't jeopardise it . . ." He was trying, rather haltingly, to explain, even to excuse.

But even yet I could think of only the one thing. It burst out of me in outraged indignation. "You promised I should see Robert!"

He shook his head slowly. "I promised only that you would not see him if you created any disturbance. I had to keep you quiet, it would have been senseless to cause another death when the man could not have helped you. As it is, he will probably suffer no more than a sore head when he recovers consciousness."

He turned, taking Victor with him, to stand talking quietly at the far end of the room. Only the murmur of his voice reached me, the words unintelligible. A part of my mind was still too numbed to accept the truth of his preposterous intention but those whispered words held a menace that frightened me.

"I want to know what you're saying," I said.

The colonel looked at me over his shoulder. "Better not. You wouldn't like it, my dear."

He was being considerate, trying to spare me. The situation was utterly incongruous.

"I want to know," I insisted. It was obvious he was going to refuse again. Anything, whatever they were saying, was preferable to those whispered words. "Please tell me." However hard I tried, it came out as a pathetic little quaver. "I'd rather know . . ."

"Very well," he complied, but his face was stiff with distaste for my persistence. "I was explaining to Victor that it is not necessary to appear accidental. To the knowledge of the police, Robert has already made one attempt on your life; they will be only too eager to accept him as the culprit."

"That wasn't Robert," I cried. "You know it wasn't!"

"Nevertheless, once again he makes an excellent scapegoat. I shall, of course, be questioned. My presence here will not have gone unnoted but that man, when he recovers consciousness, will also know that it could not be I who knocked him out as I was in the cottage with you. You had better give me a little time, Victor —say half an hour—to return to Coplands and establish an alibi with Mrs. Cooper for the exact time of—" He had been expounding with an impersonal flatness but he couldn't bring himself to the point of saying the word. That failure on his part brought the first real terror striking home. He could plan it, coldly and inexorably; at my insistence he could discuss it impartially; but the fact that even he could not utter the word death in connexion with me produced stark realisation at last.

"How can you?" I choked on it. "How can you . . . ?"

But he had turned to Victor.

"I have made all the explanations necessary to Mrs. Grayson. There is no need to go into any more detail or answer questions. You understand?"

Victor nodded. For all the emotion he displayed he could have been taking orders for a dinner menu. I looked at him in horror, still finding it impossible to believe that the colonel would leave me with him.

But the colonel was already moving to the door. As he reached it he said, "I think that is all, Victor."

At the last moment, with the door already open, he spared a look at me. I saw then that his face was grey and that a vein high on his left temple was throbbing with uneven violence.

He didn't speak. The glance was almost cursory, sweeping fleetingly over me as though he had been compelled to give that last look against his will and would have preferred to leave without it.

And then the door closed quietly behind him.

If I made some movement to follow him it was entirely without my own volition. My mind was still too stupefied, even if I hadn't realised the uselessness of appeal to him. Any such attempt would have been forestalled by Victor, in any case. I believe he thought I had that intention; perhaps I had moved, because with the lithe sinuosity of a cat he interposed himself between me and the door. There was nothing threatening in his action; it was preventive only, but it caused me to shrink convulsively away from him.

"Why don't you sit down, Mrs. Grayson?" he suggested.

He was as deferential as ever, even to the point of pulling round the chair so that I should receive the benefit of the full warmth from the electric heater.

The absurdity of the situation made me have difficulty in subduing the inclination to burst into hysterical laughter. He would be servile to the last, seeing to my comfort. But in the end he would have no compunction whatever about putting those strong fingers round my throat and squeezing until he had choked the life out of me.

The thought that Victor would be as politely urbane in that act as he was in his other duties was too much. Suddenly weakened legs made me comply with the suggestion. When I had done so he seated himself, but at a distance. Even now, his training would not allow him to encroach on his position as a servant.

As he sat down I saw him glance unobtrusively at the clock and followed his gaze. It was exactly eight o'clock.

I looked dazedly round, still not quite believing what was happening here. This room that was so dearly familiar to me was the condemned cell. I knew now what the condemned prisoner felt, with the last minutes ticking away into eternity.

An execution for which Robert would be blamed; and fear was lost temporarily in despair for the evidence accumulating against him. It seemed the most bitter of ironies that now, at last, when I knew without shadow of doubt that he was innocent of murder, not only could I not prove it but my own death would also be laid at his door. Even if, in time, he managed to furnish proof of the colonel's guilt as a spy, what evidence could be put forward, beyond his own word, that it was Victor's hands that had dealt out death.

I looked at those hands, and fear returned. They were lying passively in his lap, with nothing in the almost slender contour of them to suggest the strength of which they were capable.

For a time I had overcome the earlier revulsion of that supernormal strength. Those hands had tended to me with gentleness, rendered service to me. It was a mockery that the very hands which, only two nights ago, had pushed me aside at the crucial moment, should now be waiting quietly, dormantly, to deprive me of the life he had perhaps saved then.

I watched Victor now with a dreadful fascination; trying to detect some sign of perturbation in him. It was inhuman that he could sit there so calmly, watching the minutes tick inexorably away, knowing what he must do when the time limit was up. But there was nothing to suggest any sense of strain in him. That calm immobility hypnotised me into a feeling of unreality, lulling me into a false security.

This just was not happening. It was some ghastly, macabre nightmare. If it had been real, I should have been screaming, trying to escape, instead of sitting here bound by inertia. I should have been reasoning with Victor, pleading with him, trying to bribe him, fighting him with every means in my power.

There would have been mounting terror as the last minutes of my life flowed relentlessly past, not this quiet, fatalistic acceptance.

It was not acceptance. It was only tiredness and confusion of mind which had found hallucinatory relaxation in the peaceful quiet.

Victor himself put an end to the illusion. Apart from an occasional flickering of his eyes towards the clock he had been motionless. When, with a final glance, he moved at last, rising to his feet, the macabre scene attained reality.

I had never experienced such terror. It held me spellbound, immobile, so that I could only watch him in wordless horror. I could not have screamed now if I had tried. My whole body was so frozen with fear I was unable even to cringe away from him as he approached. His movements were so fluently deliberate to my dilated eyes, it was like observing a film in slow motion. But no amount of slowing down of the film could forever delay the moment when he would reach me, when those hands would stretch out towards my throat.

If I had not been watching him in such ghastly fixation I would have noticed earlier the opening of the door. I think that a part of my mind had noted that cautiously widening aperture, but it was not until I saw Dale Merrick framed in the doorway that I believed the evidence of my eyes.

The first, the only, sensation was one of profound relief. I forgot my former fears, the uneasiness that he had roused in me. Everything was submerged beneath the thankfulness of his presence.

I found my voice now, even although it was only a wobbling quaver. "Oh, Dale . . ." I said.

Victor thought I was bluffing. Over his shoulder I saw Dale grimacing frantically but even that warning couldn't prevent me from uttering his name again, but with a more positive conviction that alerted Victor into realising that I was not just offering up a helpless abortive appeal against fate. He glanced uncertainly round. When he saw Dale he straightened, turning to face him.

I would have run past him to seek the refuge Dale offered, but without taking his eyes off the other man Victor's hand shot out, the fingers closing in a cruel grip on my arm. He seemed to exert no effort at all but the wrench he gave to my arm flung me across the room, to crash in the corner with a heavy jarring that sent the pain searing through my injured back.

I wasn't sure whether for brief moments I lost consciousness or not. Through a haze of agony I became aware that they were fighting. I watched them in a state of pain induced trance, unable even to move when their exertions brought them hurtling towards me.

Dale was trying to deal a knock out blow. I wasn't quite experienced enough to be sure, but I thought he could also be attempting to employ judo. Victor appeared to have no such qualifications. He didn't need them, he relied wholly on his colossal strength, but he was adept in evading many of the vicious blows. Not all of them. There were signs on his face to show the effectiveness of Dale's proficiency; one eye was already swelling and there was an angry red patch on his jaw.

It seemed an unequal battle. Dale was unmarked; but if Victor's injuries caused him pain he was impervious to it. He was obviously waiting the opportunity to get in close through the flurry of blows the younger man was dealing out, accepting what punishment he received stoically until the propitious moment arrived.

I waited breathlessly for it to happen. Dale was tiring. Whereas Victor had been occupied mainly in evasion, he had been exerting himself strenuously. I knew that once Victor got his hands on him, it must be finished.

The moment came. Dale must have realised that he was tiring, that his legs were not as nimble and the punches landing on the other man were lacking power. He could not have known of Victor's strength or he would not have ventured into close combat. I tried to warn him but the words came out only in a strangled whisper, lost in the tumult as furniture broke and ornaments shattered beneath their onslaught. The warning was too late, anyway. Dale's face registered complete surprise and consternation as the biting strength held him in a vicelike grip. But he was lucky. Victor's balance was precarious, unabling him to extend the full effort. As his feet shifted, Dale seized the chance to break his hold. The violent extrication flung him headlong, practically at my feet, so that briefly as he lay there we were gazing face to face.

He looked at me as though he couldn't quite believe what he saw, almost as if his mind had been so intent on the fight he had forgotten my presence. I noted the signs of distress which proclaimed near exhaustion, and the dismay that was still there from that first encounter with Victor's strength. He had started the fight with confidence but he was uncertain now, knowing he had underestimated his opponent. The respectful, fearful awe which the power of that seemingly slight frame had roused in him could have been comical under other conditions.

As he scrambled to his feet he was shouting to me, but I

couldn't make sense of what he said. The words were delivered disjointedly through his laboured breathing; and then he had no time for anything but wary evasion of those crushing arms.

But Victor had been craftily biding his time until the first vigorous assault should be spent. Dale was too slow now in his withdrawal and the older but still fresher man moved in with the lightning tensility of the released uncoiling of a steel spring. And once again Dale was lucky; the powerful hold had failed to encompass both arms. At that close range even failing strength could not diminish the ferocious effectiveness of the free fist he sent crashing to the point of Victor's jaw.

For a second Victor's eyes glazed as his head jerked back under the force of it. He recovered immediately but in that fraction of time his hold had relaxed, so that the second blow delivered in the same vulnerable place caught him before he had time to renew it, sending him reeling to the ground. Dale followed him down, flinging himself with such a deliberately savage intensity that the remaining breath was knocked from the only half conscious body beneath him. His exhaustion was overcome now by a passion of vindictiveness. It was not enough that his adversary was defeated. His face was a mask of hatred, distorted with the savagery of a man who knew no quarter for a fallen antagonist.

Victor struggled feebly, moaning as the hands round his throat squeezed pitilessly, his face already dangerously suffused.

I had never witnessed a fight before, especially a contest of such primeval deadliness. It had been necessary; my own life had been at stake. To fight in defence of someone in danger, even using any foul means to attain victory, was justifiable, but what I saw now in Dale Merrick's face terrified me. I was submerged suddenly in sick horror for what he was doing to a defenceless man.

The pain pierced through my back, making my head swim as I dragged myself dizzily to my feet, picking up the first thing that came to hand. It was only afterwards that I knew it was my Tudor lady I had smashed beyond repair, but it would not have deterred me from using it to prevent Dale Merrick from carrying out his murderous intention.

The movement of the lifting of my arm caused flashes of agony to stab through my back again, diverting my aim. Instead of delivering the blow on the back of Dale's head, the deflection of pain brought the figure down sickeningly on Victor's temple. He was fully unconscious even before the blood started to flow.

I looked down horrified at what I had done. At first Dale didn't seem to realise what had happened. He stared stupidly at the wound on Victor's head, and then slowly the insanity left his eyes. He gave a long, shuddering sigh and rolled off the inert form, too exhausted to make the effort to get to his feet; just looking up at me with his chest still labouring and an unutterable weariness in his face.

I backed away. I couldn't bear to be near him. It seemed unimportant that had events been reversed, Victor would have crushed the life out of him with cold blooded impassiveness; and me, too. I was still too badly shaken by the primitive, naked passion I had just beheld. He had not even any longer been fighting for survival; Victor had already been defeated. It had been the sadistic instinct of a predatory animal inflicting torture on its helpless prey.

Drained of strength and emotion, he looked incredibly young, inoffensive. But I had seen it. I had seen the vicious mercilessness in his face. It sickened me even to look at him, knowing the murderous depths which lurked beneath that innocuous, very ordinary outward appearance.

I caught my breath, suddenly, unbelievingly. It wasn't possible . . . and yet why not?

He had known Lya; and not, as he had told me, only through insurance formalities because of the changed name. Dale Merrick was not in the insurance business; he could not have had any such information about her by that means.

I was aghast at where my thoughts were leading me. But how else could he have learned of that assignation on Oxton bridge? And of that slight injury to my arm due to the incident with the motor cycles, when I had been experiencing no discomfort to disclose it to him the following day. Lya would never have confided in someone who was not inextricably involved in her plans. Someone whom she had used in the perpetration of them. Someone who was of the same height and build as the man on the bridge last night!

It didn't make sense. Only a few minutes ago, Dale had fought a deadly battle with Victor to prevent him from killing me. He would not have done that, if he belonged to the colonel's organisation. He would have allowed Victor to carry out the heinous task, to complete what he himself had already failed to accomplish in two attempts. Unless . . .

I didn't want to follow that line of reasoning but my mind travelled inexorably on it. Unless, as the colonel had explained, he personally knew no one higher in the hierarchy than Lya and was ignorant of the colonel's superior position, he wouldn't know that categorically he was also answerable to the colonel.

It wasn't possible. Not this very ordinary but kindly man. This *kindly* man . . . ?

Dale stirred, raising himself tiredly on one elbow. "Thanks," he said. "But what kept you? I could have done with that assistance earlier." He glanced at the recumbent form beside him and remarked, "That wound looks as though it will need stitches. Still, he can count himself fortunate at that." His face was sober. "If you hadn't knocked him out when you did . . ."

"I meant that for you," I said. His blankly innocent expression angered me suddenly. "You needn't pretend any longer. I know all about you."

I was surprised to see that he looked ashamed. I would have expected him to be annoyed, cautious. Instead, he said, "You know? I'm sorry. I guessed you'd feel that way about it."

"You *guessed* . . . ?" Words failed me.

"A man has to do what he has to do," Dale said quietly. "In view of your loathing of me it can only be counted as providential that you laid out our murderous friend here, instead of me."

"And how different is he from you? You tried to kill—"

"Yes, I did," he agreed. "I can't even be sorry I failed."

I hadn't known how much I had wanted him to deny it. All my ghastly suspicions had not really allowed me to believe him capable of such diabolical conduct. Even so, his callousness made me run cold. He was flexing himself gingerly preparatory to getting up. I couldn't fear him in such a weakened condition but I was wondering frantically what I could do to prevent him, whether I could bring myself to the point of laying him out with a better aimed blow, when the problem was solved for me.

My intention had been clear. Dale was eyeing me with some alarm. "For God's sake, Rosanne—" He stopped, interrupted by the sharp squeal of brakes in the lane. "Saved by the bell! I really believe you would have tried to scatter my brains over the carpet, wouldn't you? And after what I've just gone through for you!"

"For me? Why did you bother, when—?"

"You have a point there," he said caustically.

The footsteps approaching hurriedly up the path drew my attention. "Who's that?" I demanded suspiciously.

"Palmer, I expect." He sounded neither concerned nor dismayed. "Too late to have rescued you, but at least in time to prevent you from making a further effort to do me some damage," he said with some acerbity. "Well, come in, Superintendent," he invited, as Palmer appeared in the doorway in company with two police officers and Sergeant Mollett, and stood surveying the disorder of the room in consternation. "The first battle is over. The second was just about to commence. You took your time getting here."

"You all right, Mrs. Grayson?" Palmer asked sharply.

"All right, but not grateful," Dale Merrick answered for me.

It had not been necessary when we were alone without witnesses, but he was going to bluff it out now. I looked at him with loathing.

"That's why you had to stop Victor, because you knew the superintendent would be here any minute."

Before Dale could speak the superintendent said, "That's Haldane's manservant, surely?"

The faint doubt was understandable. Beneath the blood which had flowed from his temple, Victor's face was swollen and distorted almost beyond recognition. Drawing my attention to him diverted me temporarily from Dale Merrick.

"It's Victor," I said. I rushed headlong into explanation. It was probably rather a garbled account but Palmer seemed to follow me without having to make too many interruptions when I deviated too distractingly. Dale broke in once but I ignored him beyond fixing him with a look of scathing contempt.

When I had finished the superintendent nodded. "It fits in. It was Haldane's car . . . He could be the man Special Branch have been trying to lay hands on for some years."

"He took the ticket away with him," I said. "If he destroys it—"

"Oh, he won't destroy it, Mrs. Grayson," he assured me. "He'll want to claim whatever your husband left there. Although I doubt there'll be any mention of him personally in it. At the time when Grayson deposited those papers he wouldn't know of Haldane's involvement; but if he's what he admits to be we'll find plenty of incriminating evidence in his home."

He spoke sharply over his shoulder to Sergeant Mollett, issuing orders about a search warrant and reinforcements from the village constabulary. I waited impatiently, barely containing myself until the man had left before I pointed an accusing finger at Dale Merrick.

"Why don't you arrest him, too?"

Palmer looked surprised. "Well, later perhaps," he said with caution. "If I find just cause . . ."

"He'd have killed Victor just now if I hadn't stopped him."

The two men exchanged glances. There was concern in the superintendent's face as Dale nodded. "She's right," he said curtly. "I understand how you feel, but a fine mess you'd have been in—"

"I know, I know. I should be grateful that Rosanne intervened."

The feeling of camaraderie between the two men amazed and annoyed me.

"He tried to kill me, too," I declared. This seemed to be my night for exposing murderers and would-be murderers. "He admitted it just before you came."

In blank amazement Dale said, "I did no such thing! What on earth are you talking about?"

I glared at him furiously. "You did! You even said you were sorry you had failed."

Helplessly Dale said, "I was talking about Victor . . . Whatever put this idea into your head?"

His air of innocence was superbly done. It would have deceived anyone. It was deceiving Palmer, that was obvious, rousing impotent anger in me that made me stutter.

"You *did* try to kill me and you *did* admit it—"

Superintendent Palmer broke in quietly, trying to subdue my agitation. "Just a minute, Mrs. Grayson. When and where is Mr. Merrick supposed to have made an attempt on your life?"

"At Oxton bridge last night. And the night before, the motor cycles outside my flat, that was him, too. Someone tried to shoot me then and—"

"Easy, easy," Palmer interrupted gently. "I have no knowledge of Mr. Merrick's whereabouts two nights ago but we can establish that later, with certainty and to your satisfaction, I dare say. But at the time you are claiming he was trying to throw you off the bridge Mr. Merrick was seated in one of our patrol cars farther down the lane."

The quiet assertion shook me. "He couldn't be," I faltered.

"You have my word for it," Palmer assured me. "As well as that of several other police officers in whose company he was waiting. You can be grateful to Mr. Merrick. If he hadn't warned us that from your manner earlier in the day something was afoot, we might not have been extra vigilant in keeping watch of your movements. You would have been at the bridge unguarded if you had succeeded in eluding only one car on your trail."

"He couldn't be," I reiterated. "Why would he be with the police? He was working for Lya. Ask him what he was doing outside her flat this afternoon, if he's not supposed to know her—"

"I know what he was doing there, Mrs. Grayson. He was waiting until I was free, so that he could tell me what you had remembered doing with your lighter. After I'd finished at Lya's apartment I was further detained making inquiries into that."

"Was it . . . ?" Dale broke in to ask and the superintendent nodded.

"Almost certainly, I'm afraid." He continued to regard me with the same sombreness with which he had spoken before going on, "Mr. Merrick tried to get you on the phone here when you weren't at home. He was terribly anxious when no one spoke although the receiver was lifted. He felt something was wrong, he phoned me to say he was coming here. I told him I'd follow as soon as I could, but fortunately for you he didn't wait for me."

"He's not—a member of the police?" I asked.

"No—" Palmer said, and Dale interposed, "I thought you said you knew all about me?"

"I know you're not an insurance investigator. And you weren't at school with Robert, were you? That was a lie, too. Everything you told me was untrue . . ."

"Yes, it was—"

"But why . . . ?"

"Because I wanted to gain your confidence. I believed you knew far more about what Robert had been doing and where he was, than you were admitting to the police. But I had never heard of Lya Logasi until the police inquired into her background when you brought her to their notice after your first visit, and came up with some very startling disclosures. Palmer held his hand; he wanted Robert for the murder of Keith Forrester but Special Branch also wanted the man behind Lya—the colonel, as it turns out. But I was impatient, I wanted action. You were very discreet at lunch that day, very innocent—but I didn't trust your innocence. You and Robert were known as a singularly devoted couple, it was difficult to credit your story that he had deserted you for someone else. I could hardly believe you were so completely unaware of what had been going on. You'd been to see Julya Logan, so you knew of her existence and obviously in connexion with Robert, but I just couldn't make up my mind whether you knew she was Lya Logasi. So I told you. Whether you knew or not, I wanted some reaction from you, either through jealousy at realising she was not just a woman Robert had been passing information to, but his wife; or, if you already knew that, then I wanted you to pass on the knowledge that Lya's identity was not such a closely kept secret as she thought. If I knew of it, then others could also, or make the discovery in time. I hoped to make Lya—and Robert—feel insecure, so that they would be panicked into some unpremeditated action. Palmer was annoyed I had told you—"

"Agreeing to allow you to work in with us in that manner was unorthodox in the first place. I broke all rules and regulations by keeping you apprised of events as they were shaping. Your stirring the pot like that could have had disastrous results," Palmer remarked dryly, and Dale nodded sombrely.

"I know. And chiefly to Rosanne . . . But I never dreamed they would attempt to harm you. I thought you were in it yourself, Rosanne, right up to your neck. You see, at that time, like Palmer, I believed Robert had killed Keith Forrester."

I started to ask the obvious question and he forestalled me, his eyes filled with sadness.

"Keith Forrester was my half brother," he said.

18

"Dinly?" I said, and he affirmed it with a bleak nod of his head.

The sadness communicated to me. I remembered the love and admiration which had punctuated every word when he had talked about his brother; the almost love-hate relationship caused by the mother's partiality which could have resulted in hatred gaining ascendency in a lesser man, but which had not in Dale Merrick who had not allowed resentment to overrule his inborn affection.

"I'm sorry to have deceived you," he said. "I think you know how I felt about him—what he meant to my mother. You saw what the news of his murder did to her . . ."

He spoke flatly, stating his motive without really expecting understanding.

Superintendent Palmer did not give me chance to answer, even if I had known what to say.

"Save any further explanations until later, Mr. Merrick. Haldane will be expecting Victor to report; there's no need to raise his alarm by delay. Mind if I use your phone, Mrs. Grayson?"

He didn't wait for assent. He was already dialling, speaking with curt authority when the call was answered. I thought it was to the local police station, but I wasn't really heeding him; I was watching Dale.

I would have liked to say something to him but I still didn't know how to express myself. His attitude didn't help. He was holding himself aloof, as though not by any word or sign would he

expose himself to the contemptuous condemnation he still anticipated from me.

The superintendent finished his conversation, turning back to
us. "Sergeant Mollett will be waiting for us outside Haldane's
house with the warrant and reinforcements by the time we get
there. You'd better come with us, Mrs. Grayson. There's a police
ambulance on the way for Victor, so you stay with him until it
arrives," he was talking now to one of the two policemen who had
remained stolidly in the background, "and then follow us on to
Coplands. Use Morton's car. Where is Morton, by the way?" he
wanted to know. "Not still bound and gagged in the garage, I
hope."

"I went out to release him, sir, when I heard Mrs. Grayson say
what had happened," the policeman said. "He was feeling a bit
sick so he's waiting outside."

"I can't imagine why you didn't untie him, Mr. Merrick, instead
of tackling Victor on your own."

"I didn't have time. He wouldn't have been much help, anyway; he was only partially conscious."

Palmer grunted. "Well, let's get going. Searching Haldane's
house should be an interesting and revealing experience."

He got into the front beside the driver, leaving the back seat
to Dale and myself. I noticed that Dale held himself stiffly in his
own corner to avoid contact with me, but now compassion for
him was swamped under other considerations. There were more
urgent problems. My mind was churning chaotically once more.

"You're going to say it was Robert, aren't you?" I burst out
finally.

Palmer couldn't possibly have been following my reasonings;
his own mind was preoccupied with what lay ahead. I had broken
into his own trend of thought about the culmination of years of
frustrated detection of an elusive man. He was tensed with expectancy and justifiable satisfaction; it showed in the abstraction of
his query.

"What's that?"

"You're going to say it was Robert at Oxton bridge last night."

"No, as a matter of fact, I'm not." His tone told me nothing, as
he had probably intended. It was just a flat denial.

Dale moved suddenly. Palmer couldn't have seen the movement

behind him, but he had sensed it. He spoke sharply. "Leave it until we get to Coplands, Mr. Merrick."

Something in his voice disturbed me but we were already slowing down behind the car that was parked a few yards before the entrance to the colonel's drive. He was out before it stopped, running forward to confer with the occupants of the other car.

In the darkness I felt Dale's hand on mine, diffidently at first and then pressing more firmly as I made no offer to reject it. It was a gesture of comfort, even more disquieting than Palmer's voice, making me turn uncertainly towards him.

And then Palmer was back and we were moving on into the driveway.

The house was in darkness, as it usually was, except for the dim diffusion of light from one curtained window. The colonel answered the door himself and his face shocked me, even softened by the hall lights behind him which threw it into shadow. He looked haggard, aged beyond belief, the alert blue eyes dulled and sunk deeply into the sockets, and the lines of his face were so cruelly emphasised it seemed as though they could only have been effected by artificial means. Even his shoulders drooped, so that for once his size was unimpressive as he stood framed in the doorway.

The ringing of the bell might not have surprised him; he would have been expecting Victor. But he showed no dismay to be confronted by the law; he appeared disinterested even when Palmer explained their presence in politely cautionary words. The superintendent had posted men round the back of the house but his precautions had been unnecessary. Obviously, the colonel had no intention of making a run for it. He looked like a man who had suffered the ultimate defeat, leaving him broken in spirit.

He stood back. "Come in, gentlemen," he said, and his voice was as dispirited as his appearance.

And then he caught sight of me as Dale moved to allow me to precede him. He could have been expected to show utter consternation but instead he underwent a complete transformation. The years lifted suddenly from him. The lines were still in his face, his eyes were still hollow, but the impact of age was gone with the glow of life which had returned miraculously to him.

He regarded me for a few long moments in silence, seeming to search for words, and I had a feeling he had forgotten the others' presence.

"I am not a religious man," he said at last, "but I know of no other way to express what I feel than to say thank God."

It was easy to believe him. He was a man reprieved. His shoulders were straight once more with their customary military bearing as he led us through into his beautiful lounge.

"Victor?" he questioned.

"In custody," the superintendent told him.

"And the charges?"

"He will be held on the attempted murder of Mrs. Grayson while investigations are pending. Later, I have no doubt there will be other charges against him."

The colonel nodded non-committally. "And me?"

"Conspiracy in the attempted murder of Mrs. Grayson. Other charges against you, of course, will depend upon what we find here."

"Well, I won't make it difficult for you. You'd find it, anyway. No sense in your pulling the house apart." He spoke crisply; he could have been issuing orders on the parade ground. "Taking measurements would very soon confirm that my study is very cleverly divided. There is a compartment behind the east wall. I will show you the mechanism to work the door in the book shelves. My radio equipment, amongst other things, is in there. All the evidence you will need, Superintendent."

He had not yet taken his eyes from me, even while he was addressing the superintendent. I had listened impatiently while Palmer followed his correct procedure. Now I could no longer contain myself.

"He knows where Robert is," I burst out. "Make him tell me, Superintendent Palmer."

The colonel's eyes wavered now for the first time. A little mockingly he said, "In front of the police, Rosanne? When he will almost certainly be arrested on a charge of spying?"

"I don't care—" I started to say.

"I doubt he will ever answer to that charge, Mr. Haldane," Palmer said. "Do you?"

A certain wariness had crept into the colonel. "I really wouldn't know," he said, rather bored. "It depends upon how clever Grayson is in evading you. If he has a good enough hiding place—"

"He had the best of all hiding places. You chose an excellent one for him, from your point of view. But we found him."

"You did?" I cried. "Oh, where? Where is he, please? Why didn't you tell me?"

That first outpouring of joyous relief did not last. It died almost at birth, strangled by the atmosphere which impregnated the room. I looked uncertainly from Palmer to Dale. The former was striving to remain impersonally professional to cover his regret, but Dale's face was wrung with compassion. Even as I looked at him he moved over to me and put his arm round my shoulders. The action of protectiveness frightened me.

"Because there wasn't time earlier at your cottage, Mrs. Grayson," Palmer said. "And because it wasn't easy."

I knew before he said it.

I whispered, "No," as if denial would ward off the knowledge.

"I'm afraid Robert is dead," the superintendent told me quietly.

The overwhelming sorrow welled up inside me, an unbearable sense of loss. In the void of desolation that yawned before me I felt Dale's arm tighten round me, as though he would take my sorrow and make it his own. But he couldn't do that. No one could do that.

Oh, Robert, I thought wordlessly, my dear Robert . . .

"When?" I managed to articulate at last.

"The night he disappeared."

So long ago? All this time, and I hadn't known. All these weeks . . .

With one of the last intelligent thoughts of which I was capable I said piteously, "No, it couldn't be . . . I saw him, he was in the square . . ."

"That was me, Rosanne," Dale explained remorsefully. "I didn't know Robert was dead—I would not have acted so cruelly . . ." A little helplessly he said, "You'd been closely watched. You hadn't made any effort to contact Robert, but I was sure you must have known where he was—the police believed that, too. I hoped you would lead us to him if you thought he was trying to get in touch with you. When I'd told you I'd seen him there I arranged with the man watching your flat to give chase if you . . . I'm sorry, Rosanne . . ."

It didn't matter. Nothing mattered any more. Even the details seemed unimportant but one part of my mind still searched for them.

"How did he die?"

"He was killed, Mrs. Grayson," Palmer said. "When you drove down here that night you witnessed an accident. It was Robert's body that was found in that crash."

"No! I spoke to that man! Do you think I wouldn't have known that it was Robert?"

"You spoke to Keith Forrester, unless I am very much mistaken. And I don't think I am, am I, Mr. Haldane? You reported your car stolen from outside your house but it was taken by Forrester from Far End, where you were that night—either because it was faster or nearer at hand than his own. You followed him, with Victor; and Grayson, too—he had to be with you. You wouldn't be very far behind when he crashed—providently for you, although it would complicate matters when someone—Mrs. Grayson—was at the scene of the accident. But not overmuch. When she left to get assistance for Forrester you had him, hadn't you?" The superintendent's voice was hard as granite. "He was injured, the car wrecked. But why was it necessary to switch bodies?"

"Surely that is obvious," the colonel said irritably. "It was my car. I couldn't do with Forrester's body being found in any circumstances even remotely connected with me. It was bad enough that Grayson should be found in it, if he was identified, but I couldn't overlook the fortune of having a ready made accident to hand to account for the death of one of them. It was logical to assume that if you discovered the body in the crash was Grayson's, then you would come to the conclusion that he had killed Forrester at Far End and then died in an accident in his panic to get away. The difficulty in explaining why he should be in my car could have been overcome. Grayson hadn't his own car with him and he would have been reluctant to make his escape in Forrester's, belonging to the police. Being a friend of mine, he would know where to look for a good fast car. I hoped he would not be identified. I was not, of course, aware at the time that it was Rosanne who came to Forrester's assistance, but even that, as it proved, worked to my advantage. She testified at the inquest; if she had known the man to be her husband, she would have said so."

"We investigated that accident, as we investigated anything untoward in the vicinity after Forrester was missing. But we were looking for a man of his description, which didn't tally with that of the body in the car, and we had no reason at that time to believe Grayson was dead. On the contrary, we thought him very much alive. If Mrs. Grayson had remembered earlier where she had mislaid her lighter . . . You should have removed all the possessions from Forrester's pockets, as you did from Grayson's, Haldane."

"I was not concerned in concealing Forrester's identity."

"But Grayson didn't have to die because he made a convenient suspect, did he? He would have died, in any case. Why, when he was one of you? He'd wanted out, hadn't he, that was why he resigned from the Foreign Office, so that his position there could no longer be of use to you. But couldn't you have counted on his loyalty to his wife to keep him quiet?"

The colonel's face broke into a bleak smile. "Loyalty to Lya?"

"If his feeling for her was sufficient inducement, in the first place . . . But there was more to it than that, wasn't there? It's too out of character with all that is known of Grayson. You had some stronger means of coercion to get him to work for you. What blackmail did you use on him?"

"It isn't really important," the colonel said, and Palmer contradicted him gently.

"I think it is, for Mrs. Grayson's peace of mind. She has suffered a great deal in these past weeks, and more from the thought of the loss of her husband's love than from the fact of his betraying his position of trust at the Foreign Office."

His intention was kind but he was wrong, in that moment. I heard, without really hearing. I was too numbed with pain to be hardly aware of anything but that Robert was dead. Only that really registered at the time. If the colonel looked at me when he started to speak, I didn't see him. I watched him, but it was with vacant eyes.

"Lya told him of a child—a son born several months after she was reported killed in Budapest. He is in a Displaced Person's camp in Europe, behind the Iron Curtain. He was used as a lever to persuade Grayson to co-operate; he was under no misapprehension what would happen to the boy if he refused."

"The best persuasion of all," Palmer commented grimly. "You people certainly know how to get co-operation."

"Our methods get results, that is what matters."

"So Grayson got himself out of a position where he could be of further use to you. Couldn't you have left it at that?"

The colonel hesitated. "That angered me, I admit. But I meant originally only that he should leave the country. I wanted him out of the way—Rosanne will know why." I think he paused, waiting for me to speak. When I didn't, he continued, "The arrangements were made for him to leave by a private airfield not far from here. He wasn't told until he arrived at the cottage. Lya picked him up at Paddington station. Perhaps he already suspected something, felt uneasy, and that is why he left whatever documents he did leave at the left luggage office there while he waited for her.

"I had instructed Lya for him to phone Rosanne saying he was leaving the country with another woman, but he was adamant in his refusal. No further threats to his son could compel him into doing so. Lya couldn't deal with him, she had to call me in. He yielded finally only when I made it clear to him that Rosanne could meet with some accident if he continued to refuse. I believe I would still have let him go, even though he now knew of my involvement. Unnecessary killings are both messy and dangerous, they focus too much unwelcome attention. I should have had him watched; perhaps later, when he was living abroad under an assumed name, it would have been convenient for him to have died accidentally. I don't know. The question didn't arise. There was unexpectedly the problem of Forrester's presence to deal with, and later, a ready-made accident to hand. Too good an opportunity to miss. Grayson was substituted for Forrester, and Forrester disposed of down the disused well shaft. We had to wait until after Rosanne had left to do that, she was outside the cottage when we returned. Then I reported my car stolen, while Victor disposed of Forrester's car which was hidden up the lane. I really don't know what he did with it. I leave such matters to him, he is very efficient. But doubtless he will tell you himself. There is no point in refusing to accept defeat."

"No point at all," Palmer agreed dryly. "I shall have to ask you to come with us, Mr. Haldane."

"Yes, of course. I shall need my coat." He turned instinctively towards the bell and checked himself, remembering with a wry smile. "Habit dies hard. I shall miss Victor's attentions. My housekeeper, by the way, Mrs. Cooper, is entirely innocent. She has no knowledge of any of this, it will come as a great shock to her. I hope you will deal gently with her."

"She will be questioned, naturally. Now if you're ready, Mr. Haldane . . ."

But the colonel wasn't quite ready. He stood in indecision for several seconds before addressing me directly, and he appeared almost to have forgotten the others' presence.

"You may be wondering why, when I was so frank with you earlier, I didn't tell you Robert was dead. I told you I was not ashamed of what I am, and I am not. But I am not entirely without shame. The one thing I couldn't bear for you to know was that I was responsible for his death."

He waited, taking no notice when the superintendent tried to urge him into leaving. He could have been hoping for some response from me but I was incapable of giving any. I met his gaze with dulled, apathetic eyes. But he had waited only because he hadn't finished.

"I don't know what happened tonight to prevent Victor carrying out my orders after I left Far End. It doesn't matter. Whatever it was, I wish you would believe that I'm not sorry. I've known for a long time how much I've wanted you. What I didn't realise, until I waited here for Victor and thought it was too late, was how much I've loved you."

He went then, yielding finally to Palmer's insistence. His shoulders were braced, once more filling the doorway as he passed through it.

I watched him go, still without really seeing him. His exit was the culminating act of a scene imprinted on my memory even though it held no meaning. My mind had long since ceased functioning.

19

I spent long hours poring over Robert's letter, even though I knew every word by heart. Too many long hours. Dale was uneasy. When he tried to remonstrate, it was Helen who stopped him.

"Leave her alone," she advised. "She has to get over her sorrow in her own way. I know. You do, too, Dale."

They had been kind, more than kind, to me. Dale had insisted I stay at Merrick and I had been too lethargic to do more than protest feebly at intruding upon them.

"It will be good for Helen," Dale had urged. "She'll stay on instead of returning home. She needs something to occupy her, now that mother is dead."

"She won't want me," I said listlessly. "She hated me—I could tell, the day you took me there . . ."

"Because she thought your husband had murdered Dinly and you were helping him to evade the police. As I did, at that time. She didn't want me to take you to Merrick; I was afraid all the time we were there that her feelings would get the better of her."

"Why did you risk it?"

"Because I didn't like how I was using you. I thought that some-day—if you ever found out—it would help you to understand why I had done it if you saw what Dinly's death had done to my mother. She worshipped him. She had always rather despised me for having no more ambition than to run the farm, like my father;

but she saw Dinly as some sort of a James Bond. It wasn't like that, of course; his work was mostly deadly routine but he long ago gave up trying to explain that to her. It hit her doubly hard that what she had glamorised as a wildly exciting life should have resulted in his death." He waited a moment before concluding, "Helen has her own grief, too. She and Dinly would have been married by now. It will be helping her, too."

So I went to Merrick; but if my presence there helped Dale or Helen to overcome their own loss I was too selfishly withdrawn in my sorrow to know.

I had to stay somewhere until the trial was over; one place was as good as another to me. Like an obedient child that has no constructive will of its own I went through the motions of eating and sleeping, helping about the house, taking long walks with either Dale or Helen. Dale tried to interest me in the running of the farm and at any other time he would probably have succeeded.

But immediately they left me to my own devices I found some quiet corner in which once more to peruse the only thing that any longer held any meaning for me.

I had already partially learned to live without Robert during the past weeks. Unknowingly, but gradually, I had become used to him not being around; I found I didn't have to start at the beginning with the sudden blank desolation of bereavement. I couldn't look ahead to the future when the pain of loss would be dulled to wistful remembrance, but the time would inevitably come. I knew that.

But not all the time in the world could ever have eradicated the bitter hurt of knowing that the apparent happiness of the three years we had shared together had been a meaningless façade. That would always have been a festering, disillusioning wound to destroy my peace of mind. Even more than the need to get over Robert's death, I required constant confirmation that those years had been as rich in love and spiritual closeness as I had believed them to be.

Robert's letter brought me that reassurance.

He had found time, while he waited for Lya that night at the station, not only to set down a glossary of facts and events, but also to write a personal letter to me. The document of facts had been introduced at the colonel's trial but although Palmer had read the letter he had allowed me to retain it as having no bearing on the evidence.

It was an outpouring of months of strain; of fear for his son's safety, of inner torment for the acts of betrayal of his country, which he had kept concealed so perfectly from me. But mainly it was a letter of love.

What had prompted the need in him at that time to put down on paper the explanation of his actions and the reassurances of his love for me? Had he known intuitively that he would never see me again to tell me in spoken words? He didn't say, but it was not difficult to guess that some strange, lonely instinct of portending disaster had assailed him as he waited there, compelling him on into the hurried scribbling, "I couldn't bring myself to tell you we weren't married, my darling, not until I saw some way out of the problem. Lya wouldn't agree to divorce me, she is a Catholic, and not until this other ghastly mess is somehow resolved dare I take steps about divorcing her. My first consideration has had to be my son. I couldn't do anything that would imperil his safety. Whatever I feel about you, I had to do what I did for his sake. It is the only thing I have ever done for him in all his life, I couldn't deny him that right. I know you will understand that, my darling. If I could only get him away, to England . . . But whatever has happened or will happen, never doubt how much I love you . . ."

There was more in this vein, bringing warmth to the frozen region of my heart. It was too private, too intimate with love to more than whisper the words to myself. I knew that letter phrase by phrase, every word remembered in pain and anguish and tenderness, and yet in healing. I wept silently, without tears, knowing now the poignant uselessness of all that he had sacrificed in that effort to do the one thing he had ever been able to do for the son he had never seen.

There had been a photograph enclosed. A snapshot of a boy of some nine or ten years; a wan, serious little face with the solemn adultness of a child who has never experienced a real childhood. Not like Robert, and yet with something in the pale features which could have resembled a less robust, youthful Robert.

I had studied that too serious little face with pity in my heart, wanting to do for him what I had known Robert had wanted to do. But it had not been Robert's child, and the cruelty of the deception which had been played on him tore me apart when Superintendent Palmer explained.

"We've made full investigations. There was a child—a son—born seven months after Lya was reported dead. But that child died within a few hours of birth."

"How could she do that to him?" I wondered helplessly.

"He wouldn't co-operate without some strong incentive—much stronger than any lingering affection he may have entertained for her. It wouldn't be difficult to find a boy with some faint resemblance out of all those who are still in these camps all over Europe. Robert would have no reason to disbelieve her when she claimed that child was theirs. Why should he?"

Why should he? But even at the end, when he had been obligingly candid, the colonel had not been completely frank. He had confessed shame that he had been the instrument of Robert's death but he had not been able to bring himself to reveal that final piece of infamy.

But I was past feeling bitterness, or even satisfaction when the trial was over. I wasn't even in court that last day when the sentences were passed, nor was Dale. Not until Palmer came to Merrick later in the evening did we know the result. I heard it with disinterest but I would have thought Dale would have been pleased.

Instead, all he said was, in some dissatisfaction, "I would have liked it better if the man who tried to kill Rosanne had also been sentenced in that dock today. That murderous brute is still at large."

"Mrs. Grayson has nothing to fear from him. He'd be some minion employed by Lya, with no motive of his own beyond her orders. We're still working on it, but although I think we'd be lucky to get him on that charge, that type will always be involved in something unlawful. We'll get him for something, sooner or later."

He stretched his legs, relaxed in his chair; a man at ease, with the contentment of a job completed. Waiting a few minutes before adding, "I understand you're off to Johannesburg tomorrow, Mrs. Grayson. Thinking of settling there?"

"Perhaps. I haven't really thought about it, but I expect so."

"You haven't been persuaded to change your mind about going?"

"No," I said wonderingly. "Why should anyone . . . ?"

Dale made a sharp movement of interruption. "Let me refill your glass, Superintendent."

"Yes, do that, please." He smiled lazily, with some inner amusement. "I do my work and you do yours. But I did allow you to assist with mine. I should hope—"

"So should I. Let's leave it at that for now."

"As you wish," Palmer agreed urbanely.

I didn't understand that by-play of words between the two men. Not until the following morning. Not until almost the last few minutes before departure.

Helen was to drive me to the airport. As I went out to the waiting car, leaving Merrick for the last time, it occurred to me to wonder a little bleakly why Dale had elected not to accompany me on that first part of the journey. It seemed inconsistent with his thoughtfulness towards a guest during the past weeks not to grant me that last courtesy.

Helen was already in the car, gently revving the engine while Dale stowed the last of my cases in the boot. I went round to him as he slammed it firmly, not quite knowing how to express my thanks. As it happens, I never did thank him.

He took me completely by surprise by asking suddenly, "Was Palmer right, could I have persuaded you not to go?"

The hazel eyes were very serious as they looked down at me, confusing me a little.

"I don't think so," I said.

"Neither do I—yet." He nodded in confirmation. "I'm not coming with you to the airport because I don't trust myself not to try. I'm only persuasive when I'm sure of the result beforehand. You know what I'd like to tell you, don't you, Rosanne?" Despite the seriousness, his face was very appealing, very boyish, filling me with sudden consternation. "No, don't say anything. I'm not telling you—not yet. It's too soon. All I'm asking is that you'll come back."

I didn't know how to put it into words. I broke falteringly into speech, stirred too deeply with regret to do any kindly prevaricating. "It couldn't ever be the same. I couldn't have with you what I had with Robert . . ."

"I don't want that. I'm not sufficiently like Robert to expect for there to be the same between us as there was between you and him. But there are other things—worthwhile things. We could have those. I'm not asking you to commit yourself to anything, beyond coming back someday. Will you do that? Perhaps not for six months—twelve months—longer, if you need more time. You don't need to make any promises except that you will come back."

He had said he didn't exert persuasion unless he was sure of the outcome. He was persuasive now. Sure of himself and of me, too. The confidence showed plainly.

"Will you promise that?" he insisted gently. "Will you?"

I hadn't meant to. I couldn't see that it would do any good. But I knew suddenly that I would. He knew it, too, even before I nodded in slow agreement.

He was still watching me, the smile still on his face, as the car gathered momentum down the drive.